GINORTI

Book Five of the Lissae Series

R. Lennard

Ginorti

First published in 2022 by R. Lennard

Edited by Anna at CREATING ink.
www.CREATINGink.com

Published by Rebecca Lennard.
lissae.com

Check the trigger warnings by scanning the QR code below:

A catalogue record for this book is available from the National Library of Australia

To Mum,
Thank you for getting me the right glasses, for encouraging my reading,
and for picking apart the books.

To Dad,
Thank you for the teaching me how to keep going, no matter what the
odds are, and for being the best salesman without reading the books.

I put you both through even more than Shari.
Thank you for, well, everything.

PROLOGUE

Zuefie—Before Common Era

Xan could just make out the incoming storm through the thick, steel bars. It was the only view from the cold, stone room.

He hummed. To be a cloud, free from the constraints of a body. Free of pain, fear, and hunger.

The whip cracked, sliced through the air as it struck again.

It landed across the already flayed skin of his back.

Xan didn't have it in him to flinch anymore, but the pain still seared his skin, and his hum turned to a groan.

The guard laughed. "That'll show you. Think you can use your fancy magic around us? You know the law. No magic on Zuefie."

"I'd do it again," Xan rasped.

Leaning down, the guard's rank breath seared against his open wounds. "And I'll do her again once I'm through with you."

Xan's head throbbed in time with his back. A whimper reached him from the corner where Derri, his sister, his last remaining family, was huddled. Years ago, before his parents had been murdered, this guard had ridden through their tiny village and taken a shine to Derri. He'd wooed her, won her over, and made Derri his wife.

The weight of her terrified gaze was enough to ensure the cries and screams stayed trapped behind his teeth. She was protected, for the moment, by his fading Innarn.

What will happen once he had beaten me to death?

Derri had been safe with her husband when they'd come for their parents.

An image of his father, dying under the boot of a man in the same yellow uniform, came to mind. His mother screaming as they dragged her away. Just because they'd dared to be born with magic.

Burning pain struck again.

There was a whisper of his name from his sister.

Xan found he still had enough energy to flinch.

In times gone by, he and Derri had daydreamed of what they'd do if the guards ever caught them.

'*Turn to clouds,*' the younger voice of his sister said.

He smiled, bloodied teeth gleaming, as he remembered his reply.

Above him, the guard paused. "What are you grinning at?"

"Anything is possible." Stretching out his fingers, Xan wriggled them at Derri–the only movement he could make when he was so tightly strapped down.

There was the rustle of cloth, almost silent against the crack of the whip.

Twisting his neck, Xan glanced at Derri. "Time to join the clouds," he croaked.

Smiling through her tears, Derri nodded. "We'll be with Mamma."

The whip fell again.

This time, Xan gathered the energy, pulling it closer to his core.

The air in the room got thinner as Derri used her Innarn to draw the precious oxygen towards her.

Staggering under the sudden lack of air, the guard stumbled, knocking into Xan.

A fatal mistake.

"Perfect." Xan smiled as he syphoned the guard's life away.

A red haze filled Xan's vision, and Derri poked at what was left of her husband.

"Clouds?" Derri asked.

"We'll make them all clouds. And we'll drain everyone we come across."

Innarn cut through the straps holding him down, and Xan rose from the crude stone slab.

Magic was running through his veins so thick, the blood streaming from his body turned to vapour.

"Remember me," Derri whispered.

"Always." Xan reached out and grasped her hand.

He paused.

Derri stopped and looked at him. "Xan?"

"I can't feel you," he said. Wide-eyed, Xan glanced at her as the sensation of touch faded away.

"Xan..."

Whatever Derri was saying broke off. Words were lost. He could see her mouth moving, but no sound was coming out.

Xan didn't understand until Derri started to fade from view.

'Take me with you.'

It sounded like her, in his mind.

'Xan. Xan. Xan. Take me with you!'

The words were repeating.

Xan stretched out his Innarn and enveloped it around Derri.

Hard flesh and bone became weightless vapour.

The stained clothes he'd been wearing dropped to the floor as another guard slammed the door open and strode into the room.

Lightning flashed as the siblings saw he was already raising his whip.

The second guard took in the scene.

A bundle of rags in the middle of the room. Bloody trail leading from the stone slab. His dead colleague slumped where the prisoners should have been. A thick, low cloud covering the room. "What happened here?"

'*We are Xanderri,*' the siblings sent.

Shivering, the second guard looked around. "Who said that?"

Speech didn't matter anymore. Not when their very atoms were combined.

Xanderri pushed themselves towards the man's head and saw his truth.

An Innarnian hiding with the enemy.

They were here now.

He didn't have to hide anymore.

Flashes of light filled the room, as bright as the guard's screams were loud.

A uniform dropped to the floor.

'*We are Xanderri.*'

The trio would turn their Realm to clouds and vapour to keep their kind safe.

CHAPTER ONE

Zuefie

The wards were down.

Fat drops of water hit Shari's face and soaked into the pillow under her head. The icy breeze made her shiver.

Why are the wards down? It was hard to focus. Weakly, Shari pushed her Innarn out and created a shield around herself.

Fix 'em in tha mornin'.

So tired.

As the Altoriae drifted back to sleep, something niggled at her consciousness.

She didn't have a window above her bed.

Portal

Vebaday

Sixth day of the fourth week of Sunfall

"Where is she?!" Samuel thundered.

The Guardian was just as angry as his apprentice, and twice as dangerous in his silence.

'*Beyond any gateway.*' The tiny Ducibus was serene even in the face of Samuel's wrath.

"And which gateway did she last go through?" Samuel's voice dropped to a rumble.

Behind him, Jonathan sighed.

The Ducibus bowed his head. '*The one we don't guard.*'

Snarling, Samuel loomed over Pala, Innarn flaring out.

Jonathan gently pulled him back. "Can you take us to the one you don't guard?"

Pala shook his hood. '*I can show you the hallway.*'

Trying to tamper down his scowl, Samuel limped after the miniscule creature.

Shari had been right next to him.

Right by his side.

They had survived Oalark's madness, two assassination attempts, and the destruction of his home Realm, only for her to get snatched in what was supposed to be the safest place in all the Realms.

If you were in the Portal, you should be untouchable. It was practically a sacred space.

When I found out who had broken that rule, oh.

He smiled, far too many teeth showing.

He would make Oalark proud.

Pala glanced back at him and shook zir head again. 'You'll have to stay here,' the Ducibus warned.

'Why?'

'*It is too Light for you. Come, Guardian.*'

Rooted to the spot by Innarn stronger than he was expecting, Samuel scowled as Jonathan faded into the brightness that led to the very Lightest of Realms.

As the Guardian disappeared, Samuel's scowl dropped. How was he going to tell Jonathan that it wasn't just Shari he was worried about?

Clenching his fists so tight it hurt, Samuel did his best to breathe through the terror consuming him. If Shari was on a Light Realm, it was possible that she would burn. The pain would be far more than he had to deal with whilst he was on Lissae. And for the Altoriae, he worried.

But for his hatchlings? The ones Shari had put into her pocket Realm before they'd crossed through the portal? He was terrified.

If the Light Realm would burn Shari, it would turn them to cinders.

And they were all he had left.

Zuefie

Flashes of Plasma lit up the sky as the Xanderri celebrated.

Weaving through the ancient stone ruins of their city, the cloud forms took turns at diving, practising for when they would be given leave to syphon the Innarn from the prone body of the Realm's greatest fighter.

One cloud, denser than the others, moved ponderously towards the downed warrior. The other Xanderri made way for their leader.

Slowly, the leader lowered, floating just above the Altoriae's body. A wisp pulled away from the main part of the cloud and stroked against her face. Hissing, the leader drew back.

'Why is the Altoriae so Dark?'

The closest Xanderri seemed to freeze. A few dared to drift away, wanting to be out of the blast radius.

'*The influence of Altum?*' The words came from the green, fleshy form of a host.

There was a sense of questioning towards the Xanderri inside the host. Why would any of them choose to be limited in such a way? But it remained unvoiced, lurking instead on the edge of thought.

The cloud inside the body sighed. '*This host is degrading. Without our influence, the body will fail. Then, no more host.*'

Their leader bobbed. '*You may maintain the body until we secure safe passage to Lissae.*' Ze brushed against the Altoriae again. '*Dark or not, she will sustain us. It may take the younger some time to acclimatise.*'

'*We may feed?*' There was a tremble of anticipation in the thought patterns.

If the leader had a mouth, they would have smiled. '*Not yet. The Altoriae is Dark enough that her Innarn would harm us. Gather the others, travel to each branch of the Light Realms, and find a sacrifice. We can slowly acclimatise to the Darker Innarn until we can feast on the chosen one.*'

'*Feed.*'

In rapid succession, the Xanderri lined themselves up behind the one with the host, who moved jerky limbs, leading them towards the gateway.

They had sacrifices to hunt.

Chapter Two

Lissae
Hazelcrown 4060
First week of Autumn

Captain Rappen wasted no time firing the ballistae on the ships docked in Ginorti's bay. He smiled in satisfaction, as yet another fell beneath the waves.

"Reload!" he ordered.

"We're out of ammunition," a solider yelled back.

Rounding on the closest crew member, he dropped his voice. "What?"

He gulped. "It's all gone."

"Then find more," the captain growled.

Glancing around helplessly, he shrugged. "Ain't no trees to cut down here."

Rappen glanced at the tree-lined shore, before looking back at the sailor and raising a brow.

"The rocks will tear the ship apart." The sailor shook his head and gestured out to the dull grey points jutting ominously along the coastline.

Biting back harsh words, Captain Rappen snarled, "Then carve the boat up."

The skipper of the vessel stomped over to them, arms crossed as he glared. "Try it."

Growling, he thumped his fist against the railing. "We have them!"

"Ain't no way we can take the island. But we took this." He moved to the side and revealed a sodden form, clearly plucked from the waves.

Captain Rappen stepped closer, poking at the man with the hilt of his sword. Sparks leaped as the metal came into contact with his skin.

He grinned. "Well, well."

"What should we do with him?"

"Take the aberration below. Lock it in the ziom cell," he ordered.

Sailors surged forward, hurrying to do his bidding.

"Take it as a win," the skipper advised. "We can regroup, and when we come back, they'll be running scared."

"I don't want them running. I want them dead." Captain Rappen glared out at the bay where tiny figures were working hard to resurrect the downed ships.

"Don't we all?" the skipper muttered. "Full turn. Set sail for the nearest island that ain't here."

"We could return to Jinkor. Elder Chamele will want the aberration," a solider piped up.

"Jinkor is halfway round Lissae," the skipper protested.

Captain Rappen raised his brows and kept his gaze on the sailor as he slowly sheathed his sword.

The skipper gulped. "Very well," he said. Turning away from him, he started barking out orders. "Head for Jinkor!"

Belching clouds of black smoke, the ships moved off.

Staring at the shrinking island, Captain Rappen clenched his fists.

Someday soon, he'd see them all drown.

Zuefie

Someone was yelling her name.

Shari could hear them from the depths of her empty dream.

At least, she was assuming this vast blackness was a dream. If it wasn't, well... The thought didn't do to dwell on.

'*Shari.*'

There it was again.

Looking around, Shari tried to see who was hiding in the darkness.

A sound suspiciously like a snort filled her mind.

'*Open your eyes.*'

Huffing, Shari crossed her arms. Of course, her eyes were open...

Weren't they?

She blinked, just to make sure, and flinched from the sudden, blinding brightness.

'*Are you sure she's the Altoriae?*' a second voice asked. It sounded younger than the first.

'*There's something wrong with her,*' the first answered. '*She's usually not so...*'

Whatever disparaging remark they were going to utter was lost to pain as Shari's vision filled with white-hot light. It felt like thousands of needles were scraping her retinas.

Blinking, she tried to raise a hand to rub at her eyes, but the effort was more than she could bear, and her arm remained stubbornly still.

'*Shari?*' The voice inside her head was familiar.

'Yes?'

Babbling—very loud babbling—filled her mind, the two voices overlapping each other as they started nattering on about *taken* and *Sanithane* and *Altum gone.*

That.

She remembered that.

Oalark being hit by the spear.

The Queen, too proud or too broken, to accept her healing.

And the Realm of Altum, tied to the dying Queen's life force, collapsing around them.

Ignoring the shrieking in her head, Shari poked at her memory. Escaping to the safety of the Portal was but a hazy recollection. Walking by Samuel's side towards the Lissaen gateway. And something cold and wet wrapping around her before the double doors of home could open.

'*Where am I?*'

Sometimes sending was a precise art, a tool used to get delicate points across when words wouldn't do.

Then there were times like now, when sensations were all the sender was capable of.

Light, pain, bright.

'*Who are you?*' Shari asked.

The voices inside her head stopped, and there was a swiftly muffled feeling of hurt.

'*Jetonyx and Tormorylth.*'

Sucking in a breath, Shari shuddered. '*You're safe!*' She'd meant it as a question, but the exclamation seemed to ease some of Tormorylth's hurt.

'*But you aren't,*' Jetonyx reminded her.

Forcing her eyes open, Shari looked around.

A crumbling, circular pillar covered with leafy vines was the first thing she saw. From where she lay, Shari could tell she was on some sort of platform but she wasn't sure how far away the ground was. Craning her head, she could make out a canopy of trees.

Her heart sank. If she was above the tops of the trees, then she was too high to reach the ground. She'd have to save her strength in order to get them all to safety.

Before she could formulate a plan, something wet brushed against her face.

Shari's eyes fluttered closed, even as the Q'Aralides' cries echoed in her mind.

'*So tired...*'

Lissae

Adonday

First day of the first week of Hazelcrown

Sitting on the edge of her seat, ankles primly crossed, Chamele raised her teacup to take a sip. She was doing her best to ignore the other elders in the room, who were trying to sneak a glance at what lay beneath the opaque veil that covered the worst of her melted face while they discussed their latest attempt at overtaking the Shifting Islands.

As the hot, sweet tea slide down her throat, she involuntarily chuckled.

Elder Ben glanced at her. "What is funny about having to retreat?" he snarled.

Chamele opened her mouth to deny their defeat at the hands of the aberrations was amusing, but all that came out was a laugh.

The remaining elder in the room was looking at her, concerned, as Chamele's laughter took on a hysterical edge.

"I think she's cracked," Gywn said.

The clank of metal behind her was drowned out by her raucous peels.

"Leave. Now," the captain of her guards ordered.

Despite the tears streaming down her face, and the veil obscuring her view, the aides fleeing the room made her laugh even harder. Their elders lingered, taking long glances as the guards forcefully shut the heavy doors behind them.

"Elder?" the captain was kneeling before her now, gently pulling the cup from her clenched hands.

Gasping for breath, Chamele clutched at her aching sides, unable to stop the noise pouring from her mouth.

"Elder," he said again, more sternly this time. He stretched out a hand and laid it on her knee.

Chamele's head snapped back, her mouth wide as cloud vapour streamed from it.

The cloud shot to the ceiling, where it hovered. Chamele sensed it was amused by the guards in the room who were drawing their swords. Just how were they planning on fighting the vapour?

"Elder," the captain said again, dagger in his hand as his eyes tracked the movements of the wisps.

'*How easy it would be to bump him, drive the dagger right through his useless heart,*' something whispered inside her head.

Chest heaving, Chamele ignored the voice with the ease of decades of practice. Reaching under the veil, she daintily wiped her eyes. Taking a shuddering breath, she put her handkerchief away and straightened her clothing. Sitting up properly once more, she sighed. "A leftover effect from the Innarnian attack. It can cause sudden mood swings."

'*Liar,*' the voice purred.

"Perhaps you should rest," the captain said.

Remembering the look on Ben and Gywn's faces, Chamele sighed. "That may be a good idea, Captain. Do you mind terribly escorting me to my quarters?"

He nodded. "Of course, Elder."

The captain never saw the tendril of cloud as it brushed against his head, removing the memory of the morning. Instead, he helped her up and guided Chamele through the hallways of her home. The cloud followed, brushing against those who'd seen her outburst and taking the memory from them.

As grateful as she was for the help, Chamele was concerned.

The feeling faded as soon as she was in her rooms, alone, and the cloud descended to fill her head once again.

Zuefie

The next time Shari woke, Zirgha was standing over her, a hunk of rotting flesh peeling away from her cheek.

She wanted to crawl out of her skin, but when she tried to move, Shari could barely twitch her fingers.

"Well met," the words fell thickly from the dead Otike ambassador's mouth.

'*Well met,*' Shari sent back. The thought of even trying to speak was too much.

Zirgha grinned, a rictus of blackened teeth in a slack-jawed mouth.

'*Where am I?*' Shari tried.

'*Safe. You were hurt.*' Zirgha's send was far less disjointed than her speech.

Shari wasn't sure if she should be grateful or horrified.

Something about the whole situation niggled at her. Reaching out, she brushed her Innarn against the Otike. Feeling weaker than before, Shari watched in fascinated horror as the skin of Zirgha's face knitted itself back together.

She smiled down at Shari, who flinched.

'*Must heal.*' The words had an odd, song-like lilt to them. '*Rest.*'

Mind swirling, Shari's eyes slid closed without her permission.

'*Rest.*'

The whisper brushed against her mind. Sleep took over, and Shari knew no more.

Lissae

Inthday

Second day of the first week of Hazelcrown

Tania huffed, blowing her fringe away from her face.

The hair fell back into her eyes.

Sighing in frustration, she leaned over the map of the Deep Ocean, her gaze tracing Zana's finger as Rakemyst's Linked pointed out their path.

All four Linked of the joined islands had convened in the garden on Cantash as they tried to plan for the next joining. The mood was more sombre than any of the others Tania had been involved with so far, despite their beautiful surroundings.

The map was spread out over a slab of rock. They perched on boulders, staring at the parchment as if they could will it to change. Vibrant green grass smelled sweet beneath their feet, and the delicate twinkle of birdsong was soothing, if they weren't trying to figure out if they could get to the next island before another attack happened.

"Ginorti is still several days' travel away. We need to ensure we're prepared for anything once we arrive," Cyrus, Talhan's Linked, said.

"What does *anything* look like?" Tania wondered out loud.

"More fighting, probably," Cantash's Linked, Fenix, replied.

Zana straightened. "I am concerned that Ginorti has ceased calling for help."

"Maybe it means that he's okay?" Tania offered, plucking at a loose thread on the hem of her shirt. She believed that as much as the others, if their doubtful expressions were anything to go by.

"I'm more worried that Ginorti's Linked hasn't reached out to us," Fenix said. "I'm often in contact with him, and there's been no word since his isle stopped crying for help."

"Do you think something's happened to him?" Tania asked. She hated how her voice sounded so small.

Cyrus wrapped a comforting arm around her. "If it has, we'll put it right."

"Can't we just shift there?" Tania asked.

"Shifting blind is a dangerous thing," Zana said. "You could end up buried, as part of a wall, or at the crushing bottom of the ocean."

Tania sighed. "I wish Shari was back. Maybe she could convince the Guardian to use their Time Innarn to speed things up for us."

"We can't always rely on them," Zana said. "They have their strengths, but we have our own."

"I know." Tania looked away, catching sight of a draci in flight. The tiny dragon landed in a tree and used sharp claws to scramble higher until it hid in the leaves. "I guess I'm not feeling particularly strong right now."

"We all have days where strong feels hard. And staying in bed sounds like the perfect option," Fenix said. "But we have to keep going."

Tania nodded. "What happens if Ginorti's Linked isn't there for the joining?"

"Then we'll plan it with the elders," Zana said.

Fenix and Cyrus groaned.

Nodding, Tania ignored the heavy feeling in her chest that warned her something was terribly wrong.

"I'll have the Ilutri scout ahead and see if they can discover what has happened." Zana was looking at the map, the picture of calm. Only her trembling Innarn let the others know how concerned she was.

Shivering, Tania wrapped her arms around herself and quietly sighed. If Zana was worried, they all should be.

"How are the refugees from the mainlands settling in?" Fenix asked, trying to lift the mood of the group.

"Settling in surprisingly well," Zana said.

"Any issues with the locals?" Cyrus asked. "We've had a few who haven't been super impressed."

"The Ilutri have been fine. None of the refugees can get to their homes," Zana said. A brief frown marred her face.

"What's wrong?" Tania asked.

"The only place they can really get to is the tower. Many are showing up each day, asking to do work in exchange for food or goods. They seem offended when we just give it to them."

"These are proud people, who have been displaced at least twice. Some of their stories are heart-wrenching," Fenix said. "We must practice listening and have patience with them."

"We could all do with a dose of that," Tania said.

CHAPTER THREE

Zuefie

Shari blinked into consciousness.

Her gaze landed on a pale, blue-skinned being, whose four eyes only showed the whites, their body contorted in a rictus of pain. Clouds flashing different colours streamed over the being as they lay on the stone slab next to hers.

Holding still, Shari darted glances around, trying to figure out what was going on. As the clouds continued to stream past her neighbour, blue skin turned grey, and slowly, they went ashen; the life drained out of them.

'*Bring in the next.*'

The voice reminded Shari of far-off thunder, the kind that you felt through your feet before you heard the sound. It was close, but with all the clouds around, she couldn't make out the speaker.

Zirgha jerked into the room, a body too large for her to carry held in her arms.

Shari slid her eyes closed and watched the Otike ambassador from between her lashes. As Zirgha got closer, Shari wished she could create a shield around her mouth and nose. The stench of death was overpowering.

The body of her neighbour was shoved unceremoniously to the side, and a large being with peachy skin and pointed ears was dropped onto the slab in its place.

Groaning, the being opened their eyes. "Where am I?"

Shari couldn't place the accent and tried to mentally flick through the handbook to figure out where this being was from.

A cloud too dense to see through drifted closer. 'Welcome.' The voice was the same as the one she'd heard before. 'We wish to honour your sacrifice.'

"Sacrifice?" The being sat up and glanced around, his gaze landing heavily on her unmoving form. "Like her sacrifice?"

'Oh no. You are not worth nearly as much as she is,' the cloud said.

Talking clouds. There's a new one. The small, unterrified part of Shari's brain chattered at her.

The being seemed to be offended by this. "I'm not worth as much as… Do you know who I am? Lord Telnarik, leader of Sentinel Division of the Shiovion."

Shiovion, a Light Realm in the third band. One step higher than Jonathan had ever let her go. Was that where they were?

'We care not for your rank, or your Realm. We only want one thing.' The cloud drifted closer to the Shiovionian, looming menacingly over him. 'To feed.'

'Feed?'

For a moment, Shari thought there was an echo. The other clouds glided nearer and seemed to tremble. If they had been humanoid, she would say that it was in anticipation.

'Lord Telnarik, your sacrifice is honoured.' The larger cloud lifted, and the others descended upon the unfortunate lord.

Shari watched in horror as he got to his feet and ran, the clouds chasing after him. She sat up on the slab, idly noting the clank of chains, but too enthralled with Telnarik's attempted escape to do much about them.

He didn't get far. Once he reached the crumbling outer walls of what once would have been a castle, or a temple of some sort, he was swathed in mist from his pursuers.

That's when the screaming started.

'*Brilliant, aren't they?*' Thunder rumbled right next to her.

Something about this place was making her lose all sense of herself. "I'm not sure what I'm seeing, to be honest."

'*A small sacrifice for the continuation of a species.*'

"Isn't a sacrifice willingly made?" Shari asked lightly. She could feel moisture and weight over her right shoulder. It took everything she had not to turn her head.

'*Only by those who matter.*'

Biting hard enough to draw blood, Shari counted to ten before she dared to answer. "And who matters?"

'*The Xanderri.*'

"Anyone else?"

'*You.*'

She didn't feel particularly flattered. "Why me?"

'*Once we harvest all the Innarn trapped inside your fragile human shell, the Xanderri will break free of our exile and feed until we are satiated.*'

"When will that be?"

The cloud laughed. '*When we overtake Lissae.*'

Not that she needed another reason to escape, but that was a good one.

The screams had stopped, and Shari looked dumbly at the crumpled pile of the former Lord Telnarik.

"Why did you need him?"

'We find you are too Dark for our tastes.'

The weight lifted off her shoulder, and Shari sucked in a breath.

'Finished?'

The clouds drifted closer, tiny lines of lightning flicking between them, and they hummed.

'Sleep now, Altoriae. The time for your sacrifice will come.'

Shari clenched her jaw to stop it from chattering. She'd never felt more terrified in her life. Slowly, she lay down and closed her eyes, intending to feign sleep.

Her last thought before she drifted off was of wondering how she was meant to fight a cloud.

Lissae

Kerday

Third day of the first week of Hazelcrown

Jonathan slammed through the double doors of the Portal and strode through the halls, a scowl on his face.

'You will not find her like this,' Pala sent.

Glancing down, he glared at the diminutive Ducibus as ze glided serenely alongside him. "Well, I'm not going to find her at all if I stay on Lissae, am I?"

'The Altoriae is out of our reach.'

Jonathan sucked in a breath and ran a hand over his face. He wanted to stomp and growl and demand to know where in the Realms Shari could be, but that hadn't worked for him the last few times he'd tried. Samuel had been denied too and worked out his frustrations by tearing through the Dark Realms one by one, searching for any sign of her. The

Ducibus letting his apprentice do that when he wasn't allowed in the Light Realms was suspicious though.

"Can't you just tell me where she is?" he begged.

'*You know we can't. We are guides and have sworn to uphold our duties, as have you.*'

"She's *missing*, Pala. Did she leave of her own free will?"

The Ducibus shifted uncomfortably. Another one of his race joined them. This one taller than Lissae's sentinel.

"Where did you trace her last in the Portal?"

'*Just outside Lissae,*' another Ducibus, one he was sure he hadn't met before, said. This one's robes were the same shade as Pala's, but there was something wispy about them, as if they were made from pure Innarn and not cloth.

"How could she be just outside Lissae? If she was so close, she would have just shifted to safety," Jonathan said, frustrated.

'*Shifted. Yeah, maybe she did that,*' the new Ducibus sent.

There was an expectant silence.

Jonathan scowled.

'*I swear you're usually quicker than this.*' The Ducibus snorted and looked away.

There was an odd familiarity with this Ducibus. Jonathan felt like he could almost put a name to the cloaked figure, but it was stuck on the tip of his tongue. "Do I know you?"

Pala stepped between them. '*Think, Guardian.*'

"She could have shifted. But didn't. She *was* shifted. Against her will."

'*Obviously.*'

The Guardian had the impression that the new Ducibus didn't seem to know if he should laugh or roll his eyes.

"Well, we figured that. But where? The only thing you'll tell me is that she's at the gateway you don't guard."

'*Why would we not guard a gateway?*' the new one asked and yelped as a flash of Innarn streaked out and hit him. Jonathan had a glimpse of hazel eyes before the Innarn cloak fluttered back into place.

"Because it's dangerous. Why would a gateway be dangerous?" Jonathan thought aloud. "You guarded Altum, and Lissae, and a bunch of others that offer death as a main course."

'*Think, Guardian,*' the new Ducibus said.

Pala sent another streak of Innarn at him, and he yelped and skittered away, reminding Jonathan painfully of Mitch.

"If those on the other side of the gateway would hurt you, then you wouldn't guard it." Jonathan looked down a branch of the Ducibus' Hall and at the endless doors with their tiny sentinels next to them. "Guess I'll just have to find the one with no Ducibus standing guard."

He sighed and turned back to Lissae.

With all these doors, he was going to need help.

Zuefie

'*Are all Altoriaes so lazy? All she does is sleep,*' a youthful voice was complaining.

'*I don't think she has a choice.*' This one was older, but still sounded unsure.

'*I really don't want to be sleeping all the time,*' Shari grumbled. Stretching, she took stock of her body.

It felt like she was surrounded by a furnace, moments away from the flames engulfing her. The very air was hot and harsh against her skin.

'Where am I?'

'Zuefie,' the older voice said.

Shari scrunched up her eyes, her mind finally connecting the voice with the black Q'Aralide Samuel called hatchling. *'Jetonyx?'*

'Ah, so your head is working,' the hatchling said drolly.

'Feels... scrambled.'

'Well, unscramble. We need to save the egg.' It was the younger voice. Tormorylth.

'Egg?'

Before the hatchlings could answer, Shari felt moisture seeping into her clothing. Expecting to feel relief from the endless heat, she opened her eyes, only to be engulfed in fog and screaming.

'Still too Dark?' the cloud that rumbled like thunder asked.

The fog lifted away from her. Whimpering.

Drained, Shari wondered if they were doing something to her head to make everything feel like it was wrapped in wool.

'Mirror shield.' Jetonyx's send felt like he was trying to yell from the other end of the Realms.

Slowly, Shari pushed her Innarn out, creating the shield she used for so much of her childhood.

Another fog bank engulfed her.

The shield faltered. Shari reached out with her Innarn, hissing at how Light everything around her was. Gritting her teeth, she gathered it anyway, and fed it into the shield.

'Feeding from this one is hard work.' The send wasn't quite as rumbly as the thundercloud, but it still bounced around her head enough to make it ache.

'Rest. We must find another sacrifice from a lower level.' Thunder rumbled.

Before the draining fog could move away, Shari sucked a bit more Innarn out of them to power the mirror shield.

The hatchlings cheering her on were clearer now.

'What's going on?'

'You thought meat eaters were bad,' Jetonyx sent, his voice trembling. 'These are Innarn feeders. They suck the Innarn right out of you until there's nothing left.'

A flash of blue skin turning grey made Shari shudder. 'And they're gathering others from Lighter Realms until they, what? Develop enough of a tolerance to drain me as well?'

'I think so.' Jetonyx's send faded, but it didn't stop the muddy concern colouring his words from reaching her.

Gritting her teeth, Shari waited until the fog and the clouds disappeared. She didn't know how she was going to get out of this. But she had to, for the sake of the hatchlings.

Lissae

Kerday

Third day of the first week of Hazelcrown

Wolf grinned at Belfar as his mate tightened the last strap of his chest plate.

"Are we ready?" he asked.

Belfar nodded. "We should be good to go."

"I really don't like leaving Rakemyst unprotected," Varlee said, scowling into the predawn sky.

"The Linked spoke to the elders, and they've given their orders," Wolf said. "Ginorti needs our help."

"With the Returned here, Rakemyst will be fine. The wall Collis built could withstand an attack from the Altoriae herself!" Charin said, loading the last of his arrows into his quiver.

The smile slid from his face, and Wolf caught Belfar's worried glance.

They were of the few who knew that Shari was missing. For all that his niece was more than capable of looking after herself, Wolf couldn't help but worry. He'd fought with the Guardian to be one of the members who were looking for her but was denied.

Shari was important, but so were the beings on Ginorti. And with the island himself asking for help, it was vital that they answered the call.

"Let's go," Wolf said.

"Flying or shifting?" Varlee asked.

"We fly down to the base of the tower and Aharny is shifting us out. We'll be on Ginorti in moments, ready to help protect him," Belfar said.

"Perfect." The quicker they secured Ginorti, the sooner he could bring his niece home.

Shari's Sanctuary

Inside the Altoriae's pocket Realm, Jetonyx and Tormorylth looked at each other as another tree flickered and faded from view.

Each moment they spent here, another piece of the pocket Realm disappeared.

He just hoped that Shari could get out of Zuefie before they vanished as well.

Chapter Four

Lissae

Narday

Fourth day of the first week of Hazelcrown

Arilla carefully folded the cloth she'd been wiping the counter with and placed it to the side when Samuel came through the doors of the Quiver and Quill Tavern. She grabbed Calem's arm before her husband could round the counter.

He waited, muscles tense, until the Guardian's Apprentice stood opposite them. "You said you'd keep her safe."

"I did," Samuel said, golden eyes flashing.

Calem leaned forwards. "Then where is she?"

Opening his mouth, Samuel then closed it with a snap. "She... was right next to me. And then..."

Arilla willed away the tears that threatened to fall. It had been five days since Shari had gone missing. "Do you have any idea?"

"I've been scouring the Dark Realms. There's no sign of her. They barely noticed her at the conclave." He ran a hand through his hair and scowled.

"You promised," Calem growled.

"And you swore to keep her safe before she was even born. Yet here we are," Samuel drawled.

Calem banged his hands on the counter and leaned forward, drawing the attention of some of their closer customers.

The two men stared at each other intently, Calem curling his hands into a fist, knuckles white against his tanned skin. Samuel scoffed and rolled his eyes.

Sighing, Arilla picked up the cloth and started furiously wiping the counter again. *Let the Innarnians have their chat*, she thought viciously.

"I promised to keep her safe," he said. "And I will do everything I can to find her," Samuel growled.

"The Guardian says she's not on the Dark Realms," Calem shot back.

A lesser being would have thrown their hands in the air. Samuel simply scowled and turned, stomping his way through the maze of tables and slamming the door open.

If they didn't find Shari soon, she was going to look for her daughter.

Alone.

Zuefie

Shari waited until nightfall, hoping the clouds would sleep.

She should have known better.

The light of the four moons threw strange shadows across the vine-covered ruins. After slipping from the hard slab she'd been laying on for far too long, Shari crept towards the crumbling walls and grasped onto a handy vine. Carefully lowering herself down the wall, she slid into the surrounding jungle.

Slowly, she made her way through the thick vegetation. It was oddly silent—no birds calling out, or insects chattering, or rustling from nocturnal animals. Feeling clumsy from lack of movement for Lissae knew how long, Shari forced herself to go slower.

'Do you know where you're going?' Jetonyx sent.

'Away from the place they were planning to sacrifice me?' Shari shot back.

'Head for the gateway,' the hatchling advised.

'That would be great if I knew which direction it was in,' Shari sent. Flicking out the smallest tendril of Innarn she could, she sent it towards the gateway and cursed. She'd been travelling in the wrong direction.

Biting her lip, she contemplated going back through the ruins or circling around.

Squinting into the jungle, Shari started moving again, and swore when she tripped over a branch. It would be much easier if the clouds weren't covering the moon.

A sound like thunder rattled her bones.

'Going somewhere?'

"Just taking in the sights," Shari said.

The noise rose and swelled around her, loud enough that Shari feared it was possible to shatter bone just through sounds.

'We're happy to show you the sights, Altoriae.'

Thunder had never felt so ominous.

Lissae

Rasshday

Fifth day of the first week of Hazelcrown

Thunder rumbled, shaking the castle.

Raven looked up, barely able to count to three before lightning flashed, bright enough to be blinding. He glanced at the other members of the Altoriae's Guild, most of whom had their eyes trained on the ceiling as well.

"Have you ever heard a storm so fierce?" Talofa asked.

"The islands are angry," Elani said, strapping another dagger to her thigh.

"Angry?" The Uleulan looked every bit the child she was, rather than the fierce fighter of the guild Raven knew her to be.

"Missing Altoriae, attacks on one of their own. Angry, sad, it doesn't matter. But it'll affect the weather." Elani seemed unaffected, but Raven caught her slight flinch as thunder shook the sky again.

"Are we searching for Shari again?"

"Splitting in two. Some will stay on Lissae, shifting to Ginorti to help shore up his defences. The rest are going to scour the Portal with the Guardian," Asterion said, steam puffing from his nose as lightning crackled straight outside the window.

Raven smoothed down the fine hairs on his arms and stood. "Let's go then." He nodded at Elani, who was leading the searching party, and joined Asterion with those who would keep the islands safe.

He half wondered who had the worse job, but then the Realm twisted around him and he was standing in a forest. Taking a breath to centre himself, Raven could taste the decaying leaf matter and the dampness of the soil. Time of day was hard to discover when they were in the middle of the forest. Birds and insects rustled in the leaves, and Raven took the next breath to remind himself that the forest, at least, was at peace.

"You've arrived." The speaker was a broad satyr who carried even more knives than Elani.

"Well met, General Morrow," Asterion said, bowing his head.

This was Lissae's most feared general, next to the Altoriae. Morrow had protected the borders of Ginorti and some of the other islands, both Shifting and Fixed, for longer than Raven had been alive. He'd staved off the previous attack from the mainlanders, but when he'd found Ginorti's Linked missing, the General contacted the elders from the other islands to ask for reinforcements.

"Head for the shore. The Ilutri scouts have reported that the mainlanders' ships are returning." The satyr was no nonsense, not even baulking at the sight of a minotaur on his hallowed grounds.

Asterion nodded and guided them to their assigned post, where their group joined the satyrian army.

Rubbing away the bumps on his arms, Raven worked to keep the grin from his face. He'd always wanted to be part of the crack troops, but never thought he'd have the chance.

"Ready!"

Eyes snapping to the growing black cloud of the mainlanders' fleet in the distance, his smile disappeared.

They had an island to protect.

Zuefie

Jetonyx watched, helpless, as their host was recaptured.

The Innarn feeders led Shari back to the ruins and wrapped something around her ankles that made the Altoriae scream.

Another tree flickered and vanished.

Tormorylth huddled against Jetonyx's side, and the older hatchling draped his wing over her.

'What can we do to help her?' Tormorylth asked, looking up at him with wide eyes.

Jetonyx sighed. '*I'm not sure.*'

She fiddled with the cuff the Altoriae had given her, and Jetonyx's gaze snapped to it, unseeing.

'*How did the Altoriae say that worked?*' he asked.

'*She didn't.*'

'*Take it off?*' Jetonyx tried to order her, but with those enormous eyes still imploring him, the demand turned to a question.

Slowly, Tormorylth raised a claw to her forearm and slid the cuff off. As soon as the silver band was free of her flesh, she hissed, her hide gently smoking.

Hastily, Jetonyx crafted a crude shield around her. The younger hatchling sighed in relief.

'*Maybe it blocks Light Innarn?*' Tormorylth asked.

'*Shari could use it on Altum as well.*' Jetonyx frowned down at the unassuming bit of jewellery.

'*Extremes of Innarn then.*' The younger hatchling plopped to her hindquarters, one claw coming out to tap at the metal band.

Sparks sprang from her and sunk into the cuff.

Jetonyx's eyes widened. '*Did it just... absorb Innarn?*'

'*How should I know?*' Tormorylth muttered, flopping forward to rest her chin on her claws.

Humming, he sent a pulse of Innarn at the cuff and smiled grimly as it got soaked up by the cuff. '*What if... what if we feed this thing with as much Dark Innarn as we can and give it to Shari? The clouds keep complaining that she's too Dark. Maybe this will make her feel Darker?*'

'*And then they won't eat her!*' The tiny one brightened for a moment. '*But I don't have Innarn.*'

'*Well, it's up to me then, isn't it?*' he asked. Without waiting for a response, Jetonyx started blasting the cuff with everything he had.

He just hoped it would be enough.

CHAPTER FIVE

Lissae

ollis looked at the rest of the Returned and nodded at the Travel Innarnian.

"You're the fifth lot bound for Ginorti today," the man said, rubbing a button on his coat pocket with his thumb. "Bit of bad news, Oakley going missing and all that."

Smiling tightly, Collis said, "Ginorti's lost Linked is why we're going to help."

"Ah!" The man clapped his hands together. "No point in delaying any longer then!" The Travel Innarnian started weaving the ball of Air he used to lift them up to the base of the slipstream. "Ready?"

"Yes, sir," Collis said.

"Here you go."

His feet lifted off the ground, and Collis shot towards the slipstream. The suction drew him in, and he got about a body length from Ronah's shore when he was yanked to a standstill.

There were some choice words used from the shore, shouted loud enough for him to make them out as he hovered above everyone. Glancing down, Collis wished he hadn't included the jagged rocks along the former beach when he'd created the wall.

Suddenly, something shoved him from behind. Collis was propelled forward again, only for his Innarn to flare out, bright and hard, pulling him back towards Ronah.

There was a panicked yell, and a pained scream from below, and the slipstream failed.

Windmilling his arms, Collis plummeted towards the pointed rocks. A flare of green shot out of the ground and scooped him up like a giant hand, setting him down gently next to the rest of the Returned.

"What happened?" he asked.

Silently, Remmy pointed towards the smouldering Travel Innarnian. "Someone doesn't want you to leave their island."

Collis gave Remmy an incredulous look.

"Not him," Remmy said. "Ronah, or your soul-match."

The Travel Innarnian whimpered as someone doused him with a jet of Water to try and stop the embers from catching alight.

"Are you saying Ronah did this?"

Remmy laughed. "No, Collis. Your Innarn did this."

Sucking in a horrified breath, Collis turned to the others. "Find another Travel Innarnian. I'll take him to the Healers Centre."

"I'll help," Remmy said.

"Go. We'll be fine," one of the others said.

Carefully, Collis took hold of the Travel Innarnian's arm and shifted the three of them to the Healers Centre.

"What happened here?" the healer who rushed out to greet them asked.

Rubbing the back of his neck, Collis stammered for an answer and found he had none.

"Innarn flare," Remmy said, bumping his shoulder hard.

Looking over at his patient, the healer tsked. He glanced up at Collis and asked, "You?"

Collis nodded glumly.

Zuefie

Shari groaned and rolled her head.

It felt like it weighed more than Ronah.

'*Shari.*'

Someone was calling her name again, but the fog surrounding her made it hard to concentrate.

There was a sucking sensation around her middle and a shriek loud enough to make her cover her ears, despite her hands weighing more than the Shifting Islands combined.

At least there was no one to watch as she almost punched herself in the face.

The giggle inside her head dampened that thought.

'*Shari!*' The giggler was sending to her.

Shari blinked as the fog drifted away from her.

Free from its clingy grasp, her memories came back quicker. *Innarn eaters. Hatchlings. Escaping through the jungle.*

'*We have a plan,*' Jetonyx sent.

Happy she could remember his name, Shari was also worried about what the two hatchlings were planning.

'*Trust us,*' Jetonyx soothed.

Movement caught her attention, and Shari lazily rolled her head to the side.

Zirgha was jerking her way across the ruins.

Shari did her best not to flinch as the corpse collapsed to the floor and a white mist drifted out of it.

"What are you?" she hissed.

'*We are the Xanderri,*' the cloud whispered. '*And you will join us.*'

Thick fog engulfed the Altoriae. Moisture clung to every part of her body, getting up her nose, in her mouth, and soaking her ears.

Gagging, Shari leaned over the slab she was chained to and retched. Her Innarn pulsed out, slamming into the cloud, and set the atoms alight.

Shrieking, louder than before, filled her ears as they cleared of the fluid.

Clouds were flickering, hastening away from the ruins, until the red-hot sun was scorching her skin once more.

Shari had never been so glad to be burning.

Lissae

Vebaday

Sixth day of the first week of Hazelcrown

'*Apprentice. The attack on Ginorti has started.*'

Samuel sighed. '*On my way,*' he sent, shifting to Asterion's side.

Jonathan had banished him from the search for Shari once they'd cleared everything below Lissae. Despite it being only two days, it felt like he'd been resting on his laurels for an eternity. Given the chance to fight, well. How could he say no?

Arriving at the minotaur's side, he nodded as Asterion gripped the handle on his great axe tighter and scowled at the hazy outline of the battalion of ships. They were standing in a grove of trees on the headland. The grass underfoot smelled sweet compared to the bloodshed that would follow. Salt air stung his face as he stepped closer to the edge.

Asterion nodded grimly to Samuel. "Apprentice, meet General Morrow, leader of the satyrian crack troops of Ginorti. General Morrow, this is the Guardian's Apprentice, Samuel."

The two nodded at each other before Samuel turned and looked out at the ocean again. "Looks like they regrouped," Samuel said.

"Which can mean nothing good." The general shook his head. "They sank our ships last time. I'll not have them do it again."

Samuel raised a brow. "Can't you just move them?"

"They're ringing Ginorti."

What was their intent? Surely, if they had enough vessels to surround an entire island, they would have to have some serious firepower to back it up.

"Incoming!" someone shouted from farther down the beach.

Raising his gaze as a thick, arrow-like object streaked through the sky and bounced harmlessly off the wards surrounding Ginorti before falling into the water.

He grinned.

"They'll have to try harder than that!" the satyr laughed. "With the help of the Altoriae's Guild, we've strengthened the wards around our fair isle. Nothing can get through them."

Others around them were cheering, and a few yelled obscenities at their water-bound foes.

Samuel frowned. He had a feeling they were in for a lot more than one big stick being thrown at a wall.

Another oversized arrow shot across the sky, but when this one hit the wards, they shattered like a crystallised spiderweb.

The beach fell silent.

"What just happened?" someone whispered from down the line.

Stretching out his Innarn, Samuel frowned. "They've neutralised the wards."

"Neutralised?" General Morrow asked.

Something whistled as it flew. Samuel tracked its progress, jaw dropping as the ballista split apart, a huge net jumping out of the missile and plummeting heavily onto a group of fighters.

"What are they trying to do?" Asterion asked as they rushed to aid the trapped satyrs.

"Capture or incapacitate the fighters," Samuel said, attempting to slash through the thick rope with his Innarn and failing. "Asterion, break that open," he ordered, pointing at one of the dull, grey balls tied to the edges of the net.

The minotaur did as he'd asked, cracking the ball with a single swing of his axe.

Inside, orange crystal glinted maliciously.

"They've made some sort of Innarn dampener." Samuel scowled and changed a hand into a claw. It slid through the rope like butter.

"But..."

Another ballista screamed through the air. Before the net could untangle, a boulder smashed into the missile, shattering the grey, weighted balls and sending shards of crystal plummeting to the ground.

Samuel flung a shield up.

The crystal tore straight through it, the shards embedding in sand and flesh alike.

Screams sounded as more nets were descending. Fighters who'd relied on Innarn all their lives were crumbling under the weight of not being able to use it.

Panic set in, the fighters started tearing at the thick ropes with bare hands, their eyes wide and frantic.

"Anyone with a blade, cut them out!" Samuel roared. He scrambled around the net, looking at the weights.

Hidden in the tree line, satyrs and other Innarnians continued to shatter the missiles, cracking the Innarn-dampening balls.

With each shower of orange crystal, he shared a sharp, worried look with Asterion. Troops around them were falling to the ground, pain from the crystal and loss of their Innarn tearing through their bodies.

"I don't know how to stop this," Asterion grunted, using the head of his axe to bat away a hunk of glowing rock.

"I have an idea," Samuel said.

The island beneath them groaned with pain, and the satyrs on the beach crumbled as Ginorti's moan continued.

Asterion turned to him. "Better do it quick."

Zuefie

'We have to act now, while they're gone,' Jetonyx sent.

Tormorylth trembled, the silver cuff held tightly in her claw.

'I have the shield around you. You'll be safe.' He could only hope he wasn't lying.

Settling down on his haunches, Jetonyx sent the same message repeatedly. 'Shari! Open your pocket Realm. Just enough for a claw to get through.'

He ignored the pulsing squeeze that accompanied every disappearing tree now, and kept sending.

The tiny hatchling gasped, and Jetonyx opened his eyes. In front of him was a tiny portal, barely big enough for one of his claws.

And only just big enough for Tormorylth to push the cuff through.

'*Catch, Shari,*' he ordered, and nodded at the hatchling.

Stepping towards the glowing portal, Tormorylth shoved her claw into the hole, cuff grasped tightly. Hissing, she flinched.

Jetonyx's shield was faltering.

'*Hurry! Take it!*'

There was another squeezing sensation, and Tormorylth screamed.

Jetonyx's eyes widened in horror. There was stump where Tormorylth's claw had been.

'*Sorry, sorry, sorry,*' Shari was sending, her voice weaker with each repetition.

Ignoring the Altoriae, Jetonyx did the only thing he could.

He pulled a scale from his own forearm and slapped it over the bleeding stump.

The hatchlings drew together, crooning in a vain attempt to ease their pain.

Lissae

Captain Rappen gripped the edge of the railing and leaned forward, grinning viciously.

The aberrations on the beach were scrambling, but it didn't matter. All they needed was a few to remain trapped in the nets and they'd be able to take more unwilling test subjects back to Jinkor.

"Fire!" he called, and the command was repeated by the closest ships, echoing to all the vessels surrounding the Shifting Island.

This hunk of sentient dirt was about to become his.

Zuefie

Looking at the tiny claw clasping the silver cuff that was laying in her lap, Shari shuddered.

Gagging, she pried the cuff free of the limb and gently placed it to the side where the acidic blood wouldn't eat through her skin.

'*Sorry, sorry, sorry,*' Shari sobbed. '*I'll get Temira to make you a new claw. A stronger claw. You'll be whole again. Won't she, Temira?*'

'Shari?'

The Light Innarn chains clanked and scorched her ankles when she jumped. 'Temira?'

'*Where are you?*'

Pushing her view towards the Technomancer felt like the hardest thing in the Realms.

'*Stay strong. We're coming for you.*'

'No! Temira, you can't! The Xanderri... they're Innarn eaters.'

'*Xanderri?*'

And Shari's mind turned blissfully blank as the fog descended around her once again.

Lissae

Temira carefully guided the femto-crystals towards their chamber. This was the last lot to be tested for contamination from the Crystal Intelligence, and she was not about to...

'*... won't she, Temira?*'

'Shari?' Temira's head snapped up, her hands freezing into position. It would not do to misstep at this stage of the delicate procedure.

'*Temira?*' The Altoriae sounded like she was at the far edges of the Realms.

'*Where are you?*' Temira sent, pushing against Cyrus's shields. She didn't dare move, not with the potentially contaminated crystal in her hands.

Visions of ancient ruins, thick jungle, and dense clouds filled her head.

'*Stay strong. We're coming for you.*'

The link between their minds flickered. '*No... Xanderri... Innarn eaters.*'

A chill chased down Temira's spine. The Xanderri were stuff of childhood nightmares. The creatures hiding under your pallet, ready to suck the Innarn from misbehaving younglings.

Surely, they aren't real?

The connection faded, and Temira swore. Carefully, she put the femto-crystals back into their container.

"You yelled?" Cyrus said, striding into the lab with his hands in his pockets.

"We need to speak with the Guardian. Now."

CHAPTER SIX

Zuefie

Shari forced herself to watch as another sacrifice was drained in front of her.

They were lined up, one after the other. On the Xanderri's command, their new food sources were chained to slabs that had been pulled from the ruins with their own Innarn.

Beings of all types and sizes stood between her and the ravenous clouds.

She had never felt so hopeless in all her life.

'*Help me,*' the being next to her whimpered, leaning towards her for the little comfort she could offer.

What is a wikkur doing so high up in the Light Realms? Shari wondered. Through the fog in her head, she felt like she knew him.

'*Oh, you are helping. You are preparing the Xanderri for the greatest feast of all. The Altoriae.*'

Shari hated that cloud with a passion.

'*The Altoriae?*' The whisper passed along the prisoners, many of them glancing around.

What struck Shari as odd was the absolute fear in their voices.

'*Surely you have heard of her? Lissae's greatest villain? Slaughterer of innocents? The one who turns your dreams into nightmares?*' Thunder rumbled like laughter.

Something hard settled in the pit of her stomach. She'd *never* killed innocent beings.

'*Don't believe you,*' a being three up from her dared to send.

'*Why not? She's right here.*' The dense cloud drifted until it was floating in front of her.

Her tripedal neighbour flinched away, whimpering when the chains around his ankles clanked at the movement. "No," he whispered.

"I don't…"

"It's true then?" someone farther down the line asked. "You're the Altoriae?"

"Yes, but…"

"I'd sacrifice myself to see you dead," the man spat.

Shari blanched. "I've never…"

Others joined his cry, calling on the Xanderri to drain them.

Thunder rolled through her bones as Shari let the first tears fall.

Lissae

Vebaday

Sixth day of the first week of Hazelcrown

It had been mere minutes since the nets had started falling, and no matter how fast they cut through the ropes, more came flying to trap them.

An Ilutri screamed as his wings got tangled in a rope, and he plummeted to the ground.

Samuel growled as he cut the winged man free. "Don't get close to them!"

Dazed, the Ilutri struggled free of the ropes and shook his feathers out. Samuel had saved Shari's uncle from the net.

"Perhaps we should call on the Kumaru," Wolf coughed.

"The tree beings?" Samuel asked.

"I wouldn't let them hear you say that," General Morrow said. "Ginorti is the resting place for the Kumaru Elders. They'd only awaken when the situation is hopeless."

Glancing around as yet more of their people dropped from the crystal shards, Ginorti constantly whimpering beneath their feet and in their minds, Samuel scowled. "It's looking pretty hopeless right now."

"Lissaens are tougher than you think," General Morrow said, blasting a net off course without looking. "Think you can keep me from getting tangled?"

Samuel smirked at him. "I can do you one better." He stood with his back to the general, arms spread, and allowed the scales resting just under his skin free rein, delighting in the stretch and burn of assuming his natural form.

Lifting his head, he roared.

The beach fell silent, and the ships seemed to quiver.

'*Asterion, protect the general. I'm going to cause some trouble.*' Without waiting for an answer, Sanithane took to the skies.

As he winged away, he heard the general say, "Glad he's on our side."

Flying faster than the mainlanders could shoot, he soared between the ships, releasing great clouds of poisonous breath.

If he imagined every sailor who fell before him as the one who took the Altoriae, well, who was to know?

With a gap in their attackers' forces, Sanithane landed on a ship. As big as it was, it listed heavily under his bulk.

'*Who do we have here then?*' he asked, looking over at the next vessel.

A man in a tight, blue jacket with cream breeches glared back at him as he pointed and shouted something, his words lost to the wind. Not to those aboard, apparently—they scrambled to do his bidding.

Sanithane stepped closer, wooden boards creaking under his weight. 'So, *you're the cause of all this trouble,*' he rumbled. He took in the blue eyes and tightly bound blond hair. He was muscled enough to be dangerous in a fight, or delicious in a stew.

Sanithane bared his fangs. Right now, he'd prefer to grapple instead of eat.

There was a certain satisfaction to be had when the blue-coated man's voice trembled as he yelled a final command. A net launched. Leaping backwards, Sanithane pushed the ship he was on towards the blue-coat's vessel and laughed as their net fell short. Shooting into the air, he breathed out and the sailors fell to the deck, downed by the poisoned gas.

The man in blue, however, was cannier than Sanithane had given him credit for. He leaped over the side and surfaced from the water next to the ship, scowling up at the golden shape above.

Pausing, Sanithane had the feeling that he could end things right now. If he ripped this pathetic human in two, the mainlanders would stop without their commander, and he'd be able to...

These are not my thoughts. Scowling, Sanithane shook his head and pulled away from the dangerous man cutting through the waves. He hovered, debating if he should bring blue-coat to shore and let the satyrs have their fun. But with the tempting thought still resonating in his head, Sanithane dared not.

Whatever the blue-coat was, he wasn't a Blank.

Winging back to the shore, Sanithane reverted to his squishy form, and lost himself in the crowd, giving himself time to ignore the words still swirling through his head. Winding his way through the fighters, Samuel finally came to the general.

"Bought you some time," he said, knuckles white around the hilt of a black dagger.

"Could have finished them, you know," Asterion rumbled.

"Thought I'd give the rest of you a chance," he drawled, locking up the memory of the voice that wanted him to rip them all apart.

Zuefie

'I do hope you're watching, Altoriae.'

Hearing her title being rumbled by the leader of the Innarn eaters turned Shari's stomach.

Listening to the screams of their latest victim made her gag, but there was nothing left to bring up.

'Did you really think that you were doing the right thing, with all that fighting?' The Xanderri leader was like a palon with a bone, and he wasn't about to leave it alone anytime soon.

'I keep Lissae safe,' Shari gasped.

'At what cost?'

Her leathers would be perpetually wet after this, she decided. Anything to get her mind off the loathing looks and desperate screams.

Turning her head away from the dense cloud by her side meant facing those who'd rather sacrifice themselves than be in her presence.

It also meant that she caught sight of the mist floating from her neighbour's nose.

The same sort of mist that had escaped Zirgha before she'd collapsed.

It's not real, Shari realised. *The Xanderri are making them say those things.*

'Then fight them,' Jetonyx called from deep within her mind.

Steeling herself, Shari nodded.

Lissae

The Kumaru were a force to be reckoned with.

Samuel remembered Haran—a former candidate for the Guardian's Apprentice—a tall, barky being with strong Earth and Spirit Innarn. He'd been a formidable opponent until they'd been asked to fight Shari.

His elders were in a totally different league.

The woven fibres of the ropes drifted apart with a single glance from the ancient, gnarled Kumaru. The crystal designed to nullify their Innarn dropped unheeded to the sand, and beings around them found their second wind.

Samuel kept his eyes trained on the water and the tiny figure climbing aboard a ship.

He alone wasn't surprised when the enemy fleet retreated into the distance.

Cheers rose from the fighters, but Samuel stood, arms crossed, scowling out at the sea. "They'll be back," he growled.

A long-fingered hand clapped onto his shoulder. Flinching, he glanced up at one of the Kumaru Elders.

"We'll be waiting."

Shari's Sanctuary

Tormorylth shrieked as the pulsing squeezed against them.

Jetonyx flung a wing around the hatchling, grabbing her with a claw as if that would prevent her from disappearing as well. They stood, huddled amid the last of the trees, a golden egg resting between his hind legs.

His tiny sister looked up at him, acid tears pooling. *'What if we're next?'*

Gulping, Jetonyx turned his head away.

He didn't know how to answer her. All he could do was hold on tighter.

CHAPTER SEVEN

Lissae

Zoeday

Seventh day of the first week of Hazelcrown

Tania collapsed back in her seat, wiping sweat from her brow.

Fenix was beaming.

"They're safe!" Cyrus said.

"For now," Zana reminded them.

They had just received word that their forces on Ginorti had driven off the mainlanders' attack fleet.

"Where do you think they'll try next?" Tania asked.

Zana sighed. "It is not for us to wonder. We must continue to prepare for our joining with Ginorti. It's the best way to make sure that he and his people are safe."

"What else do we need to do?" Fenix asked, smoothing their hand over the map on the table.

"Work out how to create the bridge between Ginorti and the joined," Zana said.

"What about the Kumaru? Do you think they'd help?" Tania asked.

"The Kumaru won't wake up just to make a bridge," Cyrus said.

"But they helped with driving the mainlanders away," Tania argued. "Ginorti was boasting to Ronah about it this morning."

"They what? Really?"

"The Kumaru are an embodiment of Spirit and Earth Innarn. If they were to give their blessing, it would be a great boon to the Shifting Islands for them to help in joining Ginorti to us," Zana said thoughtfully, tapping a slender finger against her lips.

"Why don't we ask then?"

Cyrus opened his mouth, then stopped.

"Good idea!" Fenix said. "You should do it." Something about their tone was off.

"Are you... scared of them?" Tania asked.

"Did your parents ever tell you stories about the Kumaru?" Cyrus interrupted. She shook her head. "They're the ones who wait in forests for unsuspecting children to pass by and then use their blood and bone as fertiliser."

"They'll crush you if you cut them, snap you if you burn them, and make you their own if you try to flee," Fenix added.

Tania blinked. "If someone tried to burn me, I'd do my best to snap them in half as well."

"Huh." Cyrus rubbed the back of his head. "Good point."

"And it's not like we would just stand there while a being attempted to cut us. You'd fight back, wouldn't you?" Tania prodded. "I'll talk to them."

"And you'll take your soul's match with you," Zana said. "He will help keep you safe."

"Collis?" Tania blushed.

Zana smiled indulgently, and they both ignored the others who were sniggering at her.

"While you're gone, we'll send word to Akoren and Vannali to be on their guard."

Tania nodded and shifted away before her face flushed any redder.

Zuefie

Something in the mist was strong enough to force Shari's eyes to remain open.

Her gaze was fixed on the paling skin of her neighbour as cloud after cloud swept by, sucking the Innarn right out of his willing body.

Laboriously, he turned his head, sightless eyes trained in her direction.

Shari had the same horrid feeling that she knew the tripedal wikkur from somewhere, but the clouds fogging her mind meant she had no chance to place him.

"I die..." he wheezed. "... happy. Knowing... you're... next."

Head lolling to the side, Shari was forced to watch as the last of his life fled with the final bit of Innarn.

Gritting her teeth, she refused to cry.

But it was a close call.

Lissae

Zoeday

Seventh day of the first week of Hazelcrown

Samuel staggered through the door to his house, leaning heavily on the frame.

If he never saw another boat again, he'd be happy.

There was a rustle from down the hall, and the pounding of paws. Turning, Samuel was just in time to catch Shadow as he leaped into his arms.

"Didn't think you'd be here," Samuel said, burying his face in the creature's soft fur.

"We thought it best to wait for you," Jonathan said.

Samuel stilled. He half wanted to stay where he was, but to show such a weakness...

Perhaps it was alright around friends.

"Lizbeth left some rutenberry cookies under a stasis charm for you," Jonathan said, and Samuel heard plates clattering in the kitchen.

Heaving the wriggling palon in his arms, Samuel started forwards. "Don't you dare," he warned. "Those are my rutenberries." He froze in the doorway.

Jonathan had a hatchling clambering about in his hair.

Mind whirling, Samuel couldn't pin down a single thought as the hatchling lifted its tiny head and spotted him.

'*Mine!*' It launched itself at Samuel.

The fiercest being in the Realms suddenly had a tough choice. Did he drop the creature in his arms to save the tiny hatchling hurtling towards him? The one who could be the only other survivor of his race?

Tiny black wings spread and pumped through the air before Samuel could decide.

Not a hatchling, then. Samuel's heart seemed to rend itself in two. Q'Aralides couldn't fly until at least their second season, and this one was, now he could see it up close, far too small to be anything related to him. Not to mention, it only had two eyes.

The little beast landed on Shadow's head. Curling over, it peered between its hind legs and snorted as the palon went cross-eyed trying to look at it.

'*Mine!*' It sent again, and wandered, calm as you please, up Samuel's arm to stand on his shoulder.

"Jonathan?" Samuel's voice absolutely did not squeak. "Who is this?"

'I *Sneeze*,' the tiny one said, and promptly lived up to his name. A miniscule flame escaped his snout and lit a tuft of Shadow's fur on fire.

The Guardian flicked away the flame with a negligent wave of his hand. "Sneeze is a draci who has adopted you."

"Oh." Carefully, Samuel put Shadow on the ground, patting the palon's head to make sure the flame was truly gone. His heart squeezed painfully.

Maybe he *was* the last of his kind.

He would be if they couldn't find Shari.

"Ow!" he shrieked, hand clasping his ear. "He bit me!"

Jonathan had a twist to his lips that said the Guardian was trying hard not to laugh. "He does that."

'Not *last*,' Sneeze sent.

"And how can you tell?" Samuel scowled at the creature standing on his forearm, his hand still clamped to his ear to stop the flow of blood.

'*Can.*'

"Sneeze is a creature of few words." Jonathan was definitely laughing now, although, to his credit, was doing his best to hide it.

The tiny creature turned on the spot and blew a little jet of flames at the Guardian.

Samuel laughed in astonishment.

'*Mine!*' Sneeze stomped a foot. Samuel barely felt the movement.

Later, when his race wasn't ending, he'd ask about the best way to care for the creature. And find out what he needed to grow bigger than his thumb.

'*Am big!*' Sneeze whirled on him now.

"Yes, you are," Samuel said, reminded of the hatchlings who grew slower than the others. His chest ached at the thought of Jetonyx and Tormorylth, lost along with the Altoriae. "How goes the search?"

It was Jonathan's turn to scowl. "We know where Shari is."

"You could have led with that!" Taking a breath, Samuel eased a finger over Sneeze's leathery hide. "Where is she?" Samuel bit out.

By his side, Shadow whimpered and pressed against his leg.

"Zuefie. It's known as the Lightest Realm. The Ducibus refuse to guard it."

"Why?"

"They won't say."

Dropping his free hand to bury it in the palon's fur, Samuel said without thinking, "I'll get her back."

Jonathan nodded. "We will." He looked away from Samuel, jaw tight. "We have to. But neither of us can even attempt to storm the Realm."

"Why?"

A muscle jumped in the Guardian's jaw. "Shari contacted Temira."

"Tem... How?"

He shook his head. "I don't know. But she was able to tell us that the inhabitants of Zuefie are Innarn eaters."

"And you believe that?"

"It would fit with why the Ducibus won't guard the gateway."

Samuel wanted to growl, and stomp, and throw things, but was mindful of the creatures leaning against him. He thought hard. "We could try for unconventional, then."

"What do you mean?"

"Shari's mother. She's a Blank, right?"

Jonathan's eyes lit up.

Shari's Sanctuary

As the tree in front of them flickered, Jetonyx found he couldn't hear Tormorylth's shriek over the pounding of his hearts.

One tree left.

The hatchlings crowded around each other, next to the remaining tree, heads bowed, the egg resting in one of Jetonyx's claws.

Once it was gone, all that remained of the Altoriae's pocket Realm...

Was them.

CHAPTER EIGHT

Lissae

Adonday 5am

First day of the second week of Hazelcrown

Arilla laid her hand on the symbol carved into the double doors of Ronah's museum.

"Are you sure?" she asked the Guardian.

"It may be the only way to save Shari," he said.

Looking behind her, she caught Anika's gaze, who nodded at her grimly. Almost the entire group from her sword training sessions were crowding the room.

"You don't have to do this," she said.

They were barely ready, had only just learned the basics, and whilst they may be the best line of defence against the Innarn eaters, Arilla wasn't sure if they could deliver a fatal blow.

"Yes, we do," Anika said. The girl had at least changed into pants, even if she still wore her stilettos. Sure, she could snap the heels off and use them as daggers, but it did little to calm Arilla's racing heart.

Pushing open the doors, she said, "Here we go." Arilla stepped through.

She didn't know what she was expecting, but it wasn't endless monochromatic hallways. Or a tiny, grey-robed being pointing towards the Lighter area of the portal.

"Thanks." She straightened her shoulder, ready to lead her students towards the Realm holding her daughter captive.

Zuefie

Shari had never seen clouds so low to the ground.

The Xanderri had been so intent on draining the Innarn from as many being as possible, they'd overestimated their appetites.

If she had been anywhere else, it would have been amusing to listen to clouds snore.

Slowly, she leaned down and thrust her cuffed hand into the closest cloud. Tiny bursts of plasma jumped and sparked, and Shari could feel the strength flowing back into her limbs.

Taking care not to clank the chains on her ankles, she held the cuff next to them, hoping that it would passively absorb the Light Innarn enough to unlock them.

The glow to her bonds slowly dimmed until they unclasped and fell into her waiting hands.

Letting out a breath, Shari eased her way down from the stone slab. Stepping carefully, she made her way through the clouds.

'*Which way to the gateway?*'

Jetonyx flicked a vision to the front of her mind.

'*Hurry!*' the hatchlings urged.

Shari, free of the ruins, threw caution to the wind and ran.

Lissae

Adonday 6am

Samuel leaned against the wall near the double doors and sighed. Waiting for Arilla and her barely trained Blanks was going to be agony, but he couldn't imagine being anywhere but by the portal doors when they got back.

The last time he'd stepped through, he'd been going to the Dark Conclave with Shari, determined to keep the Altoriae, and Jetonyx, safe.

And he'd returned alone, his entire Realm gone.

"Do you want to talk about it?" Jonathan asked. He was propped against the wall as well, arms crossed over his chest.

"Altum is gone," Samuel said. The words were ash in his mouth.

"Gone?" Jonathan's brows rose.

"The Realm seems to have been tied to the Queen's life force, and when she died…" Samuel sighed again.

"The Queen is dead?"

He frowned. "Did I not mention?"

"All you said was *Shari was right here*. We've spent the last ten days frantically searching the Realms for her." Jonathan glanced at the doors. "Seeing we've got nothing to do but wait, why don't you tell me what happened?"

Sinking to the ground, Samuel kept his back to the wall and let his legs sprawl. Sneeze, who refused to be parted from his person, perched on his knee. "The conclave was a disaster. War'Jan and Oalark tried to poison everyone, but their plan backfired, and it killed War'Jan. One ambassador was trying to do the same thing to Oalark. She was under the influence of something that changed how beings acted." Samuel shuddered.

"And then... well, Helk threw his spear, stabbed Oalark through the chest. Shari tried to heal her, but the Queen said no, and the Realm collapsed. The Mountain Beast ate anyone who tried to leave and..." Samuel ran a hand over his face. "We barely escaped. Got the hatchlings into Shari's pocket Realm so they'd be safe, and we were back here. I put my hand on the door and turned to Shari, and she was just... gone."

Silence fell.

He glanced over to see Jonathan mouthing *hatchlings*.

"It's not your fault, Samuel," Jonathan said eventually.

"I could have healed the Queen, and in doing so, could have saved an entire Realm from destruction." His breath shuddered from his body. "Could have held Shari tighter. Could have shoved the hatchlings into my Realm so I wouldn't be the last."

"They're safe with Shari. You know she'll keep them safe."

"Like I kept her safe? Jonathan, you might move mountains for her, but I will unleash every beast in the Nine Realms of Hell to avenge her if she's harmed."

The Guardian shifted uncomfortably. "Let's hope it doesn't come to that."

"Why, scared?" Samuel snarled, turning his head to face Jonathan.

"No. Worried I might help you."

The pair drifted into silence.

Jonathan slapped his knees and got to his feet. "We need a distraction."

Samuel raised a brow and looked at the double doors.

"Glaring at them won't help Shari get back any quicker. Come on," the Guardian said. "Asterion had something to show me. Want to see what it is?"

Refraining from biting Jonathan's head off was becoming a habit he was tempted to break.

Zuefie

'*Faster, Shari!*' the hatchlings were yelling at her.

Shari panted, shoving away a leaf bigger than her torso as she continued her mad dash through the jungle.

'*Going as fast as I can,*' she sent, keeping one eye on the cloudless sky.

'Fa... er!'

She wanted to pause, wanted to think, wanted to stop so her screaming muscles could rest. Pushing through the burn, Shari ran on.

She was almost there—she could feel it.

Portal

Arilla squinted at the blinding white door.

"Are we ready?" she asked.

There were sounds of agreement behind her.

"Remember your formations. Keep your blade at the ready. At the first sign of Shari, we grab her and run. Got it?"

A chorus of agreement rose. Arilla glanced at them and smiled.

Steeling herself, she pulled her sword free. Pushing the door open, she said, "Here we go."

Zuefie

Something up ahead was glowing.

Pushing through the leaves, Shari almost laughed when she saw the blinding white door.

How terribly convenient, she thought wildly.

The sky above her clouded over.

Lungs straining, Shari almost tripped over her feet as the door swung open.

"Move," she tried to scream, but the word caught in her throat.

Her mother stepped into Zuefie, sword in hand, eyes widening as Shari came tearing towards her.

"Get back," Arilla cried over her shoulder.

Shari, unable and unwilling to stop her momentum, crashed into Arilla. Her hands scrambled for the handle, pulling the door closed before the clouds could get through.

Looking into Arilla's startled face, Shari beamed before she collapsed to the side.

Only one thought in her mind.

Safe.

CHAPTER NINE

Lissae

Adonday 6.30am

First day of the second week of Hazelcrown

He'd asked for a distraction, and Asterion had delivered.

One eyebrow raised, Jonathan held the jar that contained the sample of crystal Asterion had presented to him. "This is what the mainlanders were using to weight their nets?"

The minotaur nodded.

"It had some sort of Innarn-dampening field," Samuel said. "The satyrs were flinging boulders around, shattering them."

"There is corrupted crystal buried in the sands of Ginorti," Asterion said.

"Corrupted crystal." Brows furrowed, Jonathan set the jar down and moved away. His own experience with the Crystal Intelligence made it hard enough for him to use a screen, and anything that glowed orange still made his crossbow snap into his hand without warning. His Mind Healer said it would take time, but it looked like time had run out.

Samuel tilted his head. "Are you going to be able to deal with this?"

"Do I have a choice?" Jonathan said.

Asterion looked between the pair, his ears trembling slightly.

"Even with Asterion looking after the administration required, and you helping on patrol, Shari is still missing and I..."

The crystal slab on the wall chimed, and Arilla Dawn's face filled the screen. ·

"Guardian? Shari... We have Shari," she said between her tears.

Jonathan shot Samuel a look, and they both shifted to the museum.

Scrambling through the doors, Guardian and Apprentice tore through the hallways of the Portal until they skidded to a stop at Arilla's side.

'Guild, to me now!' Jonathan's send was harsh enough that half the guild members shifted in before they thought about what they were doing. Amara even had a spoon of something raised halfway to her mouth.

'Arilla has found Shari. They're in the Portal. Protect the Blanks. Protect the Altoriae,' he ordered. *'It's time to bring her home.'*

Portal

Samuel hung back, ostensibly to protect the rear of the pack crowded around the Altoriae.

It wasn't at all because he felt that his presence closer to Shari may put her in danger again. If there was the slightest chance that could be true, then he would retire to the other end of the Realms and live his life out on Altum...

Hands curling into claws, he huffed a breath.

For a moment, he'd forgotten.

A spear through the Queen's heart, death, destruction and so many teeth, snapping at all who tried to leave.

Not Altum then, but another Dark Realm, where he could lick his wounds in peace.

Despite his best attempts, a flare of hope caught in his chest.

If she survived, then maybe I'm not the last Q'Aralide after all.

Last of the Lissaen party through the double doors, he turned and nodded to the Ducibus sentinel before shutting them with a thud.

'Thank you, Guild. I'll ensure Shari is checked by the healers. You are all free to go back to what you were doing before,' Jonathan sent. "Thank you for retrieving her," he said to the Blanks.

"She did it all."

It was the one who was determined to make up for her past mistakes through needle and thread. *Anika,* if he remembered right.

"She came barrelling through the gateway just as I opened it." Shari's mother was twisting her hands, clearly aching not to be touching her offspring. "Kind of glad, to be honest, a bunch of clouds were the only thing behind her." Arilla hefted her sword. "Not sure how well these would go against water vapour."

He blinked. "We'll get her to the healers," Samuel said. "We wouldn't have returned her home without you."

Arilla nodded, gaze glued to her daughter.

Samuel shuddered. How different his upbringing would have been if Oalark had cared for them even slightly as much as Arilla did for Shari?

"I'll shift her now?" Jonathan asked as a courtesy. He barely waited for Arilla's nod before they disappeared.

With the Guardian and their Altoriae gone, the others slowly trailed away.

"I have to..." Arilla gestured.

"I can give you a lift," Samuel offered before he could stop the words from falling out of his mouth.

"Oh, shifting doesn't work…"

His lips quirked up in a short-lived grin. "Not that kind of lift."

Lissae

Arilla tried not to scream as Samuel, in his Q'Aralide form, took to the sky with her on his neck.

She scrambled to find a handhold on his smooth, scaled hide. Once she gripped his neck firmly with her legs, the terror cleared out of her veins. It was so different from flying with Calem. She'd never gone so high so fast before. Not to mention the jostling with every wing beat.

Opening her eyes, Arilla gasped at the view. All the joined Shifting Islands were on display beneath them. As much as she wanted to enjoy the sight, there was hardly a chance to. They were already plummeting towards the ground.

Between Shari's hasty return and the impromptu flight, there had been little opportunity to process everything.

But Arilla had her daughter back.

Samuel covered the distance between the museum and the Healers Centre in less time than it had taken her to clamber onto his back. She wasn't sure if she was grateful for the swiftness or disappointed the journey hadn't given her time to calm her racing heart.

The moment Samuel landed, she slid down his flank, shaking her way to Calem and SilverCloud's sides.

"Thank you," she called back, as the Apprentice, in his smaller form, nodded to her. After scrabbling to grip his scales, it was hard to be terrified of him anymore.

"Best come inside," Calem said gruffly.

Gripping Calem's arm, she raced to keep up with him as they tore through the halls to what was rapidly becoming Shari's room.

Sinking beside the bed, Arilla grasped Shari's hand. Jonathan knelt on the other side. Calem was a solid, warm presence at her back. Samuel was last in, leaning against the wall near the door, arms crossed over his chest, and looked ready to take on the rest of the Realm.

She was startled out of her thoughts as a wrinkled, age-spotted hand covered her own. Giving SilverCloud a watery smile, Arilla finally allowed the tears of relief to fall.

They would watch over Shari.

Together.

Chamele looked down at the pitiful aberration cowering at her feet and sneered.

"Do you really think yourself better than me?" she asked.

He wiped away a smear of blood from the corner of his mouth. "Anyone who doesn't rip another from their home intending to torture and beat them is better than you."

She huffed and glanced to the side.

The captain of the guard stepped forward and slammed his fist into the aberration's face, knocking the creature backwards.

"Do you know what you're good for?" Chamele said sweetly.

The creature stared at her through his swelling eye but refused to answer.

"Testing." She turned to the doctors waiting by their gleaming benches. "Find out how to break him," Chamele ordered and swept from the room, the shrieks of the captive fading behind her.

General Morrow carefully collected another shard and placed it in the specially crafted ziom box.

The satyrs on the sands of Ginorti's beach joined in the moan from their island. Ever since the attacks, there was a constant prickling of pain under their skin, like invisible needles being wriggled around.

A sound unlike anything he'd ever heard screamed through his mind and pulled at his bones, forcing him to his knees.

Keening, he looked around, only to see the others on the beach in the same state.

'*Ginorti, what's wrong?*' he asked.

'*Linked... My Linked...*' the island whimpered.

They needed to get Oakley back.

Immediately.

CHAPTER TEN

Lissae

Inthday

Second day of the second week of Hazelcrown

ollis stood, spine straight, as he silently watched the haggard guild members return from Ginorti.

"Not your fault," Remmy said.

"That shifting off Ronah caused my Innarn to lash out and wound the Travel Innarnian so severely he has yet to be released from the Healers Centre?" Collis said bitterly.

Remmy shrugged. "Well, that was kind of your fault. But you didn't know."

He leaned against the rock of the mountain range they had erected around the beach, glancing at the guild members streaming past them and nodding to the Returned as their Innarn brushed against his own. "You didn't have to stay with me." Collis crossed his arms over his chest and frowned as he looked at the wall. A tendril of Innarn snaked out and poked at it, shoring up a section which felt weaker than the others.

"Can't let you have all the fun." Remmy grinned at him and clapped him on the back. Looking over at the bedraggled group, he called out, "How did it go?"

"It was horrible. The mainlanders are using Innarn-dampening fields," Amara said, scrubbing a hand over her eyes. "And it shattered. Shards everywhere."

Collis caught Remmy's gaze.

"Sounds like your area of speciality." Remmy grinned.

Maybe those long days of being drained of their Innarn and having to come up with another way to defend themselves would finally be useful.

"What do you mean?" Amara asked.

"When we were in Anriluka's pocket Realm, she'd regularly drain us of Innarn. We had to learn how to fight without it."

"If you've got any ideas, I bet the Guardian would appreciate them," Amara said, failing to cover a yawn.

The Returned shared another look.

"The Guardian's busy," Collis said.

"Busy? Why?"

Shrugging, Remmy said, "Guardian stuff."

"Maybe we can come up with some ideas while we wait," Collis offered.

"Great idea! Except, I'm going to rest. I'm leading my first patrol tonight." Fire flared at her fingertips, and she flicked it away, scowling.

"You've been out on patrol loads," Remmy said.

"But not leading one by myself!" Amara wailed.

"Do you know the team you're leading?" Collis asked.

"Mostly." She seemed unaware of the sparks dancing over her skin.

"Use their strengths. What you don't know, ask. Your purpose is not to win, but to keep them and us safe. Remember that, and you'll be fine," Collis said.

"You make it sound easy," Amara sighed. "I'm going to rest while I can. I bid thee well." The sparks vanished, and she left with a bounce in her step, despite tripping over her own feet on the way out.

"And what about the Guardian?" Remmy asked, shaking his head at Amara's retreating form.

"We'll come up with a plan and talk with him in the morning."

"Gives you time to settle your Innarn as well."

Eying the wall again, Collis nodded. His Innarn was a building pressure inside him, and if it wasn't released, he didn't know what sort of devastation it would cause.

Anika fluffed her hair one last time, smiling into the mirror.

A final check of her lip gloss, and a quick tug to make sure her top was sitting right, and she was out the door, on her way to meet Raven.

An Innarnian.

Although she would never admit it to anyone, Anika was slightly giddy about the whole thing. Raven was *nice*. He didn't talk down to her or think less of her because she was a Blank.

Sauntering along the street, Anika waved in greeting to a few friends, keeping the smile fixed firm when Maeve rolled her eyes and turned her back with a flick of her hair. Even being the Altoriae's stylist wasn't enough to raise her to the level of popularity she'd enjoyed before.

She spotted Raven strolling along with some of the other guild members. The group looked to be heading towards the Healers Centre, probably to check up on Shari.

"Anika, well met!" Raven called.

"Well met," she said, grinning up at him. "Thank you for meeting with me."

Raven's smile was crooked, and his eyes crinkled slightly in the corners. "Have to admit, I was curious when I got your invitation."

"Oh, well." Anika fluttered her lashes out of habit as his gaze slid to her lips and back up to meet her eyes. "I was hoping you'd be able to teach me how to sharpen a sword. Arilla has been wonderful so far, but I don't want to take up all her time. Especially now Shari is home."

The easy going smile was replaced by a predatory look so quickly, Anika blinked. Had he'd ever been grinning at all? Raven licked his lips. "What do you know about sharpening a blade?"

"Aren't you going to..." Anika waved a hand in the general direction of where the rest of the guild was disappearing into the distance.

"The Altoriae has a bunch of people looking over her. I think she'll be fine. If I'm needed, someone can send to me. Besides, they're not exactly going to be upset I'm here, with a pretty girl who wants to learn more about weapons." That crooked grin was back.

Ducking her head and tucking a strand of hair behind her ear, Anika fought the rising blush. "All talk makes for a dull blade, Raven," she said.

"Best get started. The first thing you need to know..." He casually took her hand and led her over to the town square, the rest of his words drowned out by her pounding heart.

Kerday

Third day of the second week of Hazelcrown

Tania was lagging as she left Ridden Hall, her siblings skipping ahead while she waited for the other Linked to meet up with her. She had a few suggestions of what they could do with the bridge if Ginorti's Linked couldn't be located.

The sound of flapping and a stiff breeze were her only warnings of an Ilutri landing before her. "Well met, Ronah's Linked."

A few of the older girls made suspiciously squeaking noises when Voxis grabbed her hand and kissed the back of it.

Yanking away from him, she didn't even attempt to hide that she was wiping off his kiss. "Voxis," she said flatly.

His smile dimmed slightly. Eyes flickering over her shoulder, he seemed to gain his confidence again. "I was hoping to catch up with you again. I've been reading about ways to increase our defences and thought that this silly wall needs a few adjustments."

"Silly wall?" she repeated.

"Exactly. It blocks the beauty of our beaches, don't you think?" Wings flexing, Voxis hovered for a moment, much to the delight of Maeve and her groupies.

"It also blocks the ballistas from the mainland. A pretty fair trade-off."

"Perhaps if you come back to my dwelling, I can show you my other... ideas." He reached out to her, but Tania stepped away.

"Uh, no thanks." Tania looked around, hoping to spot Cyrus or Fenix. "I'm actually waiting for someone at the moment."

"Oh, really?" Silver eyes hardening, Voxis's voice turned chilly. "Waiting for your soul-match?"

"No. Cyrus, Fenix and..." She spotted the two other Linked rounding the corner in the road and heading towards them. "Zana."

"Aunt Zana?" Voice climbing, Voxis looked over his shoulder.

Throwing her Innarn to make the illusion of wings, Tania pointed to the far side of the crowd. "Look, here she comes now!"

"Oh, I just remembered. I have to..."

"Surely you can stay and greet your aunt?" Tania taunted.

"I bid thee well," Voxis said, and leaped into the sky, disappearing before Fenix and Cyrus could reach her.

"Who was that?" Fenix asked.

"A malodourous turd of an Ilutri." Tania glared after him. "And, unfortunately, Zana's nephew. He seems determined to charm me."

"Has he met Collis?" Cyrus asked, frowning at the speck in the distance.

"Yup," Tania said. "And yet, he persists."

"Wow. He's brave or stupid to go after you. Collis can have the leftover feathers for his pillow." Fenix grinned and shoved their hands into vest pockets and rocked back on their heels.

"I'm not up to that stage yet." Tania laughed. "Have you heard from Ginorti's Linked?"

"No," Fenix said, brows descending. "I think something might be blocking me from sensing him."

"Blocking? Could it be anything like the crystals they were firing on Ginorti?"

Cyrus's gaze snapped to her. "What crystals?"

Tania shrank. "Did I forget to mention that?"

Narday

Fourth day of the second week of Hazelcrown

Skye's fingers twitched as she glanced over. Grace sleeping, curled up in a ball on a pallet in the corner of the room.

The rescued Innarnian was having a hard time adjusting to life on Ronah. Not that Skye was coping any better. She'd lost count of the times she'd awoken with the slash of a sword ringing in her ears. Sometimes, in her nightmares, it was aimed at her neck instead of Suni's.

Waking with her heart in her mouth to Grace perching on the corner of the bed, peering down at her through the darkness of the room, was not something she was keen to repeat, either. Skye had shrieked, Grace had tumbled, and they'd both fired on the door when a guild member with horns had burst through to check on them.

Still, she'd made it one night without screaming herself awake. It was a pretty good start.

Rubbing her eyes, Skye yawned.

Grace stirred and stretched her spindly limbs before rolling over, her gaze locking onto Skye immediately.

"Well met, Grace. Good sleep?"

Grace nodded and stood. "Food?"

"Dressed, then food," Skye reminded her. Ever since the Guardian had invited them to help themselves to the kitchen, Grace had been keen to try new things to eat, often in combinations Skye would never have thought of.

Sighing, Grace snapped her fingers, her sleeping clothes changing into loose, flowing daywear shot through with silver.

Laughing, Skye swung her legs out of the bed. "Not all of us can get dressed so... Hey!" The tingle of Grace's Innarn swept over her, and Skye was wearing a dress to match. "Well, thanks. I suppose it is time for food."

Opening the door to the room, Skye was immediately hit with the smell of something crisp and warm. "Apple and cinnamon?" she wondered aloud.

"Food," Grace replied, shoving at her back with Innarn.

Laughing, Skye led the way to the kitchen.

Slumping into his chair in the library study, Jonathan looked glumly at the crystal in the box.

"This is what Samuel recovered from the shores of Ginorti," he said, hesitant to even touch the thing.

The Linked gathered closer, peering at the container. Temira brushed through them and stood glaring at it.

Cyrus shook his head as he bent over to examine it. "I don't understand. I recalled everything I made."

Moving to the corner of the room, arms crossed protectively over her chest, Tania said, "What if it's not something you made?"

"What do you mean?" Cyrus asked.

"A spy," Temira said flatly. "Do not touch!" she snapped, pushing the box out of Cyrus's reach.

"I'm not quite that stupid," he grumbled.

No one mentioned that his hand had been extended, fingers reaching…

"Does it have a compulsion on it?" Jonathan asked. As repulsed as he was by the crystal, there was an odd need to touch it, to hold it…

"Yes," Zana said. She nodded to Temira, and the box with the far too tempting crystal disappeared.

The tension seemed to ooze out of the room.

"Do you really think there's a spy?" Tania asked, her voice almost lost in the stillness.

"How else did the most dangerous prototype I have get into the hands of those who are waging war on us?" Cyrus snapped.

Tania shrank in on herself.

"Who do you think it is?" Jonathan asked, sending soothing vibes to Ronah's Linked.

"People are in and out of the Techno Centre all the time," Cyrus said.

"How many of them are allowed into your personal lab?" Fenix asked.

"Hardly any. The only new one is..." Cyrus shared a look with Temira and practically growled.

"Milo." They said together.

Fenix looked taken aback. "Milo? But he's..."

"Always underfoot, and I caught him rummaging through the lab," Cyrus said.

"Despite stylising himself as my secretary, he's a recognised, well-respected scientist!" Fenix argued.

"Maybe it's not him," Tania offered.

Cyrus and Temira shared a look.

"Don't go racing off just yet," Jonathan said. "Before you persecute him, we need to know what else he's passed on to the mainlanders."

The technomancer scowled at him but nodded. "There are many dangerous things in our labs that could be used by those with ill-intent."

"How do we prove..." She shot a look at Fenix. "Or disprove it's him?" Tania asked.

Cyrus grimaced. "By offering something too good to resist."

CHAPTER ELEVEN

Lissae

Rasshday

Fifth day of the second week of Hazelcrown

"She'll be fine," Samuel said, shooing Jonathan out of Shari's room. "I'll make sure she's safe."

"I know she'll be safe with you." The Guardian looked at his charge and sighed. "Seeing her like this..."

"Shari is strong. Whatever caused her pain will suffer far worse than she has." Samuel glared at the bed, half wishing he could summon the creatures and end them now.

Jonathan gave a half-hearted laugh. "I trust that you'll ensure they do."

"Go, before I call Zac in to tear you away," Samuel ordered.

"How do you know about Zac?" Jonathan said, his sharp look ruined by a gigantic yawn.

Samuel smirked. "You said his name in your sleep. Twice." He would not mention that once had been during the time he was sleeping in the Guardian's house. That would just be awkward.

"Fine, I'll go. I'll stop back later."

"After you have some rest."

"Alright!" Jonathan laughed and shifted out of the room.

Turning back to Shari, Samuel slumped in the chair, kicking his legs out in front of him. "So," he said.

Arilla and Calem had left to escort SilverCloud home not too long ago. But with Jonathan gone, he finally had the chance to see if his fears had come true.

'Jetonyx?' he asked. '*Tormorylth? Are you there?*'

There was an echoey silence.

Pocket Realms lived outside the body of their creator but were only accessible through their minds. Only the strongest of Innarnians could create them, and they were both useful to hide things but dangerous because they weren't controlled by the Ducibus.

'*Jetonyx?*' he tried again.

There was a slight sound, quiet enough that he could mistake it for a sigh on the wind. '*San...*'

Either it was his imagination, or he could hear his hatchlings.

Sitting back, Samuel steepled his fingers and stared at Shari over them.

He just had to have to hope and wait for the Altoriae to awaken.

This time, hope would be enough.

Vebaday

Sixth day of the second week of Hazelcrown

Tania found Samuel staring, unblinking, at Shari in her hospital bed.

"Okay, time for you to sleep," Tania said. Forcing a grin, she marched into the room. "I'm here to relieve you of duty. Get some rest."

"I've just told Jonathan to do the same thing," Samuel growled.

She narrowed her eyes at him. "Don't think that I don't know you haven't been sleeping since you got back. Shari is here. She's safe. And between me, Ronah, and the rest of the guild, she'll stay that way. Sleep, Samuel. She will need you when she wakes up."

"If she wakes up," he said glumly.

"That is the sleep deprivation talking. I don't know how long you can normally go without some sort of REM cycle, but us bipedal types need it at regular intervals." She tilted her head. "Wait. Q'Aralides have two legs as well. That analogy doesn't work at all."

Samuel huffed a reluctant laugh. "It really doesn't."

"You get what I mean, though," she said.

"Fine." He rose smoothly from the chair. "If she so much as twitches..."

"I'll shift you here myself," she promised.

Nodding, Samuel moved to the door. "I bid thee well, Ronah's Linked."

Tania grinned at him. "I bid thee well, Shari's friend."

Samuel ducked his head and shifted so smoothly, she barely saw him leave.

Crossing to Shari's bedside, Tania sat next to the Altoriae's legs. Tracing the patterns on the colourful quilt, with her fingertips, she hummed a tune from her childhood. "I've heard that when someone is asleep like this, they can still hear and feel." Shifting to get comfortable, Tania picked up Shari's hand and started idly drawing patterns on the back of it.

"You've missed so much since you've been gone. Let me think... You were here for the joining with Cantash... Oh, Cantash is amazing! We're touring the school soon. And Fenix, ze's Linked, is just the sweetest! They gave me and Collis a tour of the gardens. It looks so dry and desolate up the top, but, wow, Shari. You're going to love them. Speaking of love, Zana showed me some special Air Innarn and revealed that Collis was my soul-match. Everyone is making a big deal about it, but I don't really understand why."

She sighed. "And then there's Voxis. Zana's nephew. He seems... fixated on me, and I don't know what to do about it. He makes my skin crawl, really. All I want to do is shift home and have a scolding hot shower each time he touches me." Rubbing the patterns off Shari's skin, she continued. "That's not the big news, though. As annoying as he is, I'm more concerned with Ginorti."

Glancing out the window, she shivered as the sky turned grey. A storm was brewing. "The island called out for help, and his Linked is missing. And then, the mainlanders went and started a war, and obliterated our forces. They've showered the beach with some sort of blocking crystal that Cyrus thinks was stolen from his lab."

Tania gripped Shari's hand tighter. "We really, really missed you. I don't know where you were, or what you're doing now. But, Shari. Please come back."

Thunder rumbled, and Shari whimpered in her sleep.

Shari's Sanctuary

Shari flinched.

Jetonyx and Tormorylth looked at the screen, then at her in concern.

"Almost done," she said brightly. From the moment she'd collapsed in the Portal, Shari had been working tirelessly to get her sanctuary back to what it was.

The only thing that had been saved were the two hatchlings, a tiny version of the bereni tree housing *The Altoriae's Handbook*, and the last Q'Aralide egg.

'*You don't like the thunder,*' Jetonyx sent.

'*And you don't like plant matter,*' Shari shot back.

Tormorylth waddled over to her, belly bulging from her latest meal. '*Being defensive won't help. You should eat it.*'

Jetonyx rolled all three of his eyes. '*You can't eat* thunder.'

'*Can,*' Tormorylth sent stubbornly.

Shari skittered back out of the way. '*Why don't you two try? I'm going to rest.*'

'*Why?*' The two hatchlings working in sync was a scary thing to witness.

'*Because I need rest.*'

'*Liar,*' Tormorylth sent.

Shari stepped back. "Am not!"

'*Are,*' Jetonyx sent. '*Not to us. To* yourself.'

'*You just woke up.*' Tormorylth narrowed her eyes.

"No, I've been..." Shari paused. She'd been working on the stream, and then...

She sunk to the ground. Then she'd rested. And finished the trees, before grabbing in some herd beasts so her guests could eat.

"How long have we been here?" she asked.

Shuffling his bulk around so he could sit on his haunches next to her, Jetonyx let her rest against his side. '*Long enough, Altoriae. It sounds like your people need you.*'

Sighing, she looked at the screens, where Tania had resumed drawing idle patterns on her hand.

"I suppose it might be time to wake up," she said.

Jonathan forced a smile as he walked through the door of his store and greeted Eva and Lizbeth, who were standing on either side of the counter.

"What are you doing here?" Lizbeth asked. "I heard Shari was back."

Jonathan chuckled. "Just dropping by to make sure everything is okay."

"Everything is fi…" Eva dissolved mid-word, and Jonathan found himself somewhere else entirely.

A familiar room at the Healers Centre—one he'd been kicked out of not too long ago.

Wondering why he'd been shifted back, Jonathan stepped up to her bedside, and bright green, bloodshot eyes locked onto his.

"Shari?" he asked. *'Anything broken?'* Jonathan tried to ask calmly, sure the worry from the last few weeks was seeping through the placid question.

'All in one piece,' she added, attempting to ease his concerns. His Altoriae grinned at him. "Well met, Jonathan."

"Welcome back," he whispered.

Bodies filled the room. Shari's parents, Samuel, and a dozen guild members filtered through to pass on their best wishes.

The whole time, Jonathan found himself unable to tear his gaze away, in case she would disappear from his presence again.

As if she was aware of his dilemma, Shari smirked at him.

Jonathan couldn't stop his answering smile.

The Altoriae was back.

CHAPTER TWELVE

Lissae

Adonday

First day of the third week of Hazelcrown

Chamele groaned, head thrown back as white mist streamed from her mouth.

'*You are weakening,*' the mist scolded.

It felt as if she was floating outside her body. "I'm sorry," she said, trying to ignore the weird hollowness to her words. "I've found a replacement aberration, but he's not breaking."

'*We don't need him broken. We need to feed.*' The mist was hovering over a body.

Her body.

"Perhaps feeding will break him?" she asked, purposefully looking above the mantle. She'd learned long ago not to look down, lest her natural defences force the mist away.

That never ended well.

'*Bring him to us,*' the mist ordered.

"Take me to the prisoner!" Chamele called out.

Nothing happened.

"I need control back," Chamele said as sweetly as she could.

The mist grew thicker. '*Remember who is in charge,*' it warned.

Chamele gulped. "Of course," she said.

The sinking, suffocating sensation of flesh once more surrounding her made Chamele feel ill for a long moment. Something about the very nature of the mist seemed disinclined to be trapped within a singular form.

Rising on shaky legs, she wobbled her way over to the door. "Take me to the prisoner," she repeated. "I've thought of a way to break him."

The guard outside showed off his missing teeth. "As you wish."

"Alright. So. The, uh, Guardian is busy tonight. With, uh, Guardian stuff," Amara trailed off as Elani crossed her arms and leaned against a pillar.

"Right. We're going to patrol Piltarn. There have been reports that some of the Q'Aralide may be hiding there." *I got an entire sentence out without stumbling. I can do this!*

"We doubt there is any truth to the rumours," Elani added. "But it's better to disprove them than it is to dismiss them outright."

A hand rose in the back. "Will we be back in time for the joining?"

"Uh, sure," Amara began to say.

"Only if you lot don't slack off," Elani barked. "Are both groups ready?"

A bunch of wide-eyed faces nodded back at her, and she grinned at Elani. Her guild-mate twitched her lips and jerked her thumb over her shoulder. "Let's go."

Amara had never been more terrified of walking through the double doors of the museum.

The Altoriae wouldn't save her if she tripped over this time.

Inthday
Second day of the third week of Hazelcrown

Fenix sighed. There was a constant hum of sending, crawling right under their skin, as Cantash soothed Ginorti.

The feedback from the sending was making them itch, and it was harder than Fenix expected to maintain a composed front before the other Linked.

Zana's wings ruffled, and she sighed. "Are your islands trying to soothe Ginorti as well?"

"Yes!" Tania said. "It's a constant stream of comfort, but I don't think Ginorti wants to be comforted."

"I think he's missing his Linked," Cyrus said.

"Is there any news?" Fenix asked.

"There's no sign of Oakley anywhere," Cyrus said.

There was a tugging sensation, and all four Linked teared up at the same time.

"I really thought we'd find him in time for the joining," Tania whispered.

"Me too." Fenix soothingly patted her arm.

"I've been thinking, what if we leave a gap? Short enough so that everyone can cross over it, but big enough to ensure the islands aren't actually joined? That way, when we find Oakley, he can do the final bit of Innarn and will still be part of the ceremony?" Tania smiled through her welling eyes.

Grinning back, Fenix had to admire her dedication to a being she hadn't even met yet. "That sounds like a brilliant plan." Cantash's approval hummed along their nerve endings, soothing like a cold compress on a fevered brow. "Cantash approves."

"So does Rakemyst," Zana said, the corners of her lips twitching into a brief smile.

"And Talhan," Cyrus said, grinning.

"Excellent, so if we try this..." Tania pointed to a spot on the map, and the others smiled over her head before joining Ronah's Linked.

Kerday

Third day of the third week of Hazelcrown

Anika tapped on the door of the Altoriae's hospital room, half hoping that she'd be asleep.

"Come in."

Hopes squashed, Anika turned the handle. Pasting a smile on, she pushed the door open and sauntered in. "Enough lazing about in bed," she said. "It's almost time for the joining with Ginorti, and you can't be lying around on the job."

Glancing around the room, she shot a grin at the Guardian and his Apprentice. Anika was proud she managed to keep the smile when she finally caught sight of the waif who'd taken Shari's place. Pale and sweat-soaked, thinner than when she'd left on the super-secret mission, and lines of agony ringing her eyes. And her gaze...

Just what has Shari Dawn been through? A traitorous voice wondered if it was anywhere near as bad as what Anriluka had done to her. "Up. Come on." Anika summoned her bossiest tone and poked at a too-thin arm. "Everyone is waiting for you. Saying we can't do the joining without you. With Ginorti's Linked missing, we're already down one dignitary."

"Anika," the Guardian sighed.

"What? Ginorti's Linked is missing?" Shari struggled to sit up, pushing at the covers pinning her to the bed.

"Well, he's not hiding in here." Anika ignored the Guardian and hefted the garment bag in her arms. Did he really think he could keep secrets from Shari? "But you're welcome to look for him in all the hidden corners whilst you're changing." Reaching out, she made to touch the bed-ridden teen, only for a blade to appear between them.

"No," Samuel said.

"Don't *no* me," Anika snapped, hoping her tone would make them ignore the shaking of her hands. "You need to get dressed, too. I'll make sure Shari is safe, but the quicker you get ready, the quicker you'll be back."

"Anika," the Guardian tried again.

The Altoriae rolled her eyes.

She might not be able to send, but Anika could read expressions better than most, and if the two idiots didn't vacate the room soon, they'd find a dagger—or worse—thrown at their heads.

Letting her smile widen, Anika didn't take her gaze from Shari. "You aren't ready either. Go help each other. There are three female guild members ready to rush in if I so much as breathe wrong."

Grumbling, the two men left.

As the door closed behind them, Shari sighed and sank back into the pillows. "By Lissae, thank you!"

"Just because they're gone doesn't mean you can avoid this," Anika said, brushing off the comment.

Peeling back the covers, Shari swung her legs out of the bed. "Alright, what do you have for me this time?"

Anika placed the bag on the foot of the bed and carefully undid it. Lifting the gown out, she held it up by the shoulders.

Shari sucked in a breath.

The silver gown had a fitted bodice, with enough room for a flat dagger or two, a long skirt that allowed movement and hid the pants underneath, and long sleeves. That wasn't what the Altoriae was making a face at. It was the intricately, painstakingly stitched spirals, mimicking the scar patterns from Shari's aborted attempt at morphing into another creature.

"This represents your ability to keep going. To take a hit that would kill another but get back up and fight again," Anika said.

To her absolute horror, Shari started to cry.

Rooted to the spot, Anika's hand reached out, as if she could offer some sort of comfort. Whatever Shari had gone through had left her a shell of the girl who'd strode so confidently into the Ducibus's Hall. Touching her would be the height of foolishness. It wasn't as if the two of them were close, but Anika could at least try, right? "If you don't like it, there's another."

Sniffling, Shari shook her head. "It's perfect. I just..." The Altoriae looked to the side, trying to get her emotions back under control.

It was too late. Anika knew that expression. Saw it in the mirror every day since she'd been rescued from Anriluka. Knew the tightening of her jaw, the gulping breath, shoulders straightening, and... there. Ready to pretend that everything was okay in the Realms, and it was nothing more than a momentary lapse.

"It helps to talk," she blurted.

Shari looked at her and raised a brow.

"Not to me, obviously. We're not trauma buddies or anything." *Except, we kind of are.* "But a good Mind Healer can really help."

"Yeah, thanks, Anika. And thank you for the dress. It's stunning."

"As always. Still, it'll look better on than in my hands. Come on."

Fifteen exhausting minutes later, the Altoriae was dressed and ready to go. Everything looked perfect, bar the fatigue lining Shari's every move.

"The joining will be quicker than normal, I think. Ginorti needs as much comfort as you... as we do right now," Anika said lightly. "You'll be back in bed before you know it."

Reaching out, Shari grasped her hand lightly.

The strength Anika expected from the Altoriae was missing.

"Thank you," Shari said.

Anika nodded and fled the room.

She hoped Shari would get back into fighting form quickly. This new, teary version was unsettling.

Jonathan caught sight of Anika's frown as she stomped out of Shari's room, leaving without saying a word.

Straightening the hem of his pale grey tunic, he stepped back into the room, reluctant to leave Shari out of his sight for too long.

"Ready to go?" he asked.

Shari looked stunning despite her fatigue. A wave of his hand laid a glamour over her tired features. No one outside her family and the guild would know that she had been missing.

He still didn't know what had happened while she was away. There would be time after the joining to talk.

Making her way slowly to his side by grasping on to various bits of furniture made Jonathan offer Shari his arm. Before the conclave, it would have earned him a glare and had Shari rolling her eyes at him.

Now she took it gratefully, leaning on him for support.

"What's taking so long?" Samuel asked. The dark grey tunic made his shoulders look even broader. His apprentice made an intimidating figure, standing in the doorway.

"Still getting my strength back," Shari said, her voice shaky.

Instantly, Samuel was at her other side. She reached for him without hesitation.

Propped between the two of them, they walked carefully through the halls of the Healers Centre.

"Shari," Healer Holli said. "You really shouldn't be out of bed."

She pulled on his arm slightly, as if to head back to her room.

"Duty calls," Samuel said, with far too many teeth to be mistaken for anything friendly.

Holli sighed. "Don't overdo it. You'll continue to get the transfusions as long as you're on the Shifting Islands. I'll add in a low-level stimulant to get you through the joining, but once it's done, you need to be back in bed."

Shari nodded meekly.

Sending a sharp look Jonathan's way, Holli's expression conveyed her concern better than any send could have.

They stepped outside, and Shari took one look at the clouded sky and froze.

"Shari?" Samuel's voice was a rumble underneath the rolling thunder.

The bravest being he knew trembled against his side.

'*Ronah, clear the skies*,' Jonathan ordered.

The instant the bright blue was back, Shari relaxed.

Over the top of her head, he shared a look with his apprentice.

They needed to help Shari through this.

No matter what.

CHAPTER THIRTEEN

Lissae

Kerday

Third day of the third week of Hazelcrown

Shari tightened her grip on Jonathan and Samuel as the Guardian shifted them to the beach.

Except, they weren't on the white sand of Ronah's beach at all, but atop a small mountain.

"Where are we?" She hated that her voice sounded so weak. Hated that the clouds had made her stop, and the thunder made her blood freeze in her veins.

'Collis and the Returned created a wall around Ronah to prevent the mainlanders from attacking,' Jonathan sent.

Blinking, Shari was amazed at how much she'd missed whilst she'd been away.

Away.

Like she'd had a choice in the matter.

The Xanderri...

She shuddered, and Samuel took a step closer to her, trying to share his body warmth. Squeezing his arm in thanks, Shari leaned against his side.

The concern flowing from the two men was touching, but right now, they were all that stood between her and face-planting in front of the gathered crowd. At her back, she could feel her parents hovering, their nervous attention a welcome weight. The guild members were acting as a buffer between her and the rest of the curious crowd, with the Linked the only ones in front of her.

'*Where is Ginorti's Linked?*' Shari asked.

Jonathan glanced at her. '*Still lost.*'

There was a vague sense of Tania saying he was missing, but it seemed more like a faraway dream, lost in a haze of fog. Anika mentioned it too, but she'd brushed it off.

'*Oh.*' Part of her was wondering if they should be out searching, instead of joining with Ginorti. Shari wanted to stretch her Innarn out to see if she could find the lost Linked. She could feel her Innarn pulsing under her skin, but pushing it outwards was more difficult than she anticipated.

Samuel brushed against her. '*Rest. There will be time to find him after.*'

The thought niggled at Shari. Had he said the same when she was missing? She glanced up at him. By the dark rings under his eyes, he'd barely slept. That was a no, then. A tiny part of her was gratified by his concern.

A gasp from the gathered crowd brought Shari back to the joining.

Ginorti was visible on the horizon, moving sluggishly towards them. And... spinning?

Trees lined the shore a fair way from the beach. As they watched, entire chunks of sand sank beneath the waves.

'*What's going on?*' Shari asked.

'*Ginorti was poisoned, in a fashion,*' Samuel said. '*The mainlanders fired Innarn-dampening crystal onto the beaches. He must have figured it was the easiest way to get rid of the corrupted land.*'

Shari had a sense that there was more to the story than what Samuel was willing to say in public. She leaned heavier on him, as if her weight would loosen his tongue.

The incoming island continued to turn slowly, the broad side visible from where they stood. Shari felt nauseated, especially when the trees started to walk around. A breathless moment later, and the trees were not, in fact, trees at all. They were kumaru. By the size and complexity of their branches, they had to be elders.

'*The elders awoke?*'

'*We needed their help.*' Samuel's send was short, and Shari looked up as a muscle twitch in his jaw.

Jonathan patted her hand, and she glanced over to the Guardian, wishing she could clear the worry from on his face. '*The mainlanders have all but declared war on us. They aren't playing. Samuel joined the guild and some of the Ilutri to protect Ginorti.*'

Part of Shari wanted to cry, *what about me?* She huffed. When had she ever needed or wanted someone else to save her? Standing taller, she tried not to lean on the men on either side of her for a moment.

A crashing wave of dizziness made her sway. Setting her feet shoulder width apart and locking her knees, Shari stared stubbornly out as Ginorti continued to whirl. Calem's hand pressed against her back—a steady presence against the twisting thoughts.

'*You were in the Lightest of Realms, Shari. He would have died.*' Jonathan's voice was little more than an echo in the back of her mind.

Zuefie had almost killed her. Samuel wouldn't have made it through the gateway.

She nodded and sighed as the spinning slowed.

The shorter end of Ginorti came into view, lined with beings. They were close enough now that Shari could make out each individual. The gloss on the kumaru's leaves, the belted weapons on the satyrs' hips. She nodded to General Morrow, who dipped his head in return.

The Linked stepped forward as one, arms up and hands stretched wide as the Innarn of their island poured through them.

An ancient kumaru, face so gnarled it was hard to believe ze wasn't rooted to the spot, slowly stepped forward. Ze's roots didn't want to leave the earth. The kumaru stretched an arm, and vines sprang out, shooting towards Ronah and the gathered crowd. The vine twisted, flattening and broadening into a bridge that reached all the way to Ronah.

The Innarn from the Linked slipped alongside the vine bridge. Plasma and Fire created a crackling handrail, Air and Crystal weaving through the gaps in the vines to make a smooth path. Once the bridge was done, the kumaru and the Linked brought their hands down in swift synchronisation, and the bridge broke clean through the middle.

The surrounding crowd gasped.

General Morrow stepped forward, long silver hair glowing in the wake of the Innarn pulsing through the broken bridge. He made his way to the break, resting his hooves right on the edge. "Our Linked is missing. Once Oakley returns, he will finish the bridge and join us properly." He stepped across the gap. "Until then, we are free to reconnect and explore all we offer. Go freely, knowing that the Shifting Islands will continue to fight for Lissae's liberty and for our own."

The instant the general stopped talking, the ground on Ginorti's side started rumbling.

Shari clutched Jonathan's arm at the noise, her Innarn flaring around her but fading out as her fingers tightened.

From the other side of the broken bridge, a shape was forming from the earth.

The kumaru stepped up, too slowly to stop the golem from emerging.

'*The bridge is broken. Protect the bridge.*' The refrain repeated, and it Shari took a long moment to realise it was coming from the golem.

"What is that?" Tania asked, her voice wavering. "Not a hantra?"

"No," Jonathan said. "A golem. A creature of limited sentience created for a particular purpose. This one must be charged with protecting the bridge."

"It's all my fault. I wanted Oakley to join the islands together once he returns," Tania said, eyes wide as she watched the golem effortlessly bat away an ancient kumaru.

"It would take all the power of the Linked to stop it," Cyrus said.

"Or one Altoriae," Fenix added.

Biting back an incredulous laugh, Shari tightened her grip on Jonathan and Samuel. "Of course." Giving them one last squeeze, she stepped forward. Ignoring the shaking of her legs, Shari carefully made her way through the Linked and towards the bridge—only the combination of Jonathan and Samuel's Innarn swirling around her kept her upright.

As she came to the break in the bridge, Shari paused. She wasn't sure if her halting steps would be long enough to get her over a gap she wouldn't have previously considered an obstacle.

'*We've got you,*' Jonathan sent, the thought echoed by Samuel.

Bolstered by their Innarn, Shari stepped forward, allowing them to carry her over to the relative safety of the other side.

The hatchlings were whispering inside her head about *trust* and *Sanithane* and *believe*.

For the moment, Shari put their meddling to one side, and focused instead on the golem waiting for her. Slowly, she walked towards the start of the bridge and the waiting creature.

'*The bridge is broken. Protect the bridge.*'

'*I will protect the bridge,*' Shari sent to the golem.

The creature of earth shambled around on legs thicker than her body. '*Protect the bridge?*'

'*Yes. I will.*' Shari wanted to glance back at those waiting behind her but stood her ground. '*We will. The beings of the Shifting Islands will ensure the bridge is safe while we wait for Ginorti's Linked to return.*'

'*I am Ginorti.*'

Sucking in a harsh breath that rattled her lungs, Shari chanced a glance at General Morrow, who was standing off to the side, bow at the ready. '*Ginorti?*'

'*Want Oakley.*'

"I know," Shari said aloud. "I know you want your Linked back. I've been... away. But now I'm back, I'll do everything in my power to bring him home."

The golem nodded its misshapen head. '*Hurt.*'

"He's hurt? Do you know where Oakley is being held?"

'*You.*'

Shari wrinkled her brow. She wasn't holding the Linked. '*Do you mean I'm hurt?*'

The golem nodded again.

'*I...*' Years of ignoring that she was in pain made the denial spring immediately to her mind. Shari took a breath. '*Yes. But I have help. And friends to make sure I'll get better. Just like Oakley when he returns.*'

The golem frowned, dirt crumbling from its face. '*Not child.*'

'*I know you're not. You're older and wiser than any of us. Communicating in such a cumbersome way must be difficult. And we appreciate the effort. Can you sense your people?*'

Head twisting, the golem regarded the kumaru it had so unceremoniously flicked to the side, and General Morrow, standing with his ever-present bow at his side. 'Yes.'

"While we search for Oakley, we will all protect you as best we can," Shari said, mostly for the others present.

'*Hurt.*' The golem sent again.

This time, there was the instant awareness that the isle himself was in pain.

'*Is it the crystal?*'

Another nod.

If ever there was a time to trust those around her, it was now.

'*I'll do what I can to remove it,*' Shari said. '*We all will.*'

The golem nodded and plodded off to the side. Crouching, it lowered its head and resembled nothing more than a lumpy boulder. Another golem sprung up opposite the first. One on each side of the bridge. From the rolling exclamations, more golems had appeared.

'*Safe.*' The golem's send was sluggish, as if the creature was going back to sleep. Or had spent all its energy in communicating.

Shari felt much the same, but the weight of watching eyes prevented her from sagging. Without turning, she let the vibration of footsteps on her side of the broken bridge soothe her.

Silently, the four Linked joined her.

There was a warmth at Shari's back, and a brush of fingers along her arm. Samuel had returned to her side, Jonathan only a half-step behind his apprentice.

General Morrow returned to his place at the foot of the bridge. "It is customary for the Linked of a Shifting Island to offer the Altoriae a tour." He glanced at the golem, who remained still. "It would be my honour as one of Ginorti's elders to escort you around our island in our Linked's place."

Part of Shari wanted to look at Jonathan to see what the right thing to do was. Being alone with strangers, even if they were of Lissae, was quite beyond her capabilities at the moment. Her Guardian's Innarn brushed against her own, bolstering Shari once more.

"It would be our privilege to join you, General Morrow," Jonathan said, filling her silence.

The general glanced at her. "Perhaps..."

"We should greet the kumaru first," Tania butted in.

A deeper voice behind Shari said, "I've always wanted to ask the kumaru how they stand still for so long."

Trying to stifle her laughter, Shari looked over her shoulder at her uncle. "Maybe they'd like to know why you prefer the air to the ground?"

He grumbled at her but was betrayed by the corner of his lips turning up.

"Very well." General Morrow's gaze rested on Shari for a moment longer, but he stepped aside, allowing the decidedly unconventional group to pass.

For once, Shari was glad her newly acknowledged status came with fewer questions. The Linked, the Altoriae and her Guardian, then the elders, should have crossed the bridges first. As it was, her parents, Wolf, Belfar, and a sizeable chunk of the Altoriae's Guild had trooped across the bridge unimpeded.

Samuel held his arm out to Shari, who grasped it with a grateful smile. The Guardian fell into step on her other side as they followed the satyr for a tour of the latest Shifting Island.

Oalark's promise to divide the landmasses up between the beings of the Dark Realms floated through the back of his mind as the satyr led them from the much narrower beach through a majestic forest. The canopy overhead was dense enough to filter out the burning light, and he almost wished that Shari would make her home here.

The general was motioning to things, his mouth moving as he was no doubt spouting pleasant facts about Cylanthar knew what. All of Samuel's focus was on the heartbeat of the Altoriae.

The way it was racing.

Half-sure it was in fear, he glanced down at the top of her head. She looked up at him and smiled easily.

Samuel wasn't sure he deserved that.

Shari had seen the things he'd done at the Dark Conclave and heard stories of far worse deeds. How could she smile at him so complacently?

The trees split apart, revealing a clearing around a bunch of... other trees.

Helping Ginorti protect his shores had shown Samuel that the other beings of Lissae weren't necessarily afraid of him. He wasn't sure if the lack of fear was due to limited brain cells or even less understanding. Or perhaps, they all thought the Guardian had tamed him to an extent. Maybe he needed to eat a few to ensure the proper level of fear was maintained?

"Although there are bereni and rezems scattered through the forests, our main settlement is here," General Morrow was saying.

Is this all Ginorti is? Twigs and leaves?

Something sharp stung his ear, and Samuel hissed, making the general pause in his speech. Muttering an apology, he raised his hand and pulled Sneeze off his shoulder.

'No *biting*,' he sent to the tiny draci.

'*More than leaves,*' Sneeze huffed, a double ring of smoke puffing out his nostrils.

'*Apologies,*' he said.

"Who's this?" Shari whispered, her gaze fixed on the draci.

Sneeze sneezed, tiny sparks stinging against Samuel's skin.

"Shari, meet Sneeze."

The draci looked up and beamed at the Altoriae, showing his minuscule fangs.

"Awww, he looks like a tiny Tormorylth," Shari cooed.

"Who?" Jonathan asked. "Was ze a delegate?"

"No," Shari said. "She's one of the Q'Aralide hatchlings in my sanctuary."

CHAPTER FOURTEEN

Lissae

Kerday

Third day of the third week of Hazelcrown

The Guardian shook his head, certain he'd heard wrong. "I'm sorry, what?" Jonathan said. There was no way she could so calmly say...

"The hatchlings we saved. They're in my sanctuary."

When Samuel had mentioned them before, he'd been half-humouring him. It hadn't occurred to him that Shari would bring them back. In a daze, Jonathan rubbed a hand over his face as Samuel turn and grasp Shari by her biceps. "Are they alright?"

"Mostly." Shari's head dipped. "It was touch and go for a moment. Back on Zuefie."

"But now?" Samuel's voice dropped and his eyebrows drew together.

"Just..." Jonathan's voice cracked. He soldiered on. "Just how many hatchlings are we talking here?"

"Two," Shari said. "And the egg."

"You have an egg?" Samuel squeaked.

When Jonathan finished processing the idea that there were now *four* deadly Q'Aralide inhabiting Lissae, he'd make a note to tease his friend about it. Carefully.

Samuel could be so sensitive.

"There are three Q'Aralide in your sanctuary. Right now?" Jonathan asked. They were drawing the attention of the others.

"Everything okay, Guardian?" Calem asked, his gaze fixed on where Samuel held Shari.

"Fine. Shari's feeling a bit faint," Samuel said idly.

Jonathan felt like laughing. If anyone was feeling faint, it was him.

Four Q'Aralide.

On Lissae.

Right now.

He breathed in, counted to four, and breathed out again.

If Shari could survive in the Lightest of Realms, he should be able to contain himself in the middle of Ginorti's main township.

Under Samuel's hands, the Altoriae trembling.

'*Faint?*' she asked.

At least she was nowhere near any sort of fainting spell.

"I am not feeling faint," she hissed.

Maybe the trembling was more out of an intense urge to maim him?

Right this second, he didn't care.

His hatchlings had survived.

I'm not alone.

Relief washed over Samuel like a wave, his knees going weak. Half holding Shari up, and half leaning on her, Samuel's cheeks hurting from grinning so much.

Not alone. The words echoed through his head, chasing the cobwebs away. It was as if knowing he wasn't the last member of his race cleared his thoughts.

"Samuel?" Shari asked. "My dad is about to separate you from your hands."

Sneeze bit his ear again. Hastily, Samuel removed his hands, lost in the idea that his hatchlings were safe. And there was an *egg*.

Not alone. Not the last.

'*I'm not sure that Lissae is the right place for two Q'Aralide hatchlings,*' Jonathan sent.

Rounding on the Guardian, Samuel clenched his jaw so he wouldn't snarl. '*Where should they go then? Back to what's left of Altum? The Realm we destroyed? Or perhaps we should let them loose on the Portal, leave hatchlings to fend for themselves and hope for the best?*'

Shari reached out and touched his arm, soothing the coiled muscles. '*We can't send them away, Jonathan,*' she sent. '*So long as Samuel is around, the hatchlings are safe.*'

'*But would they survive outside of your sanctuary?*'

General Morrow approached the trio. "Is Ginorti not what you were expecting?"

Samuel stared, dumbfounded, as Shari lied. "I'm feeling a little worn. The Guardian and Apprentice are trying to convince me to return and rest, but I'd like to continue with the tour."

"Worn?" the general looked over the Altoriae, prodding at her with his own Innarn and making the threads which held Shari upright jump and spark. "I see." He looked at the Guardian for a moment, before returning his gaze back to Shari. "Even the strongest of our warriors need to rest."

Nodding, Shari lowered her head.

Jonathan caught his gaze. Neither of them knew what to do with this new, passive Altoriae.

"Rest, Altoriae. We would be honoured to give you a private tour at a later time."

"My thanks, General," she said.

"We bid thee well." Jonathan dipped his head, and Samuel followed suit.

Before he knew it, they were back in Shari's hospital room.

The Altoriae swayed slightly, the little colour she had falling away.

"Rest," he said, pushing her lightly.

She fell backwards onto the bed. "But I can…"

Shari was asleep before she finished the sentence.

Narday
Fourth day of the third week of Hazelcrown

Jonathan nodded to Asterion as he entered Shari's room. She was still stuck in bed at the Healers Centre.

"Well met, Altoriae, Guardian, Apprentice," the minotaur said.

"Well met. Do you have news?" Jonathan asked.

Shari sat up, wriggling against the colourful pillows. "News?"

Ever since Shari had formally recognised him as her Guardian, they had shared a stream of consciousness. The moment Shari had stepped onto Altum, the connection had been severed. After being able to communicate to Shari for so long, it was disconcerting to have her not know something he did.

"Asterion is working as my assistant. He's been talking to Ginorti's elders to see how we can aid them."

"They have been quite welcoming." He gave Jonathan a significant look.

The Guardian nodded, acknowledging the unspoken message. Those in Ginorti didn't share the same prejudices that Asterion had found in other places.

"The kumaru elder, now ze has awoken, has refused to return to zir rest. Ze fears the contaminated crystal in the soil."

'Contaminated crystal?' Shari asked.

Jonathan's smile became fixed. Shari had never asked him to repeat information like this before. 'Mainlanders fired Innarn blockers at Ginorti's beaches,' Jonathan replied.

Shari frowned.

Jonathan fought to keep his expression clear. In the furrow of the Altoriae's brow, the Shari he knew returning. "Did the spinning not help?" the Guardian asked.

"It did, but there are still shards present. To return to zir rest, Gangar would risk zir roots coming into contact with the shards, which could kill zim," Asterion said.

An indrawn breath made them look at Shari. To cover how uncomfortable she was, Shari asked, "What can we do to help?"

"Find the shards. Some are as small as a grain of sand."

Green swirled in Shari's eyes. For someone who didn't know better, it would be easy to mistake the colour for her healing Innarn. Having been on the receiving end of Shari's healing more times than he'd like to admit, Jonathan felt certain the colour was different. More like the lightest of spring leaves than the deeper winter greens.

"What are you thinking?" Jonathan asked. He ignored the thought that itched at him. Before the Dark Council, he wouldn't have had to ask.

"Something like the net when Rakemyst was attacked by the Chirea," Shari replied.

"To find the feather?" Jonathan checked. Shari had woven a massive sieve out of fallen branches to find a golden feather held dear by one of the fallen Ilutri.

"A feather is significantly larger than the crystal shards we're looking for," Asterion said.

"It's a start." Samuel glared at the minotaur, as if not agreeing with Shari was a crime worth eviscerating him for.

"I could…" Shari pulled the covers to one side.

A healer appeared in the doorway, frowning. "You could stay right there."

Jonathan had to hide a smile. Holli Donovan had an uncanny knack of knowing when one of her patients was causing trouble.

Shari sighed.

"You have a guild for a reason, Altoriae, and they want to *help* you get better. Why not set them this impossible task?" Holli suggested as she firmly tucked the blankets back around Shari.

"But…"

The send was an echo in his mind. '*Hyper-independence isn't healthy, Shari. Learning to trust is going to be hard for you, but something well worth practising. And now, when you need to rest, is the perfect time to practice.*' Holli gently smiled at Shari. The message was as much for him as it was for his charge. Even if neither of them wanted to admit it.

The Altoriae pouted, and Jonathan felt like joining her.

"We can help," Samuel said. "Tell me more about this net."

Settling back to get more comfortable, Shari began explaining her plan.

Holli locked gazes with Jonathan. '*You'll need to watch both of them. The guilt he carries for her disappearance will drive your apprentice to push himself beyond what he is capable of.*'

'*And who will watch me?*' Jonathan sent wirily.

Grinning, Holli nodded at the doorway. Looking over, Jonathan caught sight of Zac and practically melted at the goofy smile the other man wore.

"Anyone for a cup of azehal?" Zac asked, lifting a steaming copper jug.

"Oh, I…" *love you.* Jonathan stopped himself before the dangerous words could slip past his teeth. "I'd love one," he finished lamely.

Zac poured him a cup and pushed it into his hands with a wink. Bounding over to the bed, he started nattering on about the delights of Cantash and Ginorti that Shari just *had* to see.

Staring into his cup of azehal, Jonathan wasn't sure what he was going to do about this latest revelation.

Zuefie

Thunder and lightning flashed through the bodies of the Xanderri as they mourned the loss of their biggest meal and their chance to take over Lissae.

'*We need more Innarn,*' the biggest cloud sent.

The Otike puppet, formally known as Zirgha, jerked to a stop in front of zim. '*Join with me.*'

'*We dislike this,*' the biggest cloud rumbled.

'*We have a way to travel through the portal.*' Zirgha's limbs jerked, a flap of useless flesh falling from a limb.

'*Will your host survive?*'

'*We have many hosts.*' An upper limb jolted to the side, showing the sacrifices they'd gathered.

The largest cloud dove towards the most recent one, and the grin the body wore split the facial skin of the puppet. '*We do indeed.*'

CHAPTER FIFTEEN

Lissae

Rasshday

Fifth day of the third week of Hazelcrown

Chamele frowned at the headline in the local newspaper.

Erupting volcano causes township to flee.

This was the third natural disaster in as many weeks.

Her contemplation of the news was interrupted by the doors of her suite being flung open. Captain Rappen strode in as if he owned the place.

"Elder," he bowed his head—just.

Setting aside the newspaper, Chamele shooed the guards out of the room. Once the door was closed behind them, she adjusted her veil and neatly folded her hands in her lap. "Captain. What news of our... experiment?"

"It refuses to talk... so far."

"I assume you have applied appropriate force?" Icy prickles started dancing over her skin. Clouds swam in Chamele's vision, and the elder would have groaned aloud if it weren't for her current company. "Not now," she hissed.

Too late.

She was looking down at her body as the cloud filled the room.

'*You were strong,*' her cloud said.

'Yes, I *am*,' Chamele said.

The cloud drifted away. They stroked the captain. '*We need someone stronger.*'

'*No. No, you can't leave me. Not after so long,*' Chamele implored.

'*But we want—must. Captain?*'

"Yes?" Captain Rappen knelt and rolled her body over far less gently than she deserved.

'*You will be our new host.*'

"I'm host to no..." The captain didn't have time to refute. Flinging his head back, Captain Rappen would have screamed if it weren't for the cloud pouring into his mouth. Shuddering, he fell.

Chamele was sucked into her own body once more. As she pushed herself off the floor, the elder looked at the captain. It had been so long since the cloud had taken her over, it was hard to remember the first time.

An age later, Captain Rappen's eyes flung open, and he took a great, gasping breath. Jerkily, he rose. "It is time for us to go." His voice echoed, as if many beings were speaking over the top of one another. "You are fading." The sword hanging from the captain's hip sang as he withdrew it.

The tip was at her throat before Chamele could blink.

"But you were a suitable host." The multiple voices seemed confused, and the point of the sword wavered, as if the captain was warring with himself.

Or the thing that now controlled his body.

Chamele didn't dare breathe.

"We will let you die." The sword lowered. "Alone."

Sheathing his blade, Captain Rappen turned away.

"Wait!" Chamele cried. Without the cloud, she could already feel her limbs weakening. "What will become of me?"

He didn't turn back.

"I still command the armies! I can still get you the aberrations!"

The captain paused and looked over his shoulder at her. "And yet, you remain here, talking, while this body goes and does the things you command."

Chamele's jaw fell as Captain Rappen left the room.

Clouds no longer in her vision, the elder dropped to the floor and sobbed.

Vebaday

Sixth day of the third week of Hazelcrown

There was a rustle of fabric outside Shari's door.

"Are you ready?" Fenix asked, poking their head through the opening.

"Ready for what?" Shari asked.

"Your tour." They slid into the room, looking amazing in tight pants, a long-sleeved red shirt with black cuffs and chains that looped through holes at the bottom of the shirt and attached to a longer, asymmetrical piece that moved like a skirt, but wasn't.

"I don't think I'm allowed to leave," Shari said. It still stung slightly that Holli had told her off last night.

"Privilege of being a Linked. I'm breaking you out." Fenix winked and whipped back the sheets.

Shari blushed as Fenix whistled.

"Someone was already planning on sneaking out, it looks like."

"Say it louder for the healers on the mainland, why don't you," Shari grumbled.

Laughing, Fenix held out their hand. "Come. Run away with me."

"Gladly," Shari said. She took their hand, and Cantash's Linked pulled her up with surprising strength. Swaying, she stumbled before regaining her balance.

"Ready to escape?" Fenix said in a mock whisper.

"You did clear this with Holli." There was a squeezing sensation, and salt air with a touch of brimstone hit her nostrils. The Healers Centre had disappeared. It had been replaced with a brightly decorated room with a low table off to the side. Colourful cushions were scattered on the floor, and a plant with pale, green leaves hung by the door. "Right?"

"If it makes you feel better, sure." Fenix winked again and turned, almost tripping over a diminutive man with curly, white hair. "Milo!"

"Well met, Fenix, Altoriae. I was unaware you were back on Lissae."

Shari stopped, looking around the place they'd shifted to, and tilted her head. "Where else would I be?"

"Oh, far be it for me to know," Milo blustered. "I was just checking in with today's schedule."

Fenix reached out and swiped the clipboard in Milo's hands. "Schedule's been cleared. Look at that."

"But... I..."

"Go. Enjoy your day off," Fenix said, pointing to the door.

He shoved a vial with blue liquid into Fenix's hands. "At least take your medicine first!"

Sighing, they uncorked the vial and tipped their head back, swallowing it easily.

Right as Shari noted the glowing yellow motes, the hatchlings piped up.

'Bad...'

The word echoed in her head, and Shari's gaze flicked between Milo and the vial, wondering which one they were referring to.

"I have a spare for you, Altoriae," Milo said, lines creasing his face as he smiled a tad too brightly. "Fenix's mother swore this helped her grow stronger. Perhaps it will aid you?"

'*Don't drink.*' Jetonyx's voice sounded louder.

"Ah, the healers have me dosed to the eyes," Shari said easily. "But I can check with them first?" She made to take to the proffered vial.

Milo pulled it back. "Secret family recipe, I'm afraid," he said.

"Day. Off." Fenix grumped and bodily moved the tiny man out the door.

"Fenix!" he grumbled. Still blustering, Milo made his way outside with only a bit of helped from the Linked's Innarn.

As the tiny man disappeared, Fenix sighed. "Got to love him, but Milo doesn't do subtle at all," Fenix said. "Now, the tour can begin!"

"And where are we?" Shari asked, trying to brush aside the slimy feeling of Milo's Innarn rubbing against her own. '*Jonathan, does Milo feel weird, or is it just me?*'

'*No just you.*' Her Guardian sounded tired.

'*He tried to give me something to drink.*' Shari sent.

'*Shari?*' Jonathan sounded far more away, her name practically quivering in his mind.

She scoffed. '*I didn't have any.*'

Jonathan's sigh echoed down their link. '*Stay safe. And if he tries anything, kick him, hard.*'

She stifled her giggle and turned her attention back to her host.

"My house," Fenix said.

Looking around, Shari was charmed by how warm and inviting everything was, and said as much.

"Wait till you see outside." Fenix opened the door and bowed, gesturing for her to go first.

Slowly, Shari made her way outside, the heat seeping into her bones. Combined with the sea breeze, it finally felt like she was home. Buildings were crowded all around them at different angles. The layout of Cantash made no sense at all, but she could vaguely remember being told that was the whole idea.

Dry and warm, with pale-coloured buildings all over the island, Fenix took her on a tour that stopped at two massive, steel double doors. Despite looking nothing like the ones at Ronah's museum, it still reminded Shari of them, and she reached out a hand, stroking the metal.

The doors hummed and slid open.

"Huh," Fenix said. "Never done that for me."

Shari laughed. "I must just have the right touch." Stepping through the doors and into the metal box, she grinned at Fenix as they joined her.

"Has the Guardian told you anything about Cantash's gardens?"

"A little," Shari said. "And Tania says there's a school down here as well, but she hasn't seen it yet."

"Yes, our exchange program was kind of... side tracked," Fenix said. Their smile became strained, and Shari blanched. Did she have to smooth any sort of hurt feelings over?

Before she could think about what to do, the metal box slid to a stop, and Fenix stepped out of it, into a veritable jungle.

"By the life of Lissae," Shari breathed. A direct contrast to Cantash's surface, the gardens were lush. She could hear creatures of all types and spied a few winged ones flitting from tree to tree.

"If the Guardian has spoiled my fun with this, then you'll just have to make do with the other half of the garden."

"The other half?" Shari said faintly.

"It's where we work and learn. Surely you can't expect kids to pay attention when there's an active volcano spitting at them from their classroom window?"

"Course not," Shari murmured. She was barely paying attention now, her head swivelling this way and that to take in all the sights. Draci were flying above them. A caelonis was burning bugs for an arustos. Plants with the juiciest apples she'd ever seen hung from low boughs. "Do you come down here often?"

"Every day. Got to get our green time," Fenix said cheerfully.

Shari could see why the gardens had earned the nickname.

Cantash's Linked led her to the far end, where buildings were carved out of the rock walls. They pointed to a large archway with stylised flames etched around it. "Welcome to our school," Fenix said.

"Shari!" Tania was grinning at her, and other students from Ronah poured out and crowded around.

The press of bodies that would have once sent her reaching for her weapons was now a welcome reminder that there were tangible beings close enough to touch, or to help.

"Well met," she grinned. An unfamiliar Innarn wrapped around her, helping her to stand tall. Shari's blood pounding through her veins as she searched out the source.

'Easy, Altoriae. My little sister asked that I watch over you.' The voice was soothing but not one she could remember hearing before.

'Cantash?'

'Well met, Altoriae.'

Sagging into the Innarn around her, Shari sighed.

"It's so good to..." Tania stopped, flushing.

"Finally get a tour of Cantash! Patrols have kept me so busy," Shari said, easily filling in the blanks. *Some things are ingrained, like lying about where I've been.*

"Cantash has been so excited to formally meet you," Fenix said, bouncing on their toes.

Shari smiled. "I'm sorry I had to go before the feast started."

A Daen pushed his way forward. He looked slightly too old to be a student, but not old enough to be a teacher. "Not to worry. We're always ready to feast!"

"True," Fenix laughed. "Altoriae, meet the Head of Ignis Academy, Professor Ember Sparks."

Biting the inside of her cheek to stop herself from grinning at his name, Shari dipped her head. "Well met, Professor."

"Well met. Are you joining us for classes today?" The Professor beamed at her, like he knew exactly what she was thinking.

Glancing at Fenix, she shrugged.

"'Fraid not, Professor. The Altoriae has a few duties to attend to before returning to class," Fenix said, slinging an arm around Shari's shoulders.

Seems she wasn't the only one able to lie so easily.

The Professor slumped and looked significantly older than he had moments before. "Maybe next time?"

"I'll see what I can do," Shari said. The idea of going back to class was tempting, if only as a distraction from the thoughts clattering around in her head.

"Excellent! All right, students, call time! We have learning to do."

Everyone filtered back inside, Tania waving at Shari before disappearing.

"Come on," Fenix urged. They guided her along the wall, stopping to point out different things along the way. "There are four schools on Cantash. One for littles, one for younger teens, another for older teens, and the fourth for adults who want to continue their education. Professor Sparks looks after all of them. They sit on the main compass points at different parts of the isle. Each has a door to get to and from the other quickly, in case of emergency, or if a prank war is called." Fenix grinned.

"A prank war?" Shari asked.

"Tradition dictates on the last week of the school year, a prank war is called. Most of the time, it's the younger teens who win," Fenix was beaming now.

"How does a prank war work?" Shari wondered.

"Three rules: nothing permanent, nothing harmful, and don't get caught."

"So...?" Shari broke off. The only things she could think of would violate at least two of the three rules.

"Things like buckets of flour perched carefully atop ajar doors. When the next being, usually a teacher, walks through, they're covered in flour."

Shari chuckled. "I can see how that would blow off a bit of steam after exams."

"Between each of the schools is a range of restaurants, businesses, and services, including libraries, museums, galleries, and way more. We provide the only source of calromata and eobustus in Lissae, and our crafts people have workshops set up along the wall as well. It would take half a day to walk around the entire island, but a lil draci told me you like museums?"

Shari nodded.

"Perfect. Come this way!" Fenix bounded along, their enthusiasm contagious. Stopping before two charcoal black doors, they said, "Welcome to Cantash's Museum."

Tania smiled as she slipped out of the doors of Ignis Academy to find Collis waiting for her.

Collis grinned back. "Have a good day?"

"Yes! I love that Cantash has students separated by age and ability, rather than everyone at the same school. I kind of wish we could do the same thing on Ronah."

Eyeing the students pouring into the garden, Collis said, "Cantash has a much larger population than Ronah. All the other Shifting Islands seem to."

"Well—" Tania felt a phantom twinge of pain, and knew Ronah, despite getting her people back, still mourned for all the years they had been separated. "Now there's a whole heap more, with the refugees."

"Who are going to other islands." He offered his arm to her, and Tania tucked her hand into the crook of his elbow, letting Collis guide her through the masses.

"Some will stay with us," Tania said weakly. Between the Returned and the influx of refugees, Ronah's resources were pushed to the max. She'd had a meeting with the elders, who had promised to put out notifications for everyone to be supportive and limit their consuming to what was necessary, but some were still bitter.

"Most will go. They are used to having space and being able to create their own communities." Collis smiled down at her.

"True." Tania just wished that she could do more.

"Tomorrow, Ginorti's students will sit in Ridden Hall. Are you going to attend their school as well?"

The change of subject was as obvious as it was welcome. "Yes, I think so. Will you be there?"

His Innarn brushed hers, and Tania smiled. Something about Zana announcing that they were soul-matched had eased a longing she hadn't wanted to acknowledge.

They reached the doors of the lift, which would take them back to the surface. Tania wrinkled her nose at the massive crowd ahead of them.

Before she could say a word, they had been sucked into the soil and spat out in front of Collis' rezem. Laughing, she shook the soil from her hair. "Benefits of being a Linked?" she asked.

Collis grinned and rubbed a smudge of dirt from her cheek.

Hindsight would say that Shari could have timed things better.

The line for the lift out of the gardens was massive. She felt like a giant amongst the tiny students pouring out of the closest school, which had to be for the littlest Daens.

"You could just shift away, you know?" a voice murmured.

Looking to the side, Shari spotted the girl with blue hair and a burn mark where her ear should have been. They'd met on Talhan and patrolled together. "Eva, right?"

Eva grinned. "The one and only. What brings you to Cantash?" Hanging onto her arm was another girl, who was staring sightlessly into the distance.

"Finally had time for a tour," Shari said.

"Wow. So, it's true then?"

"What's true?" Shari asked.

Lowering her voice and stepping closer, Eva whispered, "We're at war?"

Shari wanted to deny it, but the rumblings she'd heard said otherwise. "I've been off-Realm. What war?"

"The one with the mainlanders?"

"Eva." The other girl tugged on her friend. "Don't."

"Have we met?" Shari was eager to avoid talks of war until she'd spoken to Jonathan.

"I'm Reah." She ducked her head. "Well met, *Altoriae*."

Rolling her eyes, Eva stepped back. "Fine, I'll behave."

Reah grinned and kissed Eva's cheek. "Thank you."

"We're going to see Lizbeth," Eva confided.

"Oh, Lizbeth is lovely. Please remind her to send to me when she's free," Shari said.

"When you're free, more like it," Eva laughed, and tugged Reah onto the lift. She gave Shari a jaunty wave as the doors slid shut.

Slumping, Shari wished she could do more. She needed to heal faster and stop this war before it properly started.

But first, she needed to talk to her Guardian.

Arilla flexed her fingers around the handle of her sword.

If she hadn't promised to be here, she'd be... what? Shadowing her almost adult daughter? Surely, as a mother, it was her right to ensure Shari recovered from her capture in a safe, loving environment?

Taking a breath and relaxing the death grip she had on the handle again, Arilla tried to shake the thoughts out of her head. "Well done, Anika! A little higher next time, and block with your daggers, not your arm. Steel can take the blow much better."

Shari had been independent since she was tiny. If Arilla had the timing figured out, it was around when Lissae had asked her daughter to be the Altoriae that it had all started. Some days, she considered asking the Guardian to wind time back and give Shari an easier childhood.

"Excellent! Now, swap partners and go again," she called.

The students swapped, and the clash of steel on steel started up, peppered with the occasional curse as a blow landed.

Was it wrong to want to keep the Altoriae wrapped up in the softest of blankets, safe at home while everyone else fought the oncoming war?

If it was anyone else's child, she would have said yes.

But Shari was hers.

And she would do anything to keep her safe.

"You are an excellent teacher," a deep voice said, making her jump. "Even when you're distracted."

Arilla turned, the point of her sword sweeping up until she registered who was speaking.

General Morrow.

Leader of the crack troop of satyrs.

"Well met, General."

"Well met, Arilla." He looked over the rows of students feinting and blocking. "I heard of your lessons and had to see for myself. Are they only for Blanks?"

Her smile became fixed. "We don't have anyone else to teach us, so I figured I'd step up."

"A few of my troop are Blanks as well," the General said.

Out of the corner of her eye, Arilla noted that those closest stopped and stared, unashamedly listening in.

"Not all care to wield a sword. I'm sure they'd be happy to introduce your students to a few alternative methods."

"That is a generous offer, General," Arilla said, touched.

"More than an offer—a promise, if you wish to take them up on it."

"We would be honoured," Arilla said.

"Yes!" one of those closest said. "Ow!"

"Remember to block," Arilla called out, turning back to the class.

"I'll send word when they are free. I bid thee well." The General bowed and strode away.

"I bid thee well," Arilla said faintly. She'd never thought a general would bow to her. A Blank.

Maybe the Realms were changing.

And maybe she'd find the strength to help Shari and not just hide her away.

'I want to go out!' Tormorylth grumbled.

Jetonyx sighed. *'We can't. The Altoriae has to let us out.'* He was perched at the top of a sturdy tree; one Shari had constructed just for him. Although Tormorylth liked to nestle under his wing as often as he'd let her.

Tormorylth's frustration was understandable. She'd seen Altum collapse and had their supposed haven start imploding with them in it.

Just because it was understandable, didn't make it any less annoying.

'But...'

He growled and stared down at her. An old trick that Sanithane had used when Jetonyx and his nest mates had been acting like brats.

The hatchling rolled all three of her eyes. *'Growling won't change my mind. I want out!'*

'Next time the Altoriae visits, we'll speak to her.'

'Like she's going to come back soon,' Tormorylth said, gesturing to the screens floating in the sky.

Shari was in a cosy room, with a fire crackling off to the side. The walls were lined with tomes, and she was idly flicking through one in her hands.

One of Jetonyx's hearts sank.

He wanted out too, and the Altoriae looked far too comfortable where she was to be coming back to her sanctuary.

Chapter Sixteen

Lissae

Vebaday

Sixth day of the third week of Hazelcrown

Jonathan smiled and fell into step with her as she entered the castle. She wasn't about to admit to her Guardian she'd walked halfway to her parents' house before remembering all her things were here.

"Glad I caught you. I wanted you to meet the newest residents of the castle," Jonathan said.

Shari tried to grin back and wasn't entirely sure she'd succeeded. She felt drained after her day exploring Cantash and wanted nothing more than to curl up in her own bed, seeing as Holli had released her from the Healers Centre. "Sure."

"You alright?" he asked, frowning.

"Tired," Shari admitted, pausing at the edge of the stairs.

"We can leave it until..." He broke off, glancing upwards.

Startling green eyes looked down at them.

"Grace?" Jonathan said.

"Sorry! She heard voices and..." Another appeared, and Shari vaguely recognised her as one of the mainlander's aides she'd met on Talhan.

A low rumbling filled the foyer, and Shari's bladed glove snapped into place.

'It's *alright*,' Jonathan sent. 'It's *Grace*.'

The being with green eyes was growling at her. '*Aberration*.'

The word thrummed through Shari's head.

"Grace, come and meet Shari. She's the Altoriae," someone was saying.

Shari was too busy trying not to tremble to figure out who was talking. The rumbling was making her think of hungry clouds and dying beings spitting hateful words at her.

Screwing her eyes closed didn't help. When she opened them, the green eyes were so much closer, and Innarn almost as strong as her own–and somehow familiar–was thrashing through the room.

'*Aberration*.'

The word was so loud, a headache instantly bloomed to life on the left side of Shari's skull.

'*Altoriae*,' Shari sent back, just as loud.

The owner of the green eyes froze. '*Altoriae?*'

The aide was standing at the bottom of the stairs. "Don't let her touch you," she warned.

Grace was reaching out for her, spider-like fingers a hairsbreadth from touching skin when Shari's shield sprang to life between them. Hissing, Grace bounded away to land by the aide's side.

"Meet Skye and Grace," Jonathan said weakly.

"Well met," Skye offered.

"Why shouldn't she touch me?" Shari asked.

"I, uh, well. I don't know, really." Skye rubbed the back of her neck.

Keeping her gaze locked on Grace, Shari nodded. "Sometimes it's good to trust those instincts. Grace." She turned to the other woman.

The hunched over being snarled at her.

"What will happen when you touch me?"

"Kill," Grace said. "Kill the aberration."

Skye's eyes widened comically. "Uh, Grace, killing Shari would hurt me."

Grace tilted her head and made a curious chirruping sound.

"Because she's the Al..."

A warning growl rumbled from Grace's emancipated frame.

Hastily, Skye changed tracks. "She's the one who keeps us all safe. If you kill Shari, I'm as good as dead."

"I keep you safe." Grace's voice was painfully hoarse.

"You do," Skye said, gently running her hand over the top of Grace's head. "And Shari keeps everyone else safe. And... Oh! And Arilla would be sad!"

"Arilla?" Grace rasped.

"She's your mother, right?" Skye said, looking at Shari.

"She is," Shari said as firmly as she could.

"There we go! Arilla would be *very* sad if something bad happened to Shari," Skye said triumphantly.

The lashing Innarn disappeared from the room.

Shari blinked and looked at Jonathan before slowly lowering her shield. Another sound rumbled through the room. Eyes wide, Shari glanced at Skye, who nodded and gave a resigned sigh.

Grace was purring.

"Where did you and Grace meet?" Shari asked softly.

"On Jinkor," Skye said, a bite to her words.

Jonathan caught her gaze and images flowed through Shari's mind as he shared what Skye had told him.

Breath shuddering in her lungs, Shari pulled herself out of the slouch she'd fallen into. "I hope you're finding Ronah to be…" *How do you politely say, 'less torturous'?*

"Ronah is wonderful," Skye jumped in. "I'm so glad to have finally met you properly."

"Me too," Shari said automatically.

Grace's Innarn brushed against Shari's again, bringing back the feeling of having met her somewhere before. Her eyes were a similar shade of green to the one she saw in the mirror, and for a moment, when Grace straightened out of her hunch, Shari had a flash that rocked her.

Somehow, this traumatised stranger was related to her.

Zoeday

Seventh day of the third week of Hazelcrown

The familiar crush of her alarm clock under Shari's fist made her grin despite the early hour.

Today, she'd be travelling with all the other seniors from Ridden Hall to Ginorti and exploring the isle they'd most recently joined with.

Laying under her covers for a moment longer, Shari stared up at the ceiling. It was stained white and had none of the familiar swirls and loops that her childhood bedroom had. Shari wasn't entirely sure if she missed that or if she was glad, at the moment, to be away from the place where she'd grown up.

Sighing, Shari heaved herself out of bed and trudged through her morning routine.

Finally presentable, she slipped out of her room, almost stumbling over Grace, who was crouched by her door.

"Well met," Shari said, hand flung out to catch herself on the far wall.

Grace sniffed and scurried away.

Jaw dropping open, Shari didn't know if she should say something. Grace effortlessly slid through the shadows, an intangible being amongst the living as others from the guild strode through the hall towards the kitchen.

"Alright?" Amara said around a yawn.

Shari nodded. How did she say her maybe-relative had potentially camped outside the door in an attempt to give her a heart attack but hadn't succeeded? "Yeah," she said instead.

"Dealon's turn to make breakfast!" the red-headed Daen said, pumping a fist in the air.

"It's my turn every day," Dealon grumbled as he passed her by, a tiny grin tugging on the corners of his mouth.

The guild settled around the much-expanded table, Grace and Skye on the other end from Shari. Jonathan sat on her right, Samuel on her left, and no one said a word when Asterion slid into the spot next to the Guardian.

Platters of food filled the table, and Shari allowed the pleasant morning chatter to wash over her as she nibbled on different pieces of the feast.

"Don't," Samuel said.

Looking over, Shari grinned as a tiny draci sneezed, a jet of flame licking out and scorching Samuel's bread.

"You could have left him at home," Jonathan said lightly.

Sneeze harrumphed and turned his tail on the Guardian with a huff.

Shari giggled.

'*Like you,*' a tiny voice sent.

'*Like you too, Sneeze,*' she sent back.

"Looking forward to exploring Ginorti today?" Jonathan asked.

"I am actually. Barring any and all attacks, that is," Shari said, spreading more of the green stuff on her toast. "What is this anyway?"

"Do you have reason to believe you'll be attacked?" Asterion asked.

"It's kind of something that just happens to me these days," Shari shrugged.

"Which is why, as a teacher at Ridden Hall, I'll be accompanying you," Samuel said.

'I *fry your attackers like bugs!*' Sneeze added.

Shari stuffed some of the green-smothered toast into her mouth so she wouldn't laugh and hurt the little draci's feelings. '*Thanks, Sneeze,*' she sent.

"Looks like we have business in Ginorti today as well," Jonathan said easily.

Asterion was looking at the Guardian, rubbing his chin. "We do?"

A small part of Shari basked at the idea that whatever 'urgent' business had suddenly come up on Ginorti for Jonathan was for her benefit, and that, before Zuefie, she would have made a fuss about it. Today, it just made her feel safe.

Jonathan glanced at her casually before nodding at Asterion. "We do," he said firmly. "And with enough time to fit the tour in if we hurry."

"Oh, we're going to be so late!" Amara said. She shot up from the table, her chair clattering backwards, the bowls and glasses around her rattling ominously.

With practised moves, Dealon tugged the chair out of the way, and Raven used his Innarn to settle the things on the table.

Amara gave them a grateful smile and bolted away, presumably to get dressed.

Shari had been so distracted by the frenetic movement, she'd missed when Grace had popped up next to her.

"Son of a..." Samuel started.

Apparently, he'd missed her, too.

"Good morning, Grace. Have you tried the persea fruit?" Shari said, handing her the second piece of toast.

Grace took it and disappeared.

"Where'd she… Ow!" Samuel swore as Sneeze chomped on his ear.

"You'll end up needing a new piercing," Shari said, trying to keep her laughter contained.

From the way Samuel scowled at her, she hadn't entirely succeeded.

The group travelling to Ginorti rose from the table and made to leave, Amara meeting them in the hall with her shirt on inside out.

A bittersweet pang tugged at Shari's chest as she remembered Mitch arriving at the mayor's office with his clothes all messed up on the day she had been officially acknowledged as Altoriae. Catching Jonathan's gaze, and the suspicious sheen in his eyes. Shari sighed. At least someone else remembered Mitch the same way she did.

"Ready to go?" Raven asked.

"As we'll ever be," Shari said. Filing out the doors, she didn't say anything as the others casually crowded around, always keeping her in the centre of the group.

They made their way to the bridge to Ginorti with time to spare and waited for the rest of the school group before they crossed over.

When the Headmaster of Ridden Hall, Liza, noticed Samuel, she raised her eyebrows but didn't say anything as she waved him across with the others.

Shari grinned and leaned into Samuel slightly. When she was feeling stronger, she'd fight against the coddling. But for now, Shari was going to allow herself to enjoy it.

Waiting for them on the other side of the bridge were some of Ginorti's Elders, including one of the kumaru who'd been awoken.

"Well met, students of Ronah!" an elder called out. "I am Elder Gnarlon. This is Elder Fionn, and Prex Zini, head of Ivy Academy. Of course, you may have seen Gangar in action on our joining day."

Wood creaked and groaned as Gangar turned to glare at Gnarlon.

The beings of Ronah dutifully chorused back, "Well met."

Shari stifled a giggle. At least it would prove to be an interesting tour.

"As we are such a large group, we'll be splitting up," Elder Fionn said.

Immediately, the guild bunched around Shari.

"There are four wagons. Please climb aboard and we'll start the tour."

Caught up in the guild's tide, Shari was aboard a wagon before she could blink. Gangar creaked his way towards their wagon and clambered up so slowly the others were gone by the time he was on.

The wagon trundled off, in no hurry to catch up with the others. *'Ginorti's history is long. Made of Earth and shaped by the will of Zoemer; he is the eldest of the Shifting Islands. Although Vannali will often claim that title.'* Gangar paused and added with a creaky chuckle, *'We of Earth know patience and are happy to let them.'*

Shari chuckled , the rocking of the wagon over the dirt track making her brush against Samuel on one side and Jonathan on the other. Both Guardian and Apprentice were tense, their Innarn shimmering just under their skin.

'The forests of Ginorti are in mourning, and their leaves droop as they weep for their cousin, the beach,' Gangar continued. *'Today, your visit will cheer up the trees and coax the buds to bloom.'*

The thought that their presence could mean so much touched Shari. By the expression those who weren't on high alert wore, she wasn't the only one.

'*Of course, knowledge glides along the roots, helping to drive out the festering fear.*'

So, Gangar knew they were distracted but was trying to soothe them. Shari grinned at their guide.

Gangar creaked as he smiled back. '*Those who seek to learn inevitably end up at a school—although ours is a little different.*' The wagon was on the southernmost point of a flowery meadow. The other wagons were gathered on the compass points around the outside. Students had spilled into the middle of the field and were mingling with the teenage satyrs of Ginorti.

'*We learn outside, with our roots and hooves in the ground and our fingers and leaves reaching for the sky,*' Gangar creaked as he lowered himself to the forest floor, and the others in the wagon hurriedly did the same. '*Join in. Make friends, and learn,*' the kumaru said and froze, spreading his arms out like branches. Twigs shot out, and leaves sprouted, creating shade in the heat of the midday sun.

"Wasn't it morning when we left?" Amara asked.

"It was," Shari said.

Tania bounded over to them as the guild joined the others. "You missed all the excitement! The satyrs went to give a demonstration but found a massive chunk of the corrupted crystal in the middle of the school. General Morrow and a bunch of his troops had to come in with special gear to remove it!"

Shari looked back at Gangar, who stood peacefully in the middle of the field.

It was more important than ever that she set to work on getting rid of the Innarn dampeners on Ginorti.

Fenix slipped through the door of the white tower and quietly closed it behind them. They'd spent the better part of the morning trying to give Milo the slip.

They were meeting up with Zana and Cyrus to get a head start on the joining with Akoren while Tania was at school for the day.

'*Help.*'

Zana's head snapped up. "Did you hear that?"

'*Help.*'

Frowning, Fenix nodded. The voice, as weak as it was, reminded them of someone.

'*Help!*'

'*Oakley?*' Cyrus sent.

'*Jink...*'

The send faded.

"What was that last word?" Cyrus said, rounding on the others. In that moment, he looked every bit as intimidating as his mentor.

"Jink. Jinkor?" Zana asked.

"Could Jink be a code for something else?" Fenix suggested.

"Hardly. I will rip Jinkor apart to find him," Cyrus growled.

"Isn't this something for the patrols?" Fenix asked.

"There isn't time," Cyrus said. Items Fenix had never seen before were snapping themselves to various parts of his body. A great barrel attached to his forearm and rotated as they watched. Something glowing attached to Cyrus's other wrist, and when he moved his arm, a shield appeared. More pieces were flying through the door to cover Talhan's Linked.

Zana was serenely strapping knives to every conceivable part of herself. When she caught Fenix watching, she held one out. "Want some?"

"I thought you were a pacifist?" Fenix asked. They could feel the flush rising up their neck and flooding their face.

"A pacifist who knows when it's a good idea to protect those who need it."

"But Rakemyst is against violence," Fenix said.

"Rakemyst doesn't like forcing others to protect him," Zana corrected.

Fenix took the offered knife and looked at it. Oakley's cries echoed in their head. "I have something else in mind." They wanted to step outside and call it forward from the metal in the ground. "Is it alright if I change this?"

Looking up, Zana nodded.

Fingers running over the metal, Fenix stroked the flat of the blade and told it what they wanted. Elongating and curving, it turned into the blade of a scythe. Undoing a chain from the bottom of their jacket, Fenix whispered to it and convinced the metal to become a solid handle.

"Ready?" Cyrus asked.

"Ready." Fenix and Zana said together.

"Do you have a lock on where his last send was from?" Zana asked.

Cyrus nodded. "Time to get Oakley back." He held out his hand, and Zana grasped it.

Careful to keep the pointed end of the scythe away from the others, Fenix laid their hand over the top. "Let's go."

The Realm tilted, and they were elsewhere, in a dingy room that smelled like rotten food, sweat, and week-old urine.

In the dim light, Cyrus held a finger to his lips. With all the gear on him, the movement made a clattering noise.

"Hello?" a raspy voice called.

Fenix bit back nervous laughter.

"If that's my rescue party, you took long enough," the voice said.

'Is that Oakley?' Fenix asked.

Clattering over to the side of the room where the voice was coming from, Cyrus peered into the gloom. "How did we meet?"

"Cy? Out the front when I tripped coming off the slip stream and skinned my knee. You painted it with orange goo, and a mushroom grew out of it."

"Out of his knee?" Fenix hissed. They weren't sure if they should find the story horrifying or hilarious.

Ignoring them, Cyrus asked, "What do they have you in?"

"Ziom cell."

"Better stand back then," Talhan's Linked advised. The barrel on his arm spun, emitting a whirring noise.

"Cy, wait! Don't..."

A jet of pure light shot out, followed by the most horrific screeching sound Fenix had ever heard. Crying out, they dropped the scythe and blocked their ears, curling in on themself to escape the noise.

There was a slam of rock against rock, and abruptly, the sound was gone.

"... use Innarn. You'll set off the wailers." Oakley was climbing out of the hole Cyrus had created in the cell's wall.

"Up," Zana said, heaving Fenix to their feet.

Hastily grabbing the scythe they were desperate not to use, Cantash's Linked moaned and wriggled a finger of their free hand in their ear, willing the ringing to stop.

"There's no way out," Oakley moaned.

"I just blasted through one ziom wall. You think I can't do another?" Cyrus said.

"We're in the middle of Jinkor, in the elder's home. Escape is pointless when we're just going to be captured again," Oakley said.

Fenix felt like this should be one of those big, dramatic moments, like the ones on the crystal screens. Instead, Zana walked over and slapped Oakley.

"There's always a way out if you want to find one. Or do you want to stay here?" They'd never heard Zana speak so coldly before.

"Out. I want out," Oakley stammered.

"Then out it is. Cyrus?"

"On it." Cyrus flicked something, and the barrel whirled again. Light shot straight through the wall that had trapped them. And straight through the guards who had been waiting outside.

They had time for one horrified glance before the bodies on the other side of the wall fell, their insides melted and mixing with the liquid rock.

"Run," Fenix said. "Run!" they yelled when no one moved.

The four dove through the gap and over the liquified bodies of the guards, slipping and skidding on their remains.

Down the hall, through the door, and up two flights of stairs.

Lungs burning, Fenix would have wept with joy when they caught sight of the sky, except the way was being blocked by more guards.

Back to back, the four panted as they looked at the guards surrounding them.

'*Everyone touching?*' Zana sent. She sounded like she barely had a feather out of place.

Three yesses answered her.

The squeeze of another shifting them surrounded Fenix as the four Linked shifted away, back to the safety of their islands.

CHAPTER SEVENTEEN

Lissae

Zoeday

Seventh day of the third week of Hazelcrown

Samuel trudged along the path to his front door, only to find it ajar.

All day, he'd waited for an attack on Shari. Now would be the perfect time to strike, and Cylanthar knew, the Altoriae had enemies on all sides.

Showing too many teeth for it to be considered a grin, Samuel slid through the door, one of his knives in each hand.

He was happy to take his time with the intruder.

Slinking through the hallway, he paused at the lit up sitting area where a silver-haired being was lying on his rug with a dark shape curled up on her chest.

"You're home," Lizbeth said.

The dark beast raised its head and chirruped a greeting before all six paws scrambled to lift it upright.

Lizbeth grunted as Shadow pushed off her chest and galloped towards Samuel.

Hastily stowing the knives, he sunk down and caught the palon before he was bowled over.

"Greetings to you too," Samuel said, lifting the squirming body.

On his shoulder, Sneeze grumbled in his ear.

"How was Ginorti?" Lizbeth asked, gracefully getting up from the floor.

"Quiet," he grunted.

"And you don't trust the quiet," she said.

"Not one bit." Samuel put Zoomer down and sighed as he sunk his fingers into the palon's inky fur.

"Is tomorrow the day?" Lizbeth asked.

"Shari is well enough now to look after Zoomer," Samuel said. His fingers tightened for a moment, before resuming patting.

"I know it will be hard," Lizbeth started.

Samuel cut her off. "Thank you for looking after him."

If he ignored the pity, he'd almost say Lizbeth was smiling. "I've left some rutenberry cookies in the cold box for you."

"My thanks." Samuel bowed his head.

Lizbeth patted him on the shoulder and left the room. The soft click of the front door was the signal Samuel didn't know he was waiting for.

Water dripped down his cheeks, swallowed by the fur of the creature he'd brought back to life. The one he now had to give up.

Then he'd be all alone again.

'*Have me?*' Sneeze's claws slid through his shirt and dug into his shoulder.

Laughing through his tears, Samuel grinned. '*So I do.*'

Shari mechanically moved her legs, walking carefully back to her room.

The day on Ginorti had worn her out more than she'd expected, and dinner with the guild, while lovely, had been an energetic affair which had sapped the last of her reserves. Particularly with Grace popping by her chair to growl at her now and then.

Still convinced that there was some sort of connection between them, and knowing she wouldn't be able to sleep until she figured out what it was, Shari forewent the comfort of her bed and crossed instead to where she'd stashed the *Altoriae's Handbook*.

Flicking the pages, she came across the lineage of the Altoriaes, tracing all the way back to Kay'imi.

There had been a time, when she'd gone through the book, that a name had appeared and disappeared next to her own. For an age, she thought it had meant she was getting a sibling, but now, she wasn't so sure.

Tracing along the darker names, she stopped at Fiona MacAde, the Altoriae before her. Her sister, Danielle Williams, had been Shari's great grandmother. Family lore went that Danielle had fled the Shifting Islands after her sister's death and resettled on the mainland. Her daughter, Elizabeth, had married a mainlander and scorned anything to do with Innarn.

The way her mother told it, Elizabeth had been pleased that Arilla was a Blank, especially as her sister, Sarina, was an Innarnian who had had a child who was showing signs of Innarn when they both went missing.

Next to her grandmother's name was a line that hadn't been there before, leading to Sarina's flashing name.

And below that was something that hadn't been there before.

A new name that was changing from one word to another.

It read *Lissa.*

When Shari blinked and looked again, it read *Grace*.

As it altered again, Shari noted something else. All the Altoriaes' names were thicker than the others, right from Kay'imi to her own.

Thirteen names.

But with every change, be it Lissa or Grace, that name was bold too.

Asterion was meandering through the streets of Ronah. A feeling had told him to leave the castle and take a stroll.

He'd passed the town square and was almost at Ridden Hall when there was a tug on his pants leg.

"What are you doing out of bed?" Asterion asked.

The tiny child giggled up at him.

"Eric," Asterion sighed.

Raising chubby arms, Eric said, "Ter! Up!"

"You are too big to sit on my head," Asterion said.

"Up?" Eric asked again.

Bending, the minotaur picked Eric up. "Shall we find your parents?" He began walking towards Eric's home, the boy giggling in his arms and occasionally reaching up to tug on one of his horns.

The odd pair arrived at Eric's house, and Asterion knocked on the door.

"Coming!" a voice from inside yelled.

"Mama!" Eric cried.

"Eric?" The door swung open, bringing delicious smells of home-cooked vegetables with it. Louise Shansky, Eric's mother, was wiping her hands on a cloth. "How did you? Oh, Asterion! You're a lifesaver. I swear he can shift at will."

"It's possible," Asterion said.

"Would you like to join us for dinner? I've made far too much, as usual," Louise offered.

"Oh, it's..."

"Ter!" Eric interrupted, lunging forward. The move caused Asterion to clatter into the house, slipping by Louise sideways so he didn't crush her.

"Well, you're in now. Guess you'd better stay!" Louise said, winking at Eric.

"Did you plan this, little one?" Asterion asked, hoisting the boy up so he was at eye height.

Eric giggled and tried to shove his fist in Asterion's nostril.

After putting the child down, Asterion rubbed his abused nose and followed Eric so he wouldn't get in more trouble.

"Joining us for dinner, Asterion?" Andrew, Eric's father, asked.

"It appears so."

"Excellent! I wanted to ask you about this." Andrew tapped a finger on a crystal slab. "Go wash up, Eric."

"What is it?" Asterion asked.

Andrew handed the slab over. It was displaying yesterday's *Shifting Island Sentinel*. The headline read: *King tides across the Realm.*

"What do you think this means?"

"That Lissae has too many moons?" Asterion joked. Mentally, he was flicking through similar articles, which were all talking about significant weather problems. Rivers drying out or flooding to unprecedented heights, volcanoes appearing where there never had been one before, and winds strong enough to strip entire forests of leaves.

"Something is going on with Lissae's weather, and we need to figure out what," Andrew said grimly.

Zoeday
Seventh day of the third week of Hazelcrown

Samuel slumped through the streets, his Shadow sniffing everything as they went.

Today was the day. Shari was going to take over the care of Shado... Zoomer.

If the Altoriae was still recovering from her abduction, she may need more time before...

"Ow!"

'Not *yours*,' Sneeze sent, tugging harder on Samuel's ear.

'*I know, you pointy fanged menace*,' Samuel grumbled.

Letting go of his ear, Sneeze preened.

Sighing, Samuel strode up the path to the castle. Before he could get lost in gloomy thoughts—or have Sneeze bite him again—he pushed open the doors and entered.

Shari was waiting on the other side of the entrance, wringing her hands.

The gesture was so unlike her, Samuel wanted to ask her some sort of security question, but Shad... Zoomer snuffled his way through the door and looked up. The moment he caught sight of Shari, he bounded over to her, licking every bit of exposed skin he could find.

Sinking to her knees, Shari was laughing and crying.

"Mortals," Samuel muttered, discreetly wiping at his face.

"We grow on you," Lizbeth murmured.

Samuel absolutely did not jump. "Where did you spring from?"

Lizbeth laughed. "Felt you walking this morning and thought you might like the company."

Before he could refute Lizbeth's claim, the Altoriae was looking at him through watery eyes.

"Thank you for returning him back to a solid form," Shari said.

"How did you...?"

"Palons can send, in a fashion. Zoomer's shown me what you did. I suppose he's partial to meat now?"

"He is, rather." Samuel stuffed his hands into his pockets so he wouldn't be tempted to bury them in the silky fur.

Sha... Zoomer ignored his attempt at self-control, and barrelled towards him, knocking into his shins.

An image of the castle door filled his mind.

"He sends pictures?"

Shari laughed, a sound he'd sorely been missing since her return. "Mostly, yes."

"What does the castle door mean?"

"Perhaps," Lizbeth said. "He wants you in close reach?"

Sh... Zoomer was racing between the two of them, his thin tongue lolling from his mouth.

Rocking back on his heels, Samuel rolled the thought around. To have S... Zoomer in close reach, to be just walls away from Shari if she was in trouble, to be closer to the hatchlings... "I suppose I can. For a while."

Shari beamed at him.

Collis Iuvo had faced down pack after pack of sedolics and never flinched, but put him in a room full of elders and he turned into a quivering kid again.

Ignoring Remmy's elbow jutting into his ribs, Collis bowed slightly. "It is our continued pleasure to do what we can in defence of the Shifting Islands and Lissae," he said.

'At least you didn't forget how to speak elder in our time away,' Remmy sent, nudging him again.

'*Elder isn't a different language,*' Collis scolded.

'*Might as well be, for how formal it is,*' Remmy shot back.

With centuries of practice, Collis ignored him and bowed again.

"You had some trouble, leaving Ronah, I believe?" the Ilutri elder asked.

Gulping, Collis nodded. To be called out by the Altoriae's grandfather in front of everyone...

"And have you figured out why?" Elder SilverCloud asked.

"He's met his soul-match, Elder," Remmy butted in.

It was Collis' turn to bury his elbow into the other man's stomach.

Elder SilverCloud disregarded Remmy's noise of pain. "Ah, I remember that. When I met my soul-match, I couldn't stray more than a few wing beats from her at any time. It will pass, eventually."

"I feel like I should do more," Collis blurted. Heat rose to his cheeks, and he hung his head.

"In times of war," Elder Juniper said. "Fighters always look to do more. Do not discount finding peace in a time when others crave it."

"I will think about what you have said." Collis nodded.

"And I'll pound it into his head," Remmy said cheerfully.

SilverCloud laughed.

Collis made to move off, but SilverCloud reached out and gripped his arm. "Don't take her for granted," the elder rasped.

Looking down at the wrinkled, age-spotted hand, Collis nodded.

"I mean it. As much as we might not be ready to admit it, we are at war. Beings will die, and you are both in firing range. You take every moment you have and cherish it." The elder gave him a squeeze.

Trying to hide how shaken he was, Collis gently patted the elder's hand and slipped from his grasp. "I will," he said, and walked away.

Next to him, Remmy had dropped all pretence of humour. '*Did you see his eyes?*'

Hunching his shoulders, Collis nodded. *'Silver, like his namesake.'*

'What does the old Ilutri know that we don't?' Remmy asked.

'Trouble is coming,' Collis sent back.

'Already knew that,' Remmy grumbled, but he flicked a glance at the elders.

Hissing in surprise, Shari pulled her blade away and winced as a bead of blood trickled down Grace's neck.

"You've got to stop jumping out at me!" Shari said. Her heart was pounding so loudly, she could feel it against her collarbones.

Grace growled at her.

Sheathing her blade, Shari scowled at the other girl. "There's someone I want you to meet." Turning, she walked towards the castle door and glanced back.

At her heels, Grace bared her teeth.

Rolling her eyes, Shari strode off. Perhaps her mother could make the recalcitrant Innarnian who was her cousin behave.

An hour later, Shari was regretting the decision. Grace was perched on a chair, gnawing on a spiced roll while Arilla doted on her.

"The book says she's your sister's child," Shari blurted.

Her mother's head snapped around, and she looked at Shari in shock. "Could... could it be wrong?"

Shari shook her head. "She could have been the Altoriae. Not me."

"Oh, Shari." Arilla bundled her daughter under her arm.

Snuggling in, Shari allowed herself to feel protected. Safe. Warm. She sighed contentedly.

Home.

It occurred to Shari that she was ready to fight again.

She just had to convince the others.

Chapter Eighteen

Lissae

Adonay

First day of the fourth week of Hazelcrown

liding into the seat beside her grandfather, Shari smiled at him. The castle dining room had become a gathering place of sorts. Had it started before or after her return?

SilverCloud, looking older than when she'd left, gave her a wink and stole a rutenberry off her plate. *Did me being gone really aged him that much?* Shari's smile became fixed.

'*Don't worry about me,*' SilverCloud sent to her. '*I was old before you disappeared.*'

Shari gently bumped his shoulder with her own. '*I'm allowed to worry about my favourite grandfather,*' she sent back.

"Your only grandfather." He snorted.

"Is that because..." Shari wasn't sure what to say.

Arilla placed a platter laden with all sorts of food from the five Shifting Islands on the table—piles of purple rutenberries, and yellow osin berries, pitchers of gilfress elixir, stuffed yaqueona, and slices of persea fruit, ready for her toast.

"My parents didn't want to admit that I'd soul-matched with an Innarnian," Arilla said. "They disowned me."

Predictably, Grace popped up next to Shari and growled.

Looking straight at the unstable girl, the Altoriae nodded. "Our grandparents were fools."

The morning clatter around the castle table stopped.

"Come again?" Skye asked.

"Grace and I are cousins on our mother's side," Shari said, smearing a healthy layer of persea fruit onto her toast.

Somewhere down the table, a being started coughing.

Shari purposefully didn't look to see who it was.

Grace, however, tilted her head at Shari. Quicker than a burst of Plasma, the hunched Ilutri grabbed a knife and pierced the skin of her own thumb. Without waiting for permission, she grabbed Shari's closest hand and did the same. Bringing their hands together, both girls watched the welling red drips.

"Same," Grace rasped.

"Yes. Your mother and mine had the same parents," Shari said.

"Family?" Grace sounded so much like a child, that Shari had to clear the lump out of her throat before she could speak.

"Yes."

"Protect," Grace said, and dropped Shari's hand. She disappeared under the table for a moment, then reappeared in her assigned seat next to Skye.

"I hope this means she won't be growling at you anymore," Samuel muttered as he took the spot on the other side of her.

"Me too," Shari said. She turned back to Arilla. "Did they really disown you?"

"Oh, yes. Kicked me to the streets because I'd stood up for your father before I knew who he was. He caught me at the port when I was trying to leave." Arilla was looking at something far away.

"Skipping the bad parts, are we?" Calem said, carrying two jugs in one hand and a stack of glasses in the other.

"No point in rehashing old wounds," Arilla said lightly.

Raising a brow, Shari looked at her father, who flicked her an image of her much-younger mother, battered and bruised. Fingers tightening around her knife handle, Shari found herself grateful she did not know where her other set of grandparents lived.

"You and mum were soul-matched too, weren't you?" Calem asked his father.

"Yes," SilverCloud said. "Can't wait to see her again."

The last bit was said so quietly, Shari felt she was the only one who had heard it.

Had it been before her abduction, she would have railed against the unfairness of it, wanted to put some sort of stopper in time and prevent his death. She had a better appreciation now for wanting to rejoin your loved ones.

As she patted SilverCloud's hand, he smiled gently at her and looked up as Tania and Collis entered the castle's dining room.

"Speaking of soul-matched. Zana told me the good news!" SilverCloud said.

"What good news?" Shari asked, watching Tania blush.

"Our Linked found the next soul-matched pair."

Shari snapped her head around in time for SilverCloud to nod at the newcomers. "Tania and Collis?" she asked. A tiny part of her wondered if she should have seen it coming.

"Yep," Tania said from under the safety of Collis' arm.

"Congratulations!" Shari beamed at her.

"I still don't really understand what's so special about a soul-match," Tania said.

Collis pulled out a chair for Tania and made sure she was comfortable before claiming the one next to hers. "I've tried to explain it to her," he said.

Chewing on a bit of her toast, Shari tried to think of the best way to explain it, but SilverCloud jumped in.

"We were delighted when Calem found his soul-match," the elder said. "Not just because he had a better chance at happiness than most, but because our islands thrive on having joyful residents. I'm sure you've noticed Ronah has, despite everything going on, been more at peace lately?"

Tania nodded.

"That's because you are. The bonds of your match are strengthening, and not only helping you but your isle as well."

Taking the drink Collis poured for her, Tania frowned. "Does this mean I don't have a choice? That it was fated?"

"You always have a choice. Soul-matched doesn't mean perfect," Arilla said. "It means that particular being is your best chance of happiness. You still have to work for it, learn each other's likes and dislikes..."

Calem chuckled. How long it had taken them to figure things out?

Arilla smiled at him indulgently. "Like any other couple, some days are harder than others, but your souls, if you let them, will be drawn to each other. You are always free to ignore the call, though. It's not a happy-ever-after thing."

Tania sighed and leaned against Collis. "I'm glad. I don't want to think that this isn't real."

Collis squeezed her hand.

Shari smiled at the pair, grateful she had returned to see this.

Samuel wandered into Ridden Hall and accepted the beckoning of the headmaster.

"Feared being or not, you need to ensure you show up to class on time," Liza was saying as she walked with him to the tiny office he shared with Shari. "Shari is still not up to returning to her duties here from what I've heard..."

"Correct," Samuel said when the pause dragged on.

"So the Guardian can take over from her, or you can work a double load. You shared the classes anyway, so it just means extra marking, really."

"Marking?" He frowned.

"On the homework, and assignments and exams?" Liza said.

"It's kind of a pass or fail subject," Samuel said. "If they're alive by the end, they pass."

She blinked up at him and laughed. "Funny! Sure, alright. Still need it in writing, though."

He groaned.

"Tell me about it. Who knew being a teacher meant so much paperwork!" She paused at the door to his office. "I don't know what happened on patrol, but if you ever need..."

For the first time, Samuel purposefully blocked out a superior when they were talking to him. He nodded and made sounds of agreement until Liza patted his arm and walked away.

Just who was he meant to talk to about the loss of his Realm and his kin? Temira? That would go down faster than a hunk of falling ziom.

Opening the door, Samuel strode in and ruffled through the papers on the desk without looking at them. Distractedly, he picked up a few at random and turned and wandered to the classroom.

"You're back!" A tiny hatchling launched herself at his legs, wrapping her arms around them.

Stunned, he watched the paper, shredded by his claws, drifting down to decorate her dark head. He'd never been so glad to have wasted time on grabbing paper.

"Oooh!" She pulled back and looked up at him, fearlessly grabbing a transformed hand and studying the scales intently. "That's a neat trick! Can Shari do that?"

"No," he said, trying to temper his tone. *A neat trick. Huh.*

"Can you teach me to do that?"

A flash of Shari spiralling apart had him blurting a much stronger, "No!" He sighed as she pulled away from him. "Far too dangerous. It's an ability you're born with."

"Awww," she sighed. "Still looks cool, though. What happens if Innarn hits your scales?"

Looking around at the suddenly full classroom, Samuel sighed. Every student looked eager to hear the answer. "Why don't we go outside and you can see for yourself?"

"Wicked!"

The students rushed to pack their things, and Samuel led the eager hatchlings to the middle of Ridden Hall.

Getting them to sit on the other side of the grounds, he strode to just beyond the midpoint and changed. Shaking out his wings, Sanithane lifted his head to the sky and sighed, keeping his poisonous breath behind his teeth.

'Go on,' he sent. '*See who can fell a Q'Aralide.*'

For the rest of the class, the students flung all sorts of Innarn at him. Most did nothing, although a few bits of Lighter Innarn stung enough for him to raise his head.

And see a crowd of astounded adults watching them.

Watching him.

The tiny Dark Innarnian who'd dared to hug him was rallying her classmates with whispers they were hoping he wouldn't hear.

They were wrong.

As one, a bunch of his first-year students attacked him, roaring as they did so.

It took more effort than he was expecting not to laugh.

'*Oh no! A fatal blow!*' Sanithane sent, wrapping his Innarn around the few who stood a bit too close and shifting them to safety. Tucking his wings in, he collapsed to the side, twitching a foreleg dramatically.

Sanithane's class fell silent, the murmuring of the watching adults filling the space for a long moment.

Then his class whooped and cheered. Hollering and clapping each other on the back, they missed when Laura slipped away and prodded his head.

Opening the eye closest to her, he winked.

She hugged his maw. "I thought we'd hurt you!" Laura whispered.

'*Not a chance,*' he sent back, and changed into the squishy form. Rising, he made a show of dusting himself off and, with an exaggerated limp, staggered to the side.

Laura grinned at him as she ran to join her classmates in the celebrations.

The adults watching slowly disappeared, more than a few whispers of the *menacing Q'Aralide teaching our children* and *taken down by a bunch of kids* reaching his ears.

Samuel rubbed the back of his neck, unsure if he'd still have a job in the morning.

Still, nothing bad could happen after a day as perfect as this.

Nothing.

Inthday
Second day of the fourth week of Hazelcrown

Captain Rappen peered down his nose at the troops as they boarded the fully stocked ships.

This time, nothing was going to get in his way.

The urge to pace was squashed, but the white filling his vision demanded action.

Leaning, he pulled an aberration up by the scruff of its neck.

Aberration is a strange name for food.

Something in him shuddered. He was not about to eat the flesh of something so tainted.

Not the flesh. The white flickered for a moment, and he had the sense that it was searching for the right word. *The soul.*

"Aberrations don't have a soul," he said.

The beast at his feet whimpered.

Rappen shrugged. "Feed all you want."

It was all the permission the cloud needed. It poured from his mouth and sucked the beast dry, before hanging low over the heads of his troops.

Words were forced from his mouth. "What is our aim?" he bellowed.

"To feed!" the soldiers called back.

"And where is our feast?"

"Shifting Islands!"

Captain Rappen nodded. "Set sail at once!"

There was a round of agreement. The sailors stoked the engines, and the ships moved out.

Soldiers cheered as the land shrank behind them.

Carefully opening the door of her room, Shari held her boots in one hand, the other carrying her yellow blade.

Only to trip over Grace, who'd been sleeping across the threshold. Her cousin jumped to her feet with unnatural agility.

"What are you..." Shari asked.

Grace growled at her.

"I thought we were..."

"Protect," Grace said firmly.

"That's what I'm trying to..."

"Protect *you.*" Planting one finger in the middle of her chest, Grace pushed firmly.

Shari stumbled back into the room.

"Rest," Grace ordered and closed the door.

"Should have just shifted," Shari muttered.

'*You're dumber than a bag of rocks if you can't feel the wards around your room preventing that,*' Jonathan sent.

'*Jonathan!*' Shari whined.

'*Take Grace's advice, and we'll talk in the morning,*' Jonathan ordered.

Grumbling, Shari removed her weapons and slowly peeled her leathers off, pushing and poking at the wards as she did so.

'*Sleep!*' Jonathan sent again. '*Your mother's orders.*'

Huffing, Shari slid back into bed, her eyes closing before her head hit the pillow.

Tania rushed into the Techno Centre and flew through the halls to where Cyrus was waiting.

Bursting through the doors, she couldn't stop the scolding from falling from her lips. "I can't believe you went without me! What if there was... Oh."

Ginorti's Linked was sitting on a hospital bed, his mutilated back to her. Falling silent, Tania joined the others as Temira smeared a thick, orange paste over his wounds.

Hissing and flinching, Oakley gripped the edges of the bed, the tendons of his arms standing out as he fought not to make a sound.

The moment Temira had finished, Tania rounded the bed. "Are you okay?" she asked. "I mean, silly question, because no. Or else you wouldn't be here, right? But you're safe now."

Mossy green eyes returned her gaze steadily. "You must be Tania. The others have told me all about you."

"What?" Tania asked and looked over his shoulder. Cyrus had a fist crammed against his mouth. Zana looked as serene as ever, and Fenix was trying not to chuckle. And was failing.

"Said you'd be sore you missed out on the big rescue. Glad to finally meet you, though." Oakley winced as he shifted and stretched. "You really are a wonder," he said to Temira.

The technomancer sniffed and strode from the room.

"Was it something I said?" Oakley asked as he slid on the shirt Cyrus handed him.

"Temira's like that," Tania said. Although the technomancer's exit had felt a lot colder than it usually did. "Where's Milo?" she asked.

"Indisposed," Cyrus replied.

"I had the sudden urge to know how many draci currently inhabit the gardens. And Titch has lost the paperwork." Fenix waved a sheaf of paper. "Such a shame. He'll be counting for days." They sighed. "Still made sure I had enough medicine, though." They held up a vial with blue liquid in it as Temira came back through the door.

"What is that?" the technomancer asked abruptly.

"Restorative medicine, meant to help me connect better with Cantash." Fenix blinked as Temira snatched it out of their hand. "Hey!"

Uncapping the vial, she sniffed and handed it to Cyrus without a word.

"Who told you what this was?" Cyrus asked.

"Milo."

The two Techno Innarnians shot each other a dark look.

"He's poisoning you," Temira said.

"What?" Fenix yelped.

"Not poisoning, exactly," Cyrus said. "But he is inhibiting your link with Cantash significantly. When did you start taking this?"

"When I was a child." Fenix crossed their arms and rubbed their hands up and down, shrinking in on themselves.

"Yesterday was your last dose." Temira crossed the room and rooted through a wooden box, vials clinking as she did so. Plucking one out, she returned and shoved it at Cantash's Linked. "Take this instead. It will help wean you off and start reversing the effects. Once you take a dose, it will automatically refill. Any that the traitor gives you, put in here." Temira removed a pouch from her belt.

"Traitor," Fenix whispered.

Tania longed to hug them.

"Saying it so casually... Milo is... was..."

Heart breaking, Tania wanted to reach out as the ever-vibrant Fenix seemed to grow smaller before her eyes.

"He was my friend," they whispered.

"Not if he was treating you like that," Tania said.

"What do you wish to do about him?" Zana asked.

Fenix uncurled from their hunched position and looked up. "He needs to answer for what he's done."

"I have an idea. A way find out who Milo is working for," Tania said. "The Chirea used soul-stealer arrows when they attacked. Jonathan made sure they were destroyed, but what if they weren't?"

"Soul-stealer arrows?" Fenix asked.

"That's what Sam called them. Really, they drain your Innarn and store it. The next being to touch the arrow has it transferred into them."

Cyrus whistled. "I am so glad that I didn't think of doing that with the Innarn blockers."

"And they were actually destroyed?" Zana asked.

"Oh yeah. But our traitor doesn't know that. What if, in the cleanup of Cantash, one was found and taken to the Techno Centre to be examined?" Tania suggested.

"Oh, I like it." Fenix looked shocked by their own words. "I mean, I hate it has to be done, but I like the idea."

"I can put a bit of crystal in it that will record the Innarn signature of anyone who handles the arrow, or the case it's in." Cyrus turned away from them, breathing slowly.

"Are you alright?" Tania asked.

"I know you've spent your life with this guy, Fenix," Cyrus said. "But there are few people I would trust in my lab. Milo was someone I looked up to. I'm struggling," he admitted. "Because I feel you have more right to be angry than I do, yet I really want to just..." He made a strangling motion with his hands.

"Let's see who Milo is working for first," Fenix said. "And then we'll make sure he never does anything like this again."

"Good sleep?" her mother asked as Shari slunk into her seat at the table in the castle hall. Her parents were going to be a regular feature, not that Shari particularly minded.

"Mmmhmmm." She tried for noncommittal but didn't think it would work. From the crossed arms and the scowl Arilla wore, she was right.

"You can't go back to your old ways, just yet Shari. No patrolling until you're better," Arilla said. "This isn't just me. Healer Doonavan said the same thing."

"But..."

Arilla raised an unimpressed brow. "We let you get away with a lot, Shari. I don't question where you go late at night, or why you have as many scars as you do. But I will not see you neglect yourself. When you're ready to talk, we're here."

"What if I'm never ready to talk?" Shari asked.

"Then it will fester and develop into something worse."

Shari shuddered.

Jonathan, Samuel, Belfar, Wolf, and Calem entered the room.

"You aren't alone," Arilla said, taking her hands. "We're all here for you, Shari."

"When I woke up, the first thing I saw was clouds..." Shari started. She took a shuddering breath, and before she knew what was happening, the entire story poured from her, unbidden. By the end, she was even more exhausted than before. A hollow feeling sat in her chest, but part of her felt lighter for sharing.

Wiping away the tears, Shari looked around the room. "Thank you."

"Thank you for being brave enough to share," Belfar said. "I know it was hard."

Reaching out, she grasped his hand.

"Recovery isn't a straight line. But you're strong, and there's a great team to support you every step of the way." Belfar looked so earnest, Shari couldn't help but smile.

"You should listen to him," Wolf rumbled. "He learned the hard way."

Shari grinned and tried to block the looming clouds from her mind.

CHAPTER NINETEEN

Lissae

Narday

Fourth day of the fourth week of Hazelcrown

Chamele leaned heavily on the walking stick that had suddenly become a necessity.

The head guard had been appalled to find her on the ground after Captain Rappen's visit, and Chamele finally saw the flame he was carrying for her.

Was it too late, after twelve years of service, to ask the man his name?

Perhaps after the aberrations were destroyed, she would see if an aide knew what it was.

Limping into the drawing room, Chamele gritted her teeth. Ben and Gywn were gazing at her with a mixture of pity and disgust.

"Captain Rappen has sent reports that the troops are on their way back into the Deep Ocean," she said by way of greeting. Slowly, she lowered herself into a chair and carefully set the stick aside.

"It looks like Rappen sends more than reports," Ben said, nodding at the stick.

Taking the silently offered cup of tea, Chamele peered at him through the veil over her face. "*Captain* Rappen is in prime position to..."

"Take us out, one by one?" Gwyn asked. "These aberrations are more powerful than Vendalbara was led to believe. Time after time, they beat us."

"Oh, but we have something they don't," Chamele said, taking a dainty sip from her cup.

"What's that?" Ben asked.

"Someone on the inside."

Shari tried not to grumble as her parents shooed her out the door and into the waiting arms of Wolf and Belfar.

She'd relented, told them all about her harrowing abduction, her newfound fear of clouds, and they still weren't letting her patrol.

"You'll just have to train with us for the day," Belfar was saying.

"What's the point? The Air motus is all wrong anyway," Shari said, even as she followed their leisurely pace towards the bridge to Rakemyst.

"There's nothing wrong with the Air motus," Wolf protested.

Sneaking a glance at his face, Shari noted the tiny lines between his brows and grinned. He knew there was a problem, even if he didn't want to admit it. "Really?" she said.

"It might not flow as nicely as some others, but it works," Wolf said.

"What do you think is wrong with it?" Belfar asked.

Shari was impressed. He'd modulated his tone to be interested, rather than condescending. "The bit in the middle, after movement four. If you dip your fingers instead of raising them, it makes the sequence much smoother."

Wolf opened his mouth to say something, and Belfar nudged him. Hard.

"Show us?" Belfar asked.

Grinning, Shari nodded. They crossed the bridge and shifted to the training island, where she nervously greeted the other members of Wolf's team.

"The Altoriae has something to show us," Belfar said.

Instantly, the flock went quiet.

Sighing and brushing her hair back to hide her nerves, Shari moved through the modified Air motus she'd created whilst hiding in Jetonyx's pocket Realm.

"That... Such a slight change makes Realms of difference!" Varlee gushed. "Show us again?"

Going through the motus slowly, Shari did as she was asked, pointing out what she'd changed and why.

"Wish someone had figured this out years ago," Wolf muttered to Belfar.

Shari giggled.

Shari's Sanctuary

Tormorylth glared at the screens.

'*Altoriaes shouldn't giggle. They should slash and burn all who dare to question them!*'

Jetonyx sighed. '*You're saying that because?*'

The tiny hatchling shrank in on herself. '*Oalark used to say it about the warriors.*'

'*Is that what you think Shari is?*'

'*She's the Altoriae. Meant to be Lissae's fiercest protector.*'

Shari giggled again.

'Not *because we've been stuck in here for an age?*'

Tormorylth plopped onto the lush grass and sighed. '*Want out.*'

Eyeing the screens, Jetonyx nodded. '*I know.*'

He just had to figure out how they could escape. Stretching his wings in the same span of sky over and over again had lost its appeal the moment Oalark had died.

Lissae

Anika fluffed her hair one last time and turned her back on the mirror.

Raven was meeting her at dusk to go over some moves Arilla hadn't taught them yet. The tracker preferred daggers to swords and had seen Anika using them in the last training session.

She just hoped he meant what he said, and it wasn't a euphemism for something else.

Arriving at the training ground right on time, Anika paused at the entry. It appeared deserted, but she was used to things not being what they seemed.

Crouching, she removed the daggers from their hiding spots in the hollowed-out heel; the handles making up the back of the shoe, the steel of the blades cool as it slid along her skin.

"Raven?" she called. Her voice fell flat, lost in the vastness of the darkening grounds. "Is this some sort of training thing?"

"Yes." His voice came from everywhere—right next to her and so far away she could barely hear it.

Heat slid along her arm.

Whirling, Anika's blade cut through the air and clanged against Raven's weapon, the sound loud in the quiet of the grounds.

"How did you know where I was?" he asked.

"Body heat," Anika replied.

Raven grinned. "Could make a tracker out of you yet."

Anika stepped back. "I just want to defend myself."

"Nothing more?" he asked.

"Nothing... Do you know what it's like?" she asked. "To not be able to use Innarn to *fix* something? To make it right? All Innarn has been to me is hard work and pain."

His hand, and the blade in it, dropped to his side. "I know," he said. "Not in the same way, of course. My parents were... Well." Raven looked away. "My father was an expert tracker. I had to be better to make sure he didn't catch me."

"Catch you?" Anika asked, her voice small. For all her parents were bitterly disappointed, they were trying so hard to accept their daughter, the Blank. But she'd heard stories. They all had, of kids being forced out of the family home, made to fend for themselves, because they hadn't a speck of Innarn to their names. Others had it worse. Some had beatings to try and force the Innarn to the surface. Not on Ronah, though. Always whispers about the mainland.

Expressionless, Raven glanced back at her. He blinked and grinned. "Nothing as bad as you're thinking. Just didn't want to do my chores."

From the shadows in his eyes, she doubted that was all it was. However, now wasn't the time to question him. "Totally understand," she said, tossing her hair. "So, these moves?"

Slipping past her, Raven led the way deeper into the training grounds. "If you hold your dagger like this..." He demonstrated. "You'll have a better chance of cutting your opponent and not yourself. The showy blade-against-the-forearm stuff is only if you want to nick yourself horribly."

Adjusting her hold, Anika asked, "Like this?"

He grinned. "Perfect."

Jonathan straightened the cuff of his sleeve for the fifth time in as many minutes.

Zac had finally agreed to the date, and they were meeting on relatively neutral ground—a café on Ginorti that neither of them had been to before called Leaf and Rock.

As if his thoughts had conjured the man, Zac walked through the wide doorway, Jonathan's mouth going dry at the sight.

Sauntering over, Zac smirked at him. "Well met, Guardian."

"No Guardian here," Jonathan said, spreading his hands wide. "Just me."

"Even better."

Sitting down at the table, Zac slid along the bench seat until their thighs were touching. "This date better be one to remember," he said.

"I plan on it," Jonathan grinned. Something buzzed against his shields, and his expression fell.

"All good?" Zac asked.

"Yeah, just..." Tightening up his shields so that only Samuel or Shari could get through, he sighed.

"Saving the Realm is a full-time job, isn't it? Do we need to reschedule?" The amiable smile slid from Zac's face.

"No. Shari will come grab me if they're desperate."

"Well." Zac picked up a drink from the table. "Here's to not being desperate."

CHAPTER TWENTY

Lissae

Narday

Fourth day of the fourth week of Hazelcrown

Shari entered the classroom and waited nervously behind the desk, shielding partly as an exercise and partly to hide herself from the students filtering in.

They chatted and giggled, bumping into each other in a way that only the innocent could.

Sighing, she let the shield fade and waited until the first gasp of surprise.

"You're back!" Laura said.

Her words caught the attention of the others, who all clamoured to be heard.

"… mother said you'd died…"

"… lost my tooth!"

"… patrolling dangerous?"

"… baby chickens!"

Laura stepped up, a serious look on her face. "Have you given up?"

The class fell silent.

"No!" The word slipped out unbidden.

"Do you want to?"

Grace's name flashing in the book. Clouds low enough to cover her vision. Horrific words painting her as the villain. "No," Shari said, softer this time. "Lissae needs her protector, now more than ever."

"What if someone else could do it?" Laura asked.

Shari bit back a mirthless laugh. "For some reason, Lissae chose me. And I will continue to be the Altoriae until there is no breath left in my body."

"What if your heart is still beating, but you can't breathe?" a kid from the back of the room asked with the assured ignorance that comes with having never been on a battlefield.

"Then I'll be the hantra Altoriae and still protect your dreams. Now, who can tell me what the Guardian taught you? I know he's far too slack on little ones."

They yelled their protests while Shari ducked her head to hide a grin.

Slowly, Shari got an update and went to work on the next bit of their lesson plan.

After the class had finished, the students filed out and Shari tidied the room. A patch of Dark Innarn in the corner wavered, catching her attention.

Sending a wave out, she figured it was Laura. The giggle as she brushed by confirmed it.

It wasn't until Shari had finished and flicked her fingers that there was a gasp.

"Scared of the dark?" Shari called.

Laura popped back into the visible spectrum, scowling. "No. Are you?"

"Oh no. I'm much more scared of the Light." She'd never admit it, but she was only half joking.

Shari forced herself to smile at the eager girl looking up at her.

It was easier than looking out the window at the clouded sky.

Amara gnawed on her lip as she looked at the gathered crowd.

There was something about knowing the Altoriae had been taken from the portal that was making her, and the rest of the guild, reluctant to step foot through the double doors.

There was the conflicting side, too.

Stories of the Altoriae had been whispered for the last decade or more. She was the one parents told their children about, the one who kept the monsters out of their nightmares and away from the streets and towns by ensuring they never set foot on Lissae.

Meeting Shari had been a high point for Amara. She was so relaxed about being the Altoriae that some of the myth had disappeared. The deity-like being replaced with a teen of immense Innarn and limited fashion sense.

Shari was everything Amara wanted to be. Strong, confident in her own skin, and capable of standing up to anyone who needed it.

Until she'd returned from... wherever she'd been.

A pale figure, wandering through Ronah at the whim of others like a cloud on the breeze.

Looking up, Amara caught Raven's gaze. He nodded.

It was time to go.

Grimly, Amara looked at her patrol group.

Collis was leading them tonight. Talofa, Remmy, Eva, and Raven rounded them out.

Their first time in the portal since the Altoriae's return.

Taking a shuddering breath, Amara nodded back and walked through the doors.

Crihimos

Remmy was looking at him out of the corner of his eye. *'Have you figured it out yet?'*

'No,' Collis sent back. *'There's not a lot of precedent for being soul-matched with a Linked who is happy for you to go off-Realm but not to another part of Lissae.'*

Silently, they trudged along the path leading away from Crihimos's gateway. The two Returned circling the group to make sure all sides were guarded.

'I have a theory, even though I hope it's wrong,' Remmy sent.

Making sure he kept his gaze on the group, Collis tried not to sigh. *'What if I don't want to hear your theory?'*

'I think you do.' Remmy's send was void of the usual teasing tone.

Collis rolled his eyes but nodded.

'What if... what if Tania instinctively knew that something bad was going to happen on Ginorti, and it's not so much that she doesn't want you to leave Ronah because of the soul-match, but she knows that off-Realm is safer than on?' From the other side of Talofa, Remmy glanced at him, wearing a more serious expression than Collis had seen for at least three hundred years.

'So, Tania may think that anywhere other than Lissae is safe?' Collis asked.

'*Hey, I'm not putting thoughts in her mind, but it's a theory.*'

Across the top of Talofa's head, Collis glared at Remmy. They had more than enough experience to know that off-Realm was not safer.

The tiny girl poked his shoulder. '*What are we looking for?*'

'*Beings who are not themselves.*' Collis moved towards the front of the group, while Remmy circled to the back.

'*And how are we going to tell that?*' she asked.

A blast of Innarn shot out from the trees on the left of them, absorbed by the crystal shield Eva conjured.

'*That's one way,*' Remmy laughed even as he sent a blast back.

As the fighting began in earnest—their group of six against twice as many beings—a thick fog descended on the path.

Something prickled along the back of Collis' neck, and he felt a weakening that was all too familiar.

They were being drained of Innarn.

'*Weapons only,*' he sent.

"You feel it too," Remmy said as he slammed his fist into the temple of an orange-skinned biped with nails long enough to rend flesh.

Ignoring the *feels like home* response that trampled along his mind, Collis nodded. "Keep an eye on the others. They'll be tempted to..."

Use Innarn went unsaid, as that was exactly what tiny Talofa was doing.

Collis thinned his lips in horror as she screamed.

Fog started pouring into her open mouth.

"No!"

Something about this fog meant *danger* and *death*.

Amara whirled, her red hair standing out against the lessening fog.

"The mist is bad?" she asked.

Without thinking, Collis nodded.

"Okay," Amara said, and her fingers sparked, rising to match the flames in her eyes. The Daen flung the Fire at the fog, and it burnt, screaming.

Or the screaming could have been Talofa, as the fog inside her was seared away.

"Back to the gateway. Now!"

Once more, he scooped up Talofa's fallen body.

The bipeds didn't like the dying fog. More bodies than they had accounted for filled the clearing, menace evident in every step and hunched shoulder.

Hampered by carrying the unconscious girl, Collis wielded his staff with one hand, fighting to keep them from taking Talofa from his grasp. Back against the closest tree, he took in his patrol group.

Amara swore as two of the puppets pinned her down and others piled on to stop her flailing limbs.

All teeth and flashing blade, Eva whirled and twisted amongst them, dealing surprisingly efficient blows aimed at incapacitation rather than decapitation.

Remmy was, as always, a dark spot, stepping out from the shadows to stop those getting too close to the backs of others.

Until Raven called out and dropped to the ground on one knee after one of the downed bipeds ripped at the back of his leg.

And Remmy wasn't there.

His grip tightening on the staff, Collis was hesitant to send. With the rest of the patrollers down, the blank gaze of the orange bipeds turned on him.

Talons outstretched, the closest one was a hair's width away from him when something sailed through the air and smacked the biped in the shoulder, sending zir backwards into the others.

Stepping up next to him, a ferah grinned. "Need a hand?" Her whiskers quivering as she ran a hand down her arm, sending a wave of needle-sharp fur into the closest biped.

"Thanks," Collis said.

Out of the forest behind him, stepped others. Two mammoth cyclops, easily as tall as he was, and a being with midnight-black skin wielding a sword.

An icy skinned man holding a spiked chain grinned from the other side of the clearing where he stood next to Remmy.

"Found some new friends?" Collis called.

"The U'sala."

Collis' eyes widened. To be fighting on the same battlefield as the famed U'sala.

"You have the same expression as the Altoriae," the ferah said.

"You've met Shari?" Collis asked, as the rest of the U'sala seamlessly took down the horde in front of him.

When the last body fell, fog started pouring from their mouths.

"Run!" the ferah commanded.

They wasted no time.

As they raced towards the gateway, Collis made a mental to ask the Guardian that Talofa stayed on Lissae until they could be sure sentient fog wasn't around anymore.

U'sala and Lissaens ran as if a herd of fulni were on their tails, stampeding through the portal to safety.

Lissae

Narday 11pm

Fourth day of the fourth week of Hazelcrown

Temira looked at the tiny Uleulan lying on the table.

"Who thought it was a good idea to use fire on fog?" she asked, glaring at the bedraggled group.

Much scuffing of toes and umming later, the fiery-haired one who had given her a drink after Temira had revitalised Ronah's lode crystal raised her hand.

The technomancer pointed to the door.

The girl... 'A' something... slouched out.

"I'd be honoured to help to make up for the incompetence of others," Milo said, pushing his way through the group.

Temira caught the gaze of the ferah and tilted her head at Milo.

The ferah nodded.

Now she had someone to watch the traitor, she worked swiftly. Temira poured a vial of green goop into the girl's throat.

"What's that?" someone asked.

This was where Xani would say, '*It numbs the lining and enables us to remove and replace the damaged parts.*'

But, of course, there was no Xani.

Milo was prattling on about something entirely wrong. Temira looked up once and shook her head, causing a being to giggle.

When the Daen turned around, Temira was bent over her patient again.

'*Cyrus?*' Temira sent.

'*Is Milo there?*'

Temira sighed. 'Yes.'

'*Do you want to heal two bodies?*'

Interrupting Milo's monologue, Temira snapped, "I need the size thirteen crystal disc and a purple vial. They are kept in room twenty."

"Now?" he asked.

She glared at him, and he scurried from the room.

A shadow detached from the back wall to follow him. '*Cyrus.*'

'*If he's not gone, I'll…*' Cyrus appeared by her side. "Oh no, not a kid," he said.

"Work fast, and she'll grow to be an adult," Temira said.

Together they patched and checked, removing the burned flesh and forcing healthy tissue to grow in its place.

Stepping back, Temira wiped her brow. "She'll live."

"We've done what we can. She'll have some pain and tenderness for the next few days, but it should subside. Make sure she rests," Cyrus said.

The tallest man in the room stepped forward and scooped up the tiny girl. "Thank you," he said.

"It's not your fault," Cyrus blurted. "Whatever happened, it's not on you."

He scowled down at Talhan's Linked. "Every time Talofa goes on patrol with me, she attracts these clouds that hurt her."

"Clouds?" Cyrus said.

He shot a look at Temira right as Shari entered the room.

"How can clouds hurt you?" someone asked.

"There are clouds," the Altoriae said, "that can drain you of your Innarn. They pull apart the very fabric of who you are and take over your mind before killing you. Then they use your body like a puppet to lure others for the rest of their kind to feed on."

"Sounds more like a nightmare than a cloud," Cyrus said.

Shari looked grimmer and paler than Temira had ever seen her, and that included after the Altoriae had been killed by the training device Temira had created.

"Oh, it is. I know because I've lived it."

Chapter Twenty-One

Lissae

Rasshday

Fifth day of the fourth week of Hazelcrown

Shari looked around the room after her grim news. "Well met, Yessna, U'sala. What brings you to Lissae?"

"Murderous clouds, by the sounds of it," Kerk said.

She grinned at the cyclops twin with an old scar dissecting his eye. "Well met, Kerk, Drah."

Temira huffed.

"I think it's best if we take this conversation elsewhere?" Shari offered, gesturing to the door. "Thank you, Temira, for healing Talofa."

The technomancer nodded and crossed her arms as Collis carefully carried her patient out, followed by the others. Shari, last out the door, gave her a jaunty wave.

A tiny white hair Daen, looking rather dusty and dishevelled, was almost tripping over his own feet to get back to the room, vials clutched in his hands. "Altoriae, wait! I have the..."

Something about his presence sent her skin crawling. Shari shifted the entire group to the training group before he could come within touching distance. "Was that Fenix's aide?" she asked.

"No. That was Milo," Cyrus answered, a bitter twist to his words.

She wrinkled her nose. *'Jonathan? Who is Milo?'*

'Possibly a spy for the mainlanders.'

'Hopefully a spy for them and not something worse,' she sent back.

'I feel like we really need to talk. Meet me in my office later?'

'Sure.'

"Is Talofa alright?" she asked, turning her attention back to the group.

"She will be," Cyrus said.

"I'll take her to her room," Collis said.

"We'll guard her." Eva tugged on Amara's hand. Amara followed, tripping over her feet a handful of times.

"So..." Shari led the way to the dining room. A sitting room seemed too formal, and the U'sala all looked like they'd appreciate a good meal.

'Dad? Any chance you could send over some food?' Shari sent.

Calem shifted next to her side, his wings surrounding her.

From between a mouthful of feathers, Shari groaned. "Dad!"

"Just needed a head count," he said, patting her gently. "Any requests?"

"Roast?" someone asked. Shari wasn't sure who—it was hard to tell when one ear was pressed against her father's chest and the other was being tickled by stray feathers.

Disappearing as quickly as he arrived, Calem was gone.

Shari just hoped her face wasn't as red as it felt.

If Remmy's snicker was anything to go by, that hope was in vain.

Ignoring the Returned, she turned to the U'sala. "Murderous clouds?"

"Reports are sweeping the Light Realms. Dense, low-lying clouds followed by disappearances. If the being comes back, they aren't the same as before and often lure friends or family away," Yessna said.

'Jonathan? *You might want to join us*,' Shari sent. "Have you found a way to get rid of the cloud?"

"No." A shadow passed over Yessna's eyes. "But it seems your patrollers have, Healer."

Grinning at the mention of their first meeting, Shari looked at Collis, who seemed about to protest Yessna's incorrect title for her. "They have?"

"We have?" Raven asked at the same time.

"Fire Innarn burns it up. Looks like Dark Innarn works as well. We'll have to test it," Drah, Kerk's twin said.

Jonathan shifted into the room with Samuel in tow. They settled down on either side of Shari.

"And you were on Crihimos because?" Collis asked.

"Trying to track down the source of the clouds," Yessna said.

"Zuefie," Shari blurted. "They are the Xanderri of Zuefie."

Yessna wrinkled her nose. "Xanderri?"

"Innarn eaters," Samuel said.

The ferah blanched beneath her fur.

A slight being, who was casually cleaning his sword at the table, scoffed. "That's just a story."

"No, it's not," Shari said. "I've been to Zuefie. I've seen the Xanderri in action." She shuddered.

Carefully brushing down her fur, Yessna kicked the sword cleaner. "Lenyuu, if the Altoriae says she's seen Innarn eaters, then we will take her word."

Lenyuu nodded and put his cleaned sword back into a battered sheath. He had perfect timing, as the food she'd asked her father for appeared on the table, and the U'sala fell upon the feast.

"Where is Jeran these days?" Jonathan asked once everyone had loaded their plates.

The temperature in the room dropped as the U'sala bowed their heads.

"Yessna is the leader of the U'sala," Kerk said, his voice low.

Shari closed her eyes. "We grieve with you," she said softly.

"The U'sala celebrate the life that was. Jeran fell in battle, and we honour his sacrifice," Yessna said.

"Wait..." Something about the word *sacrifice* niggled at the back of Shari's mind. She remembered the first time she'd met Jeran. Jonathan had been healing the feisty wikkur, and he'd howled. She'd run into the room and...

Shari felt the blood drain from her face. "I watched him die."

"What?" Yessna's head snapped up, her fur bristling.

"Jeran. They brought him in with a bunch of others to Zuefie and drained them, one after the other, in front of me." Shari wrapped her arms around her waist.

"When?" Yessna asked.

Shari tried to block Jeran's last words out. There was no way the easy going leader of the U'sala would have wished for her death. "About three weeks ago."

"He was not in control of himself when he fell," Drah said.

His twin shuddered.

A being with skin pale enough to be confused with ice reached out and clasped Kerk's shoulder. "You freed him."

'*Kerk lopped his head off. Three days passed, on Pontan,*' Yessna sent.

Shivering, Shari held herself tighter. "And you think Dark Innarn kills them?"

"We did it on Nittany," Collis said. "Clouds surrounded Talofa. We…"

"You," Remmy interrupted.

"Blasted it with Dark Innarn. It exploded."

Samuel's grin reminded Shari of something more appropriate in his Q'Aralide form. "Let's go blast some clouds then."

Jonathan held up a hand.

'*Guardian? Aharny here.*'

It took him a moment to put the name to a face. Aharny was the Ilutri Travel Innarnian who had been formerly stationed at Dento. '*Yes?*'

'*There's smoke on the horizon.*'

'*Smoke?*' he asked. There were no settlements around, and smoke sounded an awful lot like…

'*The mainlanders are coming back.*'

"Before we do that, we might want to head to the shoreline."

"Why?" Eva asked.

"The mainlanders are attacking again," Jonathan said.

The Lissaen's chairs scattered as they stood. The U'sala were slower to react.

"You are fighting your own kind?" Yessna asked.

"Not something we want to do," Remmy said. "They started it by trying to drain Ginorti of his Innarn."

"Ginorti?" Lenyuu asked.

"One of the Shifting Islands," Shari said. She had stood as well but was looking decidedly pale.

"Shari," Jonathan started, but stopped at the glare she flung his way. Looked like his Altoriae thought she was back to fighting form. "Do you want to get the U'sala comfortable first?"

She scowled at him, then, smiling sweetly, turned to their new guests. "Wanna come fight?"

Yessna grabbed another roll and nodded around a mouthful.

"Perfect. Jonathan?" Shari said.

Sighing, and debating on how much trouble he was going to get in from her parents, he shifted the lot of them to the northernmost part of the wall Collis had created, at the point where Ronah joined with Ginorti.

Just as Aharny had said, there was smoke on the horizon. Above their heads, a flock of Ilutri hovered for a moment before shooting off towards the oncoming ships.

"At least now we're joined. There aren't enough ships in their fleet to ring the islands," Remmy muttered.

Beneath their feet, Ginorti was groaning.

Oakley popped up between Jonathan and Yessna, and the ferah's fur stood on end.

"We have time to plan," Ginorti's Linked said. "This time, they don't stand a chance."

Samuel looked down at the Altoriae as she started shuddering.

'No. No, *not now*,' Shari was broadcasting.

A quick glance around showed that a few looked confused or concerned, but most looked pitying, as if the being who'd been protecting them since she'd been a hatchling had finally broken.

Before he could say anything to the contrary, Shari's back arched and a dark spot appeared in the centre of her chest. A familiar-looking maw was pushing its way through, and before Samuel could stop them, Jetonyx and Tormorylth were hovering in the sky before them.

"Surprise?" Shari said weakly.

The U'sala dropped into fighting stances. Yessna was sending her fur flying already, and a spiked chain was whipping out straight for Tormorylth.

"No!" he screamed, and launched himself in the air, changing form just in time to take the blow intended for the hatchling.

Wing stinging, he turned and growled at the gathered party, only to find Shari doing the same thing.

"Don't you dare hurt them," the Altoriae was yelling.

Tormorylth was whimpering behind him. '*Burns...*'

Sanithane glanced back as Jetonyx flew higher, covering the younger one with his shadow, even as his own hide smoked.

'*Pull them back in, Shari,*' he sent, worry colouring his thoughts a muddy brown.

'No,' groaned Tormorylth.

'*Do you really want to die?*' Sanithane snapped.

"Now is not the time to get worked up over a trio of flying reptiles," Ginorti's Linked was saying.

Sanithane wasn't sure if he should be grateful or offended.

"He's a big softy anyway," Tania was adding.

When did she arrived? Another glance at the top of the mountain Collis had created showed that the Linked from the five joined islands were all there.

"We can't trust them," one of the U'sala was saying.

'*Go back to Shari's sanctuary. Now!*' Sanithane ordered.

'No,' Tormorylth sent again. Something small and sliver streaked through the air and latched on to her forearm.

Shari's cuff.

'*Jetonyx, I'm sorry. I only have one,*' Shari sent.

"You'd trust them that much?" Cyrus asked her.

Jaw set, Shari nodded. "They saved me. I wouldn't have made it back to Lissae without them."

Hanging his head, Cyrus sighed. Pulling something from his arm, he tossed it to the Altoriae. "Give this to the other one."

"Jetonyx," she said automatically. As she through the other cuff up, Sanithane felt Shari nudge it with her Innarn and fix it to Jetonyx. Instantly, the smoke stopped rising from his hide and the hatchling sighed.

"Would they help us fight?" Yessna asked.

'*Food?*' Tormorylth asked.

'*The beings on the boats are, yes,*' Sanithane sent.

Stifling a laugh, Shari nodded. "Yes. They'll help."

Uneasy truce called, the three Q'Aralide carefully landed.

In the distance, a ship's horn blew.

'*Almost snack time!*' Tormorylth grinned.

CHAPTER TWENTY-TWO

Lissae

Vebaday

Sixth day of the fourth week of Hazelcrown

Captain Rappen let the clouds pour out of his mouth, knowing they would stir the rabid troops into a further frenzy.

'*Can't you just feel their blood coating your hands? Watching their sightless eyes as they fall to your sword.*'

The sailors were screaming and pounding their feet on the deck. A few, he noted, drew the attention of the clouds more than others. As their skin turned waxen and they fell overboard, he smiled grimly.

It was the perfect way to rid themselves of any aberrations hiding in their midst.

With the clouds on their side, nothing could go wrong.

Collis gripped the handle of his staff and made sure he had enough room to move.

"Hit them with Dark Innarn!" Yessna called out.

"Before or after they use Innarn blockers on us?" someone yelled back.

"Wha...?" The ferah's question was cut off by a whistling noise.

Scenes that had only been described to Collis were happening. Something too big to be an arrow sped through the air, the weighted net flinging out.

The great, golden Q'Aralide leaped up and grabbed the missile midflight. Twisting through the air, he sent it flying back at the ships.

Who knew clouds could scream? Collis tried hard not to flinch as the two smaller Q'Aralide joined in.

The winged beasts in the sky were only a minor deterrent to the ships, smoke clogging the air as the fleet drew closer and closer, but he was still grateful they were on the same side. From the hum emanating through the rest of the Returned, they felt the same way.

More beings joined them on top of the mountain, all of them carrying some sort of weapon.

"Mum!" the Altoriae called. "You can't be here!"

Arilla laughed. "Oh sweetie," she said. "Try to stop me."

"Samuel!"

Collis hefted his staff as the golden one turned. The instant Samuel saw Arilla, the Guardian's Apprentice turned on a wingtip and flew straight for the ships.

Weaving through the barrage of ballistae, Samuel breathed out a line of noxious, green gas along the vessels. At the very end of the line, he did something, and the lot lit on fire.

Screams carried over the waves, and the beings on the islands cringed away from the Q'Aralide as he rejoined them, wrapping protective wings around the Altoriae's mother.

Shari's weakness is her loved ones.

Collis just hoped that none of the mainlanders figured that out.

Jonathan had never been gladder to have Sanithane on their side. Watching the mainlanders' ships go up in flames was both awe-inspiring and terrifying.

Sanithane had, once again, taken out an entire army.

Something moved amongst the wreckage.

Flicking Shari a quick warning, Jonathan pushed his spirit from his body and guided it towards the movement. Peering closer, he scowled. The man was one he'd seen at the attack on the Ofanahni's settlement, and by the stripes on the uniform, the cretin was a captain.

One arm wrapped around a charred plank of wood, Captain Cretin pulled on something around his neck until a device on the other end was revealed.

A portable shifting device.

Before Jonathan could call out a warning, the captain twisted the centre crystal and disappeared.

Drifting to his body, Jonathan settled his mind back into his skin, and ran a hand over his face. How were they going to stop the mainlanders? Raising his gaze to the new mountains of Ronah, the Guardian figured they had much bigger things to talk about.

Q'Aralide-shaped things.

Zoeday
Seventh day of the fourth week of Hazelcrown

Shari settled into the seat she'd conjured, Jonathan sitting on her right, and Samuel, back in his 'squishy' form, on her left. They were seated on

184

the edge of the training ground, and in front of them stood two baby Q'Aralides, each snacking on a herd beast.

"So," Shari began.

Jonathan raised a brow, and she squirmed like a ten-year-old being told off for not training as much as he thought she should be.

"Not quite the way I intended you to meet them, but here they are." She gestured at the two. Jetonyx lifted his head, intestines hanging from his maw as he smiled at them. She winced. Perhaps the sympathy card would work? "Jonathan, Guardian of Lissae, meet Jetonyx and Tormorylth, two of only three surviving Q'Aralides."

From the glare, sympathy wasn't going to win.

"What about the egg?" Samuel asked.

Oh, if looks could kill, generations of my children were already dead. "Well, technically, it's still an egg, and not, um, hatched." Shari spread her hands.

"In the middle of a battle, Shari." Jonathan's voice dipped down the way it always did when he was disappointed in her.

'Not *her fault*,' Tormorylth sent. '*Wanted out.*'

The Guardian turned his head and glared at the tiny hatchling. "I'll deal with you in a moment."

Samuel growled.

"Oh, by the life of Lissae, no! You two are not doing this with me in the middle!" Shari said and scrambled out of her seat. "Jon, they have *nowhere* to go! Where in the Realms do you think they'd be safe right now? Surely the Portal is buzzing with the news of Altum?" She winced as Samuel flinched. '*I'm sorry*,' she sent.

He gave her a tight smile.

"They can't stay here. Lissae is too Light for them."

"They're fine if they wear the cuffs," she argued. "Right, Samuel?"

The man in question was looking past her, his eyes suspiciously damp. "I thought I'd never see them again. Thought I was going to be the last one."

Jonathan ran a hand over his face. "Fine. They can stay. But if they put a claw out of line, it's on your head."

Samuel blinked. "You are far less scary than our last task master."

Tormorylth bounded over to them and laid her head on her claws at Samuel's feet. '*You look tasty.*'

Shari groaned.

'*You can't eat me, little one. Or any of those in this Realm.*' Samuel paused. '*Unless we tell you to.*'

The hatchling sighed, and Shari was surprised that no poisonous gas leaked out of her mouth.

Samuel noted her expression. "It's a learned skill. Here, you learn letters. We were taught how to milk the sacs on the inside of our throats in such a way that we wouldn't die but could inflict death on others."

"Charming," Jonathan said, but he grinned. "Still sounds better than Joshua's method of teaching."

'*Sanithane is the best teacher,*' Jetonyx agreed, carefully picking something out from between his teeth with a claw. He looked at Jonathan. '*We can stay?*'

'*You can stay,*' Jonathan sent. "I'm just going to explain to the rest of Ronah why we're now home to three Q'Aralides."

Shari pulled the egg from her sanctuary, and it pulsed in her hands. "Soon to be four," she said, passing it to Samuel.

He beamed.

Jonathan groaned.

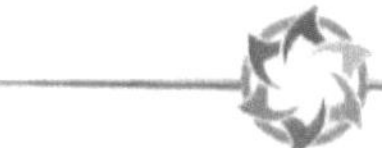

Skye rubbed her arm and wrinkled her brow.

Grace was rocking on her pallet in the corner of the room, muttering something over and over.

Twice now, Skye had tried to get close, and both times, shards of Innarn had lashed out and stung her.

Once more, then I'll get someone. Slowly, making sure that Grace could see her, Skye crept closer.

Finally, she could make out the words.

'Kill aberrations. Protect the family. Kill aberrations. Protect family.'

She half-wished she'd remained ignorant.

CHAPTER TWENTY-THREE

Lissae

Adonday

First day of the first week of Stormwake

Cyrus bounded into the training grounds on Ronah, startling Shari.

"Where are my two favourite little Q'Aralides?" he asked.

Shari raised both her brows.

"Too much?" he asked in a stage whisper.

She nodded.

Tormorylth crawled out from under Jetonyx's wing on the far side of the grounds and stretched. *'I'm your favourite?'*

"One of," Cyrus said.

'No. *Just me*,' Tormorylth sent as she walked closer.

Cyrus' throat bobbed but he nodded. "Just don't tell…"

'Jetonyx is the bigger one. This is Tormorylth,' Shari sent.

"Jetonyx. Wouldn't want him to get jealous." He winked.

Closing her middle eye, Tormorylth nodded and chuckled.

Before the miniature hatchling could melt Talhan's Linked into a metaphorical puddle, the technomancer swept in.

"Temira!" Shari said.

"Altoriae." The Head Healer's voice was flat. "Tell me why I should help the offspring of those who killed my Realm."

'*Did not,*' Tormorylth sent.

"Sorry?"

'*Did not kill your Realm. Didn't want to. Had orders.*'

"You were there?" The technomancer was finally showing Shari why everyone feared her. Innarn was whipping all around Temira, and she seemed to glow.

'*No. I wasn't even an egg. But the story of Ulnan is told as a warning, reminding us that orders are not always to be followed. And that regret hurts more than any punishment our Queen could mete out,*' Jetonyx sent. He lumbered up, so he stood between Temira and his younger kin.

'*Told you,*' Tormorylth said, and sticking her head around Jetonyx's side, she poked her tongue out.

An involuntary laugh burst from Temira, whose Innarn calmed to swirl around her calmly again. '*You stand there, some of the last of your kind, and pull faces at me?*'

'*Nothing you do—nothing—could be worse than Oalark.*' Tormorylth sank back on her haunches, and Shari longed to wrap an arm around the prickly hatchling.

"I'm sure we can be better than your Queen," Cyrus soothed. "Shari asked me here to help you, so we're already off to a good start."

'*Help?*'

"The cuff that you wear is helping you absorb some of the latent Grey Innarn from Lissae, but I'm worried that you'll outgrow it, and that just being here will hurt again," Shari said.

"May I have a look?" Cyrus asked.

Tormorylth held out her arm. Both Cyrus and Temira stepped forward to peer at the cuff that was already wrapped tight around her scales.

"Aren't you meant to have two claws?" Temira asked.

The tiny hatchling flinched. *'Gave one to Shari so she could get home.'*

"Maybe we can work on a replacement for that too?" Cyrus grinned.

The hatchling hummed and nodded.

Sitting back, Shari grinned as the Crystal Innarnians set to work. It was fascinating to watch them squabble over designs and ideas.

The sun was blocked. Shari's heart raced, and she glanced around frantically. Jetonyx gave her an unimpressed look.

'Your reflexes need improving,' he sent, and leaned his head on her shoulder to watch the show.

'Suppose they do,' Shari sent back. *'Need to get ready to fight again. Yesterday, you three did the heavy work.'*

'Mostly Sanithane,' Jetonyx sent, his thoughts sluggish.

'Are you alright?'

'This Realm is hard. Lots of energy, so I don't burn. Cuff helps, but more would be good.'

"What about one for each limb? Would that help to spread the load, rather than trying to get a single cuff to cover all of you?" Shari thought aloud.

Temira glanced at her. "Five cuffs. Arms, legs, and tail." She looked away from all of them, her expression blank. "It would work." The tail end of her coat flicked as she turned.

'Wait!' Tormorylth said.

The technomancer paused.

'Lissaens are strange, aren't they? They don't eat meat.'

Shari didn't know if she should be offended or not but held her tongue.

'But Ulnanians and Q'Aralides eat meat. Istaniern told us you eat your dead.' Tormorylth paused.

'True,' Temira sent.

Biting the inside of her cheek, Shari managed not to make a noise.

'But no one here will eat you.' Tormorylth laid her head on her claw and looked up at the technomancer mournfully.

'True.' There was a bit more bite to Temira's send.

'I will. When you're dead, I mean...'

'You... why?' Temira asked.

''Cause I think that helping us will hurt you. And it might bring you comfort to know that we care.' Tormorylth's words were said with such a childlike innocence, Shari's heart ached.

Temira slowly nodded. 'Very well.'

Tormorylth beamed.

'Only if you become my friend.' The technomancer turned once more and strode away.

"Oh, you're going to go hungry," Cyrus said. "Temira is a hard being to be friends with."

'But I care,' Tormorylth said, her bottom jaw jutting forward.

"I know," Shari soothed.

What the tiny Q'Aralide had got herself into?

Inthday

Second day of the first week of Stormwake

"You came back here, empty-handed, with half the fleet destroyed?" Chamele hissed.

Captain Rappen sneered at her. "You, safe in your haven, can do any better?"

"I don't get my soldiers killed," she said.

"No, you just order me to lead them into impossible situations and cannot mourn those who are lost when the odds inevitably turn against us." The captain smirked as the other elders in the room gasped in horror.

Only years of training prevented Chamele from growling at him. "How dare you," she said instead. "We are at *war*. And you are the one in charge of bringing our troops home safely. Something you have yet to do."

"She's right," Ben said. "You've been rather lax with that."

Fog shot out of the captain's mouth. Chamele tracked it with an odd detachment as it speed through the room and wrap around Ben's throat, slowly choking him.

"I have rather excellent control over it now," Rappen said as he strolled towards the purpling elder. "I can bend it to my will. Were you ever able to achieve such feats?"

Gywn was looking at them with wide, trembling eyes, one hand raised to cover her mouth.

Flashes of nannies and teachers cowering before her filled Chamele's mind. "Perhaps, in the beginning. But it is akin to what the aberrations are capable of."

"What's that old saying?" Rappen asked as the mist flowed away from Ben, who started coughing and rubbing his neck. Rappen came to stand directly before her. "Fight fire with fire?"

"If you think that best," Chamele said lightly, and raised her teacup to take a sip.

The Captain's gaze took in her trembling hand, and the grin he gave Chamele had her shivering and sloshing tea over the edges.

"I do," he said.

After a morning spent trying to wrangle the Q'Aralide hatchlings, Shari was exhausted.

Walking along the streets of Ronah, she nodded at the beings who greeted her but didn't stop to chat. Safely inside the Quiver and Quill, Shari made her way to the counter, where Arilla was balancing a jug and two plates of food. "Well met, Mum," she said.

"Shari! One moment. I've just got to give table ten their order and I'll..." She broke off as the order in her hands moved on air currents to the correct table. "Handy," she said.

"More time to talk," Shari offered.

"You're feeling better then?"

"I am." Shari noted the tightening around Arilla's eyes and the way she looked down.

"Shari..."

"Mum. I'm starting up patrolling again. I thought you'd like to know."

"But Healer Holli said..."

"She cleared me this morning, after I finished wrangling our newest two residents."

Arilla sighed. "I don't want to see you hurt."

"You will. It's kinda part of the job."

"No parent wants that," her dad said as he came out of the kitchen, dusting flour off his hands.

"While I was away, I learned some things that make me think I won't have to do this forever," Shari said. "Lissae is changing and..." She broke off, frustrated.

"I've felt something different for a while now," Calem admitted. "I don't know what it is exactly, but we trust you. If you think you're ready to patrol again, then we'll support you."

"However reluctantly," Arilla added, reaching out to grab her hand. Shari held on tightly before giving her a squeeze and letting go.

"If you come back hurt, tell us," Calem said.

"Dad, you know every patrol group has someone who returns with at least a scrape or graze," Shari said.

"Doesn't mean it has to be you," Arilla argued.

"I usually patrol alone." Shari winked, aiming for jaunty and unaffected.

Calem scowled. "Not anymore. Grab someone and take them with you."

"Who do you think can keep up with me?" Shari asked. "Jonathan's got so much going on, he barely has time to eat. And Samuel..."

"Will be happy to accompany you," said a voice from behind.

Hanging her head, Shari huffed out a breath. "Fine. But I'm not telling the hatchlings why you got sandblasted into a million pieces on a different Realm."

Samuel laughed.

Lifting her head, Shari caught her dad glaring at the man behind her.

"If you so much as hurt her..."

"Dad!" Shari protested. "Samuel ensured that even as his Realm was destroyed, I got out safely. How can you... wait." She frowned as a thought occurred to her. "Is this because you think he *likes* me?" Wrinkling her nose, she shook her head. "No offence, Samuel, but you're, like, four thousand years too old for me. Not to mention I don't want to kiss anyone, ever."

Calem subsided, placated. Glancing over her shoulder, Shari snickered when Samuel rolled his eyes.

"Why are you talking about kissing? You're essentially the same age as Jetonyx." Samuel looked disdainful.

"You seemed happy enough to suck face with the datzal," Shari said.

"*She* kissed *me*."

Arilla laughed at their expressions, and for a moment, all was right in the Realms.

Kerday

Third day of the first week of Stormwake

Belfar looked at Wolf as he hovered by SilverCloud's bed.

Ever since Shari's return, the elder had declined rapidly.

"Think it's time to call your brother home," SilverCloud said.

Tucking the blanket tighter around his father, as if that would delay the inevitable, Wolf said, "Sure, Dad, if you want."

"I can go get him," Belfar offered.

Wolf nodded, clearly grateful for the opportunity to spend time with his dying father. "Thanks."

Head bowed, Belfar slipped from the room. The moment he reached a balcony, he took to the sky, winging his way slowly towards Ronah, trying to give his mate as much time as he could.

"You finally told the Altoriae about your little golden secret," Yessna said.

"Yep," Samuel replied.

"How did she react?" The ferah fell backwards onto a lounge in the drawing room, putting her paws up on the arm and grabbed a rutenberry from the bowl on the table.

"About as well as you expected, at first. Had a datzal trying to impersonate her, so we had to deal with that before we got to the part where she threatened me." Samuel lent forward from his own seat and snagged the entire bowl. He was well aware of Yessna's sweet tooth and had no intention of sharing his snack.

"I'm surprised you're still here," Yessna said. "Thought you would have jumped at the chance to not have someone dictating your every move."

"Shari does not…" He paused as a shadow crossing the doorway. The guild members were forever poking their noses in when he was around, it seemed moreso since his aborted attempt to teach Shari to change.

Yessna laughed when he scowled. Samuel threw a rutenberry at her. Arching up, she caught it in her mouth and plopped back down on the couch.

"Oh, I wanna learn how to do that!" Amara said.

"It's easy." Yessna waved a paw. "Your tail does most of the work."

"I don't have a tail." Amara looked devastated. "Ah well, wishful thinking." She grinned at them and slipped away, much like the smile Yessna had been wearing.

"The Realms are dangerous now, San."

"When Shari patrols, I'll make sure she sticks to the Darker ones," he said.

Even though Yessna nodded, the ferah still looked worried.

Belfar burst into the Quiver and Quill, both wings ruffled.

"Calem, Arilla. Oh, Shari, good. You're here too." Her uncle's mate looked at the three of them and sighed.

"What's wrong?" Calem asked.

"It's time."

Shari glanced at her parents. "I'll meet you there."

CHAPTER TWENTY-FOUR

Lissae
Kerday night
Third day of the first week of Stormwake

Shari nodded to the last patroller who headed through the museum doors, torn. She had come to see off the patrols but was half tempted to step through the portal too, so she wouldn't have to farewell her dying grandfather.

She wasn't ready to say goodbye.

'*You sad?*' Tormorylth asked.

Turning to the hatchling, she nodded. The two barely fit into the courtyard outside the museum, but they ducked and kept their wings and tails tucked in, refusing to leave her side for a moment.

'*My grandfather is...*' She couldn't even bring herself to think it.

Jetonyx leaned his head on her shoulder again. '*Your memories of him feel better than anything we've known.*'

Tormorylth gave him a look.

'*Apart from Samuel,*' he added.

'*Go see him,*' Tormorylth said.

How did she say the sight of two Q'Aralides, no matter how small, might just be enough to finish him off without offending them? '*I don't think he'd be too happy with anyone who wasn't family.*'

The younger hatchling sighed, then perked up. '*We can visit Sanithane!*'

'*Uh, Samuel?*' Shari sent. '*I have a thing. A family thing. Can you come to the museum, please?*'

Before she'd finished, Samuel appeared at her side.

Samuel raised his brow at Jetonyx, who kept his chin firmly planted on Shari's shoulder.

She reached up and carefully scratched either side of his maw. "I'll be back. I'm just going to Rakemyst."

Jetonyx sighed and reluctantly removed his head.

Giving them all a watery grin, Shari shifted away to the room where she'd had the food fight with SilverCloud not so long ago.

Following the tug of Innarn, she made her way through the halls and nodded at the Ilutri guards. Slipping past, she stepped into her grandfather's bedroom.

Wolf and Calem were on either side of the bed, their mates standing with them.

Shari tried to smile but found she couldn't.

Her mother beckoned her forwards.

The vital Ilutri who'd led her on a merry chase only a few short months ago now barely made a dent in the mattress.

"Well met, SilverCloud," Shari said softly.

He opened his eyes and smiled at her. "Shari," he said. "Wasn't sure if you'd make it."

Blinking back tears, she nodded. "Wouldn't miss saying..." She shuddered, but sucked in a breath and continued, "... goodbye for all the Realms in the Ducibus' Hall."

SilverCloud laughed, a weak, wheezy sound. "It's not goodbye. Not really. So long as there are stars in the sky, I'll watch over you."

The brothers bowed their heads over his hands. "So long as there are stars in the sky," they repeated.

"I bid thee well, my boys. Take care of each other, and take care of Shari," SilverCloud said, his voice fading towards the end. He closed his eyes, and the others in the room were silent.

They watched over him until Elder SilverCloud Dawn of the Ilutri of Rakemyst took his last breath.

And then they cried.

Vebaday
Sixth day of the first week of Stormwake

Tania smiled at Oakley, whose gaze darted around the room as if he expected an attack.

Zana, who made sitting on a mossy boulder look as elegant as everything else she did, asked softly, "Shall we put up wards?"

Oakley nodded quickly. He startled when the wards hummed to life, hand twitching for something hanging from his belt.

Tray of drinks in hand, Fenix offered one to Oakley first. "It'll calm your nerves," they whispered.

"Thank you." Oakley grabbed a cup and sipped, the tension easing out of his frame almost immediately.

Giving him time to wind down, Tania glanced around the room. From what she could gather, they were in a small meeting room in

Ginorti's equivalent of Rakemyst's white tower. The building was a giant mound, the biggest rezem Tania had ever seen, with a ring of huge bereni trees on the top of it.

Like Ridden Hall, there was a clearing in the middle, and if she looked out of the window, the satyrian troops were training below.

The room itself was decorated in earthy browns and moss greens, and for a boulder, the seats were comfortable. The stone seemed to meld with her form, and she didn't want to get up. Smiling at Fenix, she took a drink from the tray and glanced at the artwork hanging on the wall.

Four stunning paintings lined the curved wall between the window and the door, all depicting leaves, but each one showed a different season. Tania allowed herself to get lost in the greens of the summer leaves before turning her attention back to her companions.

"Tell me about Ginorti?" Tania asked. "I've met him, kind of. He's..."

"I heard about the golem," Oakley laughed. "Ginorti is one of a kind."

"All our islands are," Cyrus said.

The Linked grinned dopily at each other.

"I became his Linked about fifteen years ago. Zana trained me, much as she's training you, Tania." Oakley tipped his cup to the Ilutri, who smiled. "The last Linked was a more passive personality, so I didn't have a lot of guidance from her. Without Zana, I wouldn't know half of what I do now."

"You flatter me," the Ilutri said.

Peering at her mentor, Tania startled.

Zana was blushing.

"Ginorti is... oh." Oakley leaned back, putting his foot up on the seat of the boulder and resting his arm on his knee. "All the typical things. Rock solid, stable."

The ground beneath them rumbled.

Patting the boulder, Oakley nodded. "But nothing holds a grudge like stone. He will not forget that I was taken away from him any time soon."

"How were you taken?" Cyrus asked.

"Ginorti has an inbuilt protection that I was trying to activate. I got too close to the shore and was scooped up by the mainlanders." Oakley's hands wrapped around his cup tighter.

"Is there anything we can do to make you feel better?" Tania asked.

"Keep reminding me I'm safe?" Oakley chuckled, but the white-knuckled grip told a different story. "Make sure it doesn't happen again?"

Tania's eyes welled. He sounded so lost. And for a man who was old enough to have grown up with her mother, it made her sadder than she thought was possible. "Can I give you a hug?" she asked.

Cyrus grinned. "Pile on Oakley!"

Before she knew it, all four Linked were laughing and crying, tangled together in a big heap.

Apart from being with Collis, it was the safest she'd felt for ages.

Jonathan smiled as Zac took a sip from a glass and then handed it to him.

"I thought after our first official date, you'd stop doing that," Jonathan said. They were once again in his lounge room, and for a change, he felt relaxed enough to take his shoes off. He was glad to see that Zac had done the same and was currently curling his toes into the rug.

Zac stared at him over the rim of his own glass. "Not yet. Soon, I think. How are you coping with Ronah's newest residents?"

"They are a handful," Jonathan admitted. "For all they are massive, they don't eat as much as I was expecting, and Samuel seems to have a steady supply of food for them. So at least I don't have to... What?"

Zac was staring at him, horrified. "The refugees are massive?"

The Guardian blinked. "Well, the two Q'Aralide hatchlings are."

"Wait. What? There are Q'Aralides on Lissae. On *Ronah*?"

"Where have you been hiding?" Jonathan asked. "It's all anyone has been talking about since yesterday."

"I was helping at the Techno Centre," Zac said. "Cyrus and Temira are deep in research mode, so I offered to do some of the scut work for the others. Frees them up to take over the slack from the top two."

"Ahhh, that'd do it." Jonathan sipped his drink and took a risk. "Have you seen Milo around the Techno Centre?"

"Little dude, salt and pepper hair, very officious?" Zac asked.

Jonathan nodded.

"Yeah. He follows Temira like a lost puppy. If he's not on her heels, he's in her lab."

"In her lab?" Jonathan repeated.

"Why? Is there something going on?"

In for a bead, in for a coin. "We think Milo is stealing some of the technomancer's inventions and passing them on to the mainland."

Sipping from his drink, Zac seemed to mull over the idea. "I can see why you'd think that. He's always in the right place at the wrong time. Want me to keep an eye on him?"

"Zac, I can't ask you to do that. If the spy is Milo, he's stolen Innarn blockers and Zoemer knows what else. He's dangerous," Jonathan said, leaning forward.

"But it would help Ronah," Zac pointed out.

Jonathan sighed. "It would."

"Then I'll do it," he said and put his glass down. "Now that's decided." He slid along the couch and took the glass out of Jonathan's hand, a soft grin on his face as he leaned in for a kiss.

Zoeday
Seventh day of the first week of Stormwake

Samuel felt like he was allowed to grumble.

Lizbeth and Sneeze both glared at him.

Through bribes of rutenberries, Lizbeth had talked her way into the training ground, where Tormorylth currently had the blind woman pinned gently against the outer wall and was sniffing her. Unfortunately, Sneeze had somehow ended up on Lizbeth's shoulder before said pinning and was subject to the rapid snuffling as well.

"Tormorylth, what are you doing?" Samuel asked.

'Smells sweet. Where the sweet?'

"I know you know how to form a proper sentence," he growled. "Until you do so, you won't get an answer. And stop sniffing your... guests."

'You had best not been about to call me food, Samuel Caragnton,' Lizbeth warned. *'Or you'll be fresh out of rutenberries for the foreseeable future!'*

'Of course not,' Samuel sent back, careful to make sure that his thoughts were clear and not coloured in guilt.

More glaring.

"I can give you something sweet," Lizbeth said. "But I need to get to my basket. Would you mind backing up a touch, Tormorylth?"

The tiny hatchling did as she was asked. When she sat on her haunches, the moonlight spilling over her form, Samuel was glad to see that she looked a lot healthier. She'd put on both much-needed weight and a significant amount of height.

"Here." Lizbeth was holding out a handful of his rutenberries.

"Hey!" Samuel said.

Looking him dead in the eye, Lizbeth said, "I'm sure Samuel would be happy to share."

'Mean,' he grumbled.

Sneeze blew sparks in his direction and swooped low, picking up a berry and biting into it.

Tormorylth daintily lifted one from the pile between her claw and her stump, and popped it into her mouth. She melted into a black-scaled puddle on the ground. '*Sweet.*'

Jetonyx, having met a manner, patiently waited until Lizbeth offered him one. Taking it as carefully as his nest mate, he too ate a berry and, much to Samuel's amusement, all three of Jetonyx's eyes crossed.

'*We need to learn to grow these,*' Jetonyx said.

Samuel chuckled. Maybe this generation of Q'Aralide would become farmers.

CHAPTER TWENTY-FIVE

Lissae

Zoeday

Seventh day of the first week of Stormwake

Amara looked back.

Talofa stood firmly inside the museum, wringing all four of her hands. "Be safe," she rasped.

Nodding, Amara turned back to the rest of the group. Raven was leading them this time, and they were sticking to the Grey Realms in the hopes of not running into the clouds.

"Let's go! Lamink isn't going to patrol itself," Raven said. He winked at Anika, who was standing next to Talofa, one arm wrapped around the trembling girl.

Amara rolled her eyes, and Eva nudged her in the ribs.

She didn't know how the blue-haired girl from Talhan had talked her way into Raven's patrol group, but Amara was glad.

Grinning, she grabbed Eva's hand, and they set off at the back of the group, following Raven to the gateway of Lamink.

Anika walked Talofa slowly back to the castle after they'd seen the patrollers off.

"Feels weird, doesn't it?" Talofa said. "I know I'm too young to really go on patrol, but watching all the others leave…"

Sighing, Anika said, "If you miss it, you can always help me stab stuff. I have about a *thousand* sequins I'm sewing onto Shari's dress for the Akoren joining at the moment."

"I enjoy stabbing stuff," Talofa giggled. "Tiny stuff."

"Yeah, like you," Anika teased, scuffing up the younger girl's hair.

"Hey!" Talofa squirmed away, laughing. The laugh turned into a cough, and both girls stopped. "Sorry," gasped Talofa once she had her breath back.

"It's all good. I'd forgotten that you were still recovering," Anika admitted.

"So had I," Talofa said, smiling up at her.

Adonday
First day of the second week of Stormwake

Tania made sure that the oil-coated crystals had been disposed of by the time Temira knocked on the door.

Before she could race to get it, the telltale squeak of the front door told Tania her mother had beaten her there.

"Well met?"

"Is Tania here?" Temira asked in lieu of a greeting. "We have a meeting."

Socks sliding on polished floors had Tania almost crashing into the wall. "Well met, Temira! Oh, you brought a new B.I.R.D.!"

"No more crystals," the technomancer glared at her.

"Tania?" her mum asked.

"Oh, Mum, meet Temira, Head Healer of Talhan's Techno Centre. Temira, meet Liza Hollingsworth, Headmaster of Ridden Hall."

"You do not test for Crystal Innarn," Temira said.

Tania wanted to hide her face. "Ronah still doesn't have a Crystal Innarnian. Once we do, the school will be able to test."

"Hmmm," Temira said, and brushed past to enter the rest of the house.

Flummoxed, her mum stepped to the side.

"Sorry, Mum," Tania said. "Should have warned you I had a guest coming over." She winced at the unimpressed look her mother wore.

"Dinner will be in an hour. Please let me know if your guest would like to stay."

Tania nodded and jumped at the sound of something crashing into the wall. "I'll just... ah..." She pointed toward where the sound—and Temira—was and ran.

Skidding into the sitting room, Tania's jaw dropped. The B.I.R.D. was doing laps, a dust cloth hanging from one mechanical claw and a water spritzer from the other.

"I made some upgrades," Temira said.

"I can see that." Tania's gaze was locked onto the mechanical bird as it fluttered around, cleaning anything within range.

"It can do chores. We can spend more time together."

"Once the last joining is done, I'll have loads more time," Tania agreed.

"When will that be?" Temira's tone hadn't changed, but something in her voice tore Tania's gaze away from the bird.

Temira was standing, stiff as a board, in the middle of the room, her hands clenched by her sides.

"Two more islands. At the rate we're going, by mid winter, for sure."

Temira nodded. "Very well." She turned to leave.

"You don't have to go."

"You have work to do on the joining."

"Maybe you'd like to hear some of the plans? You would have seen loads of joinings before. Let me know if this sounds silly."

"Most Lissaen ceremonies sound silly to me," Temira said, but she sat on the couch.

Tania joined her. "Well, Akoren is the water island, right? And the Wisara live *under* the island in special pods. What if we created tunnels of Air Innarn so we could actually see how they live?"

"Like they did two hundred and eighteen years ago?" Temira asked.

"Okay, not going to lie. A bit upset I wasn't the first one to come up with it. Was it good?"

Temira nodded. "It was fascinating to see the Wisara's home. They are notoriously private."

"After raising the Hantra, they owe me," Tania grumbled.

"I'm sorry, what?"

"Did I never tell you about my first ever fight?" Tania asked. She settled on the couch and patted the cushion next to her. Uncurling her fists, Temira slowly crossed the room and sank onto the offered seat, soaking up the story.

Collis stood on top of the highest peak on Cantash, panting. He and some of the other Returned had decided it was a good idea to climb the walls they'd created, and somehow, they'd ended up here.

Flopping to the ground, ignoring the bubbling lava under the ward he'd set, Collis glanced at Remmy.

The other man wiped back his sweaty hair and lifted his face to catch the sea breeze. "How do you think the ones who went to the mainland are going?"

He didn't have to question why it was on Remmy's mind. All the Returned who'd stayed on Ronah were thinking about it.

"I don't know," Collis said. "I worry about them. I don't want to reach out and put them at risk, but..."

"You still worry," Remmy said. "Me too. What if they're not okay? What if they've been taken, like Ginorti's Linked?"

They'd seen Oakley shortly after he'd been rescued, looking like he had one foot in the spirit Realm.

"I suppose there's more than one way to contact them," Collis said.

"We'll have to go the old-fashioned way," Remmy said, grinning. "Back before we were taken, my uncle used to be in charge of the Taps."

"Ah, I'd forgotten about the Crystal Taps." Collis grinned. Commonly referred to as Taps, they were crystal devices which acted as a two-way communication system. "Think the others would remember?"

"There's only one way to find out."

Chapter Twenty-Six

Lissae

Inthday

Second day of the second week of Stormwake

White clouds swirled around Captain Rappen's head.

'Must work faster. Need to feed.'

Straightening his uniform jacket, the captain looked in the mirror. "You can feed when they bleed."

Glancing around the room, he nodded in approval. After removing the clouds from Elder Chamele's head, he'd taken her rooms as well. It was only fitting that the clouds stayed in comfort, after all.

'We *are weak...*' the voice in his head trailed off.

"Did that work on the elder?" he asked scornfully. "You're as weak as I am." He took a breath. "To quiet your grumblings, we will find you a food source."

Peering into the mirror one last time, Captain Rappen startled.

His reflection had disappeared. In its place was a mop of salt and pepper hair.

"Elder?" the reflection asked.

He leaned forward. "This is Captain Rappen, head of the mainland forces. Who is this?"

"Milo from Cantash, Captain." The mop disappeared for a moment. The being on the other end retrieved some sort of stool. When he reappeared, his face could be seen. Something about the wide, tanned face sparked recognition from the cloud. "I request an audience with the elder." The tiny man lifted his nose into the air.

Captain Rappen wanted to run him through with his sword. "The elder is no longer in charge," he said through gritted teeth.

Milo sniffed. "Well, who is then?"

"I am."

The tiny man sighed, and Captain Rappen pictured reaching through the mirror and strangling him with his ridiculous tie.

"Well, you'll want this." Milo lifted a box up and held it against the mirror.

The captain mouth fell open as a long, thin box appeared on his side of the glass.

"Don't let it drop!" Milo scolded.

Automatically, his hands came up, and he caught the box before it could fall.

"What's this?" The captain wasn't sure if he was asking about the mirror that allowed objects to pass through it, or the potentially fragile contents of the box.

"The mirror is a portal that allows me to pass objects of interest through to the holder of the other piece, formally Elder Chamele and currently you. The box contains something significantly rarer. It took some effort to get to it, you know?"

Slowly, Captain Rappen opened the box. Inside was a single golden arrow. He glared at Milo. "An arrow."

"A soul-stealer arrow, leftover from the Chirean attack. It will take the Innarn from the being who is pierced with it and transfer it to the first one who touches it."

Captain Rappen smiled slowly. "Excellent. Let me know what else you get."

"Keep the mirror with you. These are the only two of their kind," Milo warned as he faded from view.

Captain Rappen was unable to wipe the smile from his face, as the cloud looped around the room. As it slid back inside his head, he carefully removed the mirror from the wall. Tucking it under one arm, and holding the box from the other, he made for the door.

Vision tinged with white, the captain strode from his rooms in search of a sacrifice to state the unending hunger of the cloud in his head.

Standing at the foot of the first bridge they'd created between Ronah and Ginorti, Tania linked arms with Zana and Fenix, who were either side of Cyrus. Oakley stood in the middle of their very squishy group.

"Now what?" she asked, her nose almost pressed against Oakley's back.

"Shuffle up to the break," Zana said.

They started moving, Cyrus or Oakley cursing every time one or the other stepped on toes.

"This has to be the most awkward thing I've ever done," Tania grumbled.

Fenix turned their head. "Once the bridge is repaired, we can figure out the next joining."

"And... stop," Zana said.

Tania had one foot on either side of the gap in the bridge. Fenix was totally on the Ginorti side, and Zana on Ronah's. Cyrus and Oakley must have been standing much like Tania was.

Oakley pulled in a breath.

Beneath Tania's feet, green mist seeped into the tear between the bridge. The mist solidified, turning to thick vines that crept to each end and pulled. There was a tugging sensation on her soul, and then Tania could stand without having to almost do the splits.

"Can we let go now?" Cyrus asked.

Zana laughed. "Yes. All the bridges have been repaired."

After unlacing her arms from the others, Tanis shook her whole body. Being that close to powerful Innarnians had her skin buzzing.

"So, the next joining?" Fenix asked.

"Actually, we have a rather important problem to take care of first," Cyrus said. "We planted the fake arrow. Now all we have to do is wait."

"And while we wait, we can plan," Zana said, trying to smooth the metaphorically ruffled feathers of the others.

"Akoren's main element is water, isn't it?" Tania asked. "How are we meant to craft Water into a bridge?"

"How did you craft Plasma, or Air, or Fire?" Oakley asked. "It's much the same way."

Tania bit her lip. She felt as if she was always the one asking questions. "How do we see the Wisara's city beneath the waves though?"

"Huh," Cyrus said. "We've never really... They usually just meet us on land."

"Well, that's rude," Tania said without thinking.

"It's also something we could change. Air bubbles that automatically refreshed cast over a being's head or breathing apparatus would take care of airflow," Zana said.

"I could make special crystal devices to help beings get around."

"And we can work on the designs for the bridges," Oakley said, gesturing to Tania and Fenix. "Assuming Zana wants to gather the high-level Air Innarnians. We don't want anyone suffocating."

Zana smiled. "I will. It would be nice to have a break from organising the joining. They seem to be happening faster than in the past."

Tania fiddled with her hem. Shari had mentioned what the Q'Aralide Queen had said about the Shifting Islands becoming a whole new Realm, and Tania still wasn't sure if she should tell the other Linked or not.

Kerday

Third day of the second week of Stormwake

Jonathan smiled gratefully at Asterion and accepted the offered cup of azehal.

"You know you don't have to do this," Jonathan said.

Asterion tilted his head. "It's polite, is it not, to get a cup for someone else if you're already making one?"

"True. Thank you." Jonathan took a sip and sighed. "Perfect."

Someone knocked on the door, and Amara poked her head through. "My turn?" she asked.

Today he was checking in with the regular patrol leaders and making sure they were handling the responsibly alright. If there was something they wanted to change about the roster or their group, this was their chance to raise it.

Amara was next to last on the list.

"Well met, Amara. Come on in," Jonathan said.

The Daen slid into the room like smoke and perched right on the edge of the chair.

"Tea?" Asterion offered.

"I'd probably just spill it," Amara said.

"I'm not going to bite." Jonathan grinned. "I want to check in and see how you were going."

"Oh! Right, well. I kinda don't feel like I'm patrol leader material, to be honest." Amara shrugged. "I have enough problems watching where my own feet are going, let alone keeping an eye on everyone else."

"I've noticed you've been partnering with Eva a lot," Jonathan said.

Amara blushed, her face turning the same colour as her hair. "Well... I... We..."

Jonathan smiled. "I just want to make sure that you and Eva will not be putting others at risk by sneaking off."

"We'd never!" Amara said. "Well, not on patrol, at least."

Lifting his cup to hide a smile, Jonathan took a sip. "I'm glad. Having someone to come back to is important."

Narday

Fourth day of the second week of Stormwake

Shari sniffed but refused to let her tears fall.

All the Ilutri on Rakemyst had gathered, and the sky matched the fallen's name, the silvery clouds weeping along with the rest of them.

Her grandfather's body rested on a slab crafted from Air Innarn. All morning long, Ilutri and the other Innarnians had been going up, bowing their heads over him, and whispering their private goodbyes, then joining into a circle around his body and laying a wreath at their feet. Once the circle was full, an end opened up and a spiral was created.

Calem, as the oldest child, had been the first to say goodbye. And now Wolf, as the youngest child and final mourner, stepped up and knelt.

He spoke to SilverCloud for a long time, whispers none but the Spirits could hear.

If Shari squinted just right, she could make out the wisp of soul that was SilverCloud. He was cavorting around another, her grandmother, who was smiling at his antics.

Wolf stood and tipped his head back. For a moment, Shari thought he was going to howl. Instead, he opened his mouth and breathed, eyes closed and tears falling as he paid homage to the Spirits dancing about far above their heads.

SilverCloud's wisp slipped down to the mourners and hovered before his sons. He bounced between one being and the next, as playful as he'd been in life.

When his soul brushed against Shari, she smiled, a ridiculous grin on her face despite the solemn occasion. A soul this fresh didn't always use words, but SilverCloud's intention was obvious.

Smile. Be glad. Remember the happy times.

Scrubbing at her face, she turned to track his progression through the spiral, beaming the whole time.

As one of the first, she hadn't realised how many had come to say goodbye but was honoured by the number of lives SilverCloud Dawn had touched.

When he reached the end of the spiral, all the Ilutri took to the air at the same time, their wings fanning out to create a corkscrew leading higher and higher. His soul sped towards the waiting Spirits, safe in the arms of those who had come before him.

Then and only then did Shari allow herself to cry.

CHAPTER TWENTY-SEVEN

Lissae

Rasshday

Fifth day of the second week of Stormwake

Someone knocked on the door.

Skye looked up as Grace growled. "Grace, we are safe in the castle. Occasionally, some of our friends might drop by to catch up with us."

She was having to dredge up endless wells of patience to deal with the decades of abuse Grace had faced, and she really didn't feel like she was qualified to give the sort of help Grace required.

That didn't mean she was going to foist the girl off to just anyone else, though. She needed to find someone who Grace trusted.

The knock sounded again.

"Coming!" Skye said. Getting off the bed, she smiled at Grace before opening the door.

The girl with the daggers stood on the other side, a bundle of material held in her arms. "Well met," she said.

Grace growled louder.

"Don't know if you remember me, but I'm Anika. Arilla told me you had to flee with, well, hardly anything," she said. "I had some practice pieces that I thought might fit."

"Practice pieces?" Skye asked.

Anika breezed into the room and started placing the clothing into two piles on the bed. "These look like they'll fit you. They go with your colouring, for sure."

With another comforting smile at Grace, Skye walked over and gasped. The top item of clothing was the most beautiful green dress. Light and flowy, with carefully embroidered flowers, it was perfect.

She stroked a trembling hand over the gauzy outer layer. "May I try it on?"

Anika beamed. "Sure!"

Grabbing it, Skye squealed and darted to change behind the screen stationed at the side of their room. After swiftly dragging her tunic off, Skye flung it aside and pulled the dress on over her head.

Smoothing the skirts down, Skye stepped out. "What do you think?"

Grace's mouth dropped open. "Pretty!"

"Just a practice piece, hey?" Skye asked, running her hands along the perfectly fitted bodice.

"Fine." Anika rolled her eyes. "You got me. But seriously, that green was just calling out for you."

"And the flowers?" Skye asked, stroking the elaborate blooms.

"Practice," Anika said, grinning.

"You made these for Skye?" Grace rasped.

"Yes. Here, Grace, have a look at these," Anika said, patting the second pile. "Promise I won't bite," Anika said gently when Grace didn't move.

Skye wandered back to the bed and started picking through the outfits on the second pile, holding them up so Grace could see them. Half of them were loose and flowing, like the green dress that was making her feel like something out of a story, and the others looked like they would be skintight. "These are like nothing I've seen before, Anika. You're amazing! How do you come up with the ideas?"

"Did you hear about Shari's test?" Anika asked.

"Yes? She killed Anriluka, right?"

They both ignored the way Grace was creeping closer to them.

"She did. But not before Anriluka literally tore away strips of my skin. It's been hard to come back from that. My Mind Healer suggested doing something with my hands, and I felt the need to stab things. A lot. What better way than to make something pretty in the meantime?" Anika shrugged like it was nothing. She pulled a dusky blue tunic out and held it up to Skye. "Through trial and error, I learned there were days where I craved the pressure of tight clothing–it makes me feel safer. Other days, it's restrictive and makes me feel smothered, but loose and stretchy gives me at least the illusion of control."

"Today's a stretchy day?" Skye asked, taking in the slouchy pants that ended in a tight band at the middle of Anika's calf, and the cropped top with a band around her waist.

"Most days are now." Anika grabbed a jewel-bright top and a grey skirt. "What do you think of this, Grace?"

Grace tilted her head, slowly reaching out to take them from Anika. Skye blinked, and Grace was gone.

Startled, Skye scanned the room.

Anika jerked her thumb at the changing screen, then started laying out different combinations of tops and bottoms across the bed.

Skye became absorbed in looking at the wonders Anika had brought them until Grace cleared her throat.

She looked up and her jaw dropped.

For the entire time Skye had known Grace, she'd been dressed in dirty, threadbare rags that looked like a sheet had been wrapped around her and tied at the shoulders.

Now...

"You look like a person," Skye blurted.

Anika beamed.

Grace smoothed her hands over the skirt—the same movement Skye had made. "I feel like a person," Grace whispered.

"Then my work is done. If you don't like something or it doesn't fit, let me know. I'll leave you to experiment." One more smile, and Anika left before they could stop her.

"Thank you!" Skye called after her.

Spine straight, Grace walked over, her fingers plucking at the hem of the red shirt. "So many."

"So many clothes," Skye agreed, rummaging through the pile.

Belfar rubbed Wolf's back.

His mate held the robes SilverCloud had worn when doing official elder duties. "Calem has refused. Years ago. They want me to take up the mantle when it's time." His voice, normally gravelly, sounded thicker due to how much Wolf had cried.

"You're far from being an elder," Belfar said.

"I'm the oldest Dawn on Rakemyst," Wolf said. "They should know that tradition doesn't mean a lot to me."

"Says the head of the elder's guards," Belfar snorted.

Wolf sighed. "Is that what I am now? Zana will take on the role of elder while the others squabble about who was born first. Whoever it is will choose their own guard."

"And you'll be free to do what you want to do," Belfar said.

"What if I don't know what that is? What if I've spent so long trying to please others, that I don't know who I am without..." Wolf sniffled.

"Then we'll find out. Together," Belfar said.

If it didn't have connotations of *chickens* and *eggs*, Shari would have said her father was brooding.

Mind you, he had every right.

After the funeral, her parents had moved back into her childhood home. The timing was perfect, as the dwelling for the family who'd been staying there had been completed last week.

Now the kitchen was filling with the smells of her father's baking again, and Shari didn't know if she should be happy or worried.

Tray after tray lined the benches with pastries and cookie combinations that she didn't recognise.

Leaning against the doorframe, Shari embraced the wave of peace. Her dad baking when he was stressed or upset was a reminder of a time when all she had to worry about was strengthening her shield, and not getting caught by the Guardian.

Despite Calem's frenetic energy, he moved with care as he took one tray out of the oven, put another in, and set a bowl to stir itself. Dough was being kneaded by Air Innarn on the table, and he was pulling out more ingredients for something else.

Arilla stood next to Shari and wrapped an arm around her waist.

Leaning her head on her mother's shoulder, Shari sighed. "Will Dad be..." *Alright* felt like the wrong word to ask. The death of anyone was hard, but a parent? Shari didn't even want to imagine it.

"He did the same thing when his mother passed," Arilla said. "Fell into a baking frenzy and fed the entire island for a week."

"There are a lot more beings on Ronah now," Shari said.

Arilla sighed. "SilverCloud would have trailed his fingers through the flour and be putting designs on the back of Calem's shirt by now." She gave a watery laugh.

Shari grinned through her tears. Flicking her fingers, she drew a heart on the back of her father's shirt.

Hiccoughing, Arilla covered her mouth.

"Okay, love?" Calem asked, turning around. He wiped his forehead with the back of his arm, leaving a streak of white behind.

A shake of Arilla's head, and Calem descended, wrapping them both in his arms.

She'd thought there were no more tears. Surely, she'd cried enough to fill an ocean or two? Apparently, Shari's body disagreed, and they started falling again.

"We might miss him," Calem said above their heads. "But he lives on."

Shari held her parents tighter.

✦

Vebaday

Sixth day of the second week of Stormwake

Samuel walked through the town with his head held high, trying to ignore the winces and beings skirting him. Some crossed to the other side of the road just to avoid his presence.

Or they might just have been avoiding the shadows cast by the two hatchlings flying overhead.

Carefully holding the egg in his hands, he traversed the stream and into Ronah's cemetery, where Asterion was waiting for him.

"Well met, Apprentice," the minotaur said. "Ronah has been busy." He gestured to the edge of the cemetery near the forest, where there was a new, twisted version of a bereni tree towering over everything else. It had to be, as it was large enough for four Q'Aralide to comfortably inhabit.

'Ronah has outdone herself,' Samuel sent.

A happy hum filled his mind, and he patted the closest tree.

'I knew I liked you.' Ronah's voice felt smug.

"Thank you, Asterion," Samuel said.

The minotaur bowed but stayed where he was as Samuel turned and walked towards the massive structure. 'Welcome to your new home,' he sent. The hatchlings slowly circled downwards until they landed.

'This is a home?' Tormorylth crept forward, peering at the wide doorway. 'I've never had one before.'

Jetonyx blinked away suspiciously damp eyes.

'What do you do with a home?' Tormorylth asked.

Samuel kept a smile fixed on his face while his hands fisted at his sides. 'Like your cave, but warmer. Safer.'

'I miss my cave,' Tormorylth said mournfully.

'Still better than pretending I'm a sand dune,' Jetonyx said, and pushed the door open.

Tormorylth gasped. 'It has an inside! Do all trees have an inside?'

'Not like this.' Jetonyx rolled his eyes, but glanced at Samuel, who nodded in confirmation and tried not to smirk.

'Most trees have solid insides, but the bereni trees of Lissae are hollow, so beings can live in them.'

A strange noise came out of the tiny hatchling.

She was squeeing with excitement.

'I've never seen a tree before Shari's pocket Realm, and now I'm living in one!' She skipped through the door.

Jetonyx rolled his eyes but followed so closely behind he almost tripped over her tail.

Samuel glanced down at the egg. "I suppose we'd better go, or they'll destroy the place before we get a look in."

In response, the egg quivered in his hand and a crack appeared on the side.

CHAPTER TWENTY-EIGHT

Lissae

Zoeday

Seventh day of the second week of Stormwake

ac glanced around Cyrus' lab but stayed put. After the last time, when he'd poked a shiny box and it blew up in his face, he was reluctant to touch anything.

They were waiting for the results of the crystal embedded in the fake soul-stealer arrow.

Minutes later, a device went *bing*.

He glanced at Cyrus, who sighed and leaned back in his seat.

Scrubbing his face, Cyrus sighed. "It's him. Milo stole the arrow. I don't know how, but it's on Jinkor at the moment."

After pushing to his feet, Zac brushed off his pants. "Suppose I'll go see where Milo is now."

"Milo is right here," the being of the hour squeaked.

Zac turned around, his hand slamming out, palm up. Thick chains rattled across the room and wrapped around Milo's torso.

Arms pinned to his sides, the Daen hopped a few steps before he toppled over, head hitting the ground hard.

Milo groaned and tried to wriggle. The chains tightened.

"You... can't..."

Grimly, Zac stepped forward. "Watch me."

"What are you going to do with him?" Cyrus asked.

"Take him to the Guardian."

What colour was left drained out of the traitor's face.

Samuel stared in shock at the egg. '*Shari. Shari!*'

The Altoriae blinked into existence by his side, her weapons at the ready.

Sneeze, nestled on his shoulder, bit his ear, pulling him out of the daze he'd been in. "The egg," he whispered.

Shari frowned, but glancing around and seeing there was no threat, she put her blades away. "What about the egg?"

There was a cracking noise.

Gasping, Shari reached out, putting her hands on the shell above his own.

A tiny Q'Aralide burst out, golden scales gleaming as it shot into the air. Samuel darted forwards and caught the newest and final hatchling as she fell.

A golden hatchling.

'*No fair! Ze got colours and I haven't even moulted yet,*' Jetonyx pouted.

Samuel crooned at the baby, while Shari rubbed the side of Jetonyx's maw.

"Just think of all the things you'll be able to teach both of them," Shari said soothingly. '*I thought these two were both black? Do they change their colours?*'

'*Yes. But I don't know when it will happen now. It was a meteorological phenomenon for me and my nest mates.*'

'*Do you think it could still happen?*'

'*I'm sure it will,*' Samuel sent as he looked down at the tiny creature in his arms.

He would move the heavens and travel through all nine hells to get these hatchlings whatever they wanted.

Adonday
First day of the third week of Stormwake

Shari glanced around the room instead of staring at Yessna over the rim of her cup.

The U'sala had set up camp in the rooms under the castle that the Returned had first used whilst they were waiting for their dwellings to be ready. They had asked her to a meeting, and when she arrived, there had been a veritable feast laid out on the table.

Yessna had immediately pushed a cup into her hands and all but shoved her into a seat before taking the one opposite.

"What's all this about?" Shari asked.

"You know there's more of us than this." Yessna gestured to the group, who was watching avidly. There were nine U'sala including the ferah, but the wisest course of action was to ignore the rest. She'd already taken one of their crew out, and Kodan had apparently been their best. The others would be hardly any trouble.

"I remember there being far more at your camp," she said nonchalantly.

"We want to settle down," Yessna said. "The others? They're happy to rove, but we... I... grow tired."

"The last U'sala who said something like that to me tried to murder my entire town," Shari said.

Yessna pulled back, a hiss on her lips. "I can't deny an action by one of ours."

"But would you..." Kerk started.

"... deny us?" Drah finished.

Shari hid her grin behind a hand. "What would you do on Ronah? There's hardly a plethora of baddies to defeat."

"We've noticed dreams throughout the Realms becoming more unpredictable. It's harder to control the crossover points when that happens," Nerina, the healer, said.

"Crossover points?" Shari asked.

"You know, the point where the dream fades and melds with reality? That's the way Anriluka exploited, so she wouldn't have to use the portal," Yessna said.

"Huh." Shari knew what it was but hadn't heard the term before. But she wasn't going to let them know that. "And you want to, what? Patrol the crossover points?"

"Essentially, yes. We've trained for years and can spot a crossover before it happens. With a fixed population like Ronah's, it shouldn't be any trouble to stay on top of it all," Wubi, wielder of the spiked chain, said.

Shari tried not to take their idea personally. The dreams of Ronah's residents had been her childhood training grounds, but since Anriluka's defeat, she hadn't really visited them again. And it was dangerous to leave dreams unguarded. "Sounds like a plan."

The U'sala grinned and clamoured around her.

"If you can convince Jonathan," she added.

Yessna groaned.

Inthday

Second day of the third week of Stormwake

Jonathan scowled at the map of the Realms he was pouring over. A distant clanking distracted him, and he tried to focus on the matter at hand. He and Asterion had been going over the patrol schedules, trying to cover for the mainlanders who refused to come to the Shifting Islands, but they weren't having much luck.

Their official reason was the relocation of the Travel Innarnians, but from what others had heard, the Innarnians stuck on the mainland were concerned about the flaring tempers of the neighbours endangering their families.

No matter which way he looked at the map, they simply didn't have the numbers they needed to patrol safely.

"What if some of the higher-level Innarnians took on Realms by themselves?" Asterion suggested.

Before he could answer, the clanking and cursing he'd been trying to block out got closer.

"Brought you a present!" Zac said, wiping sweaty hair away from his forehead as he stepped through the doorway.

"Sorry?" Jonathan asked.

Reaching behind him, Zac swore. "Don't even try to..." he growled.

Dropping his pen, Jonathan leaned back in his seat, trying to figure out what was going on.

Muscles straining, Zac heaved a weight wrapped in metal and pushed it towards the desk.

Not a weight. A being.

"Who's this?" he asked.

"Milo," Zac said lowly.

"He's the one who took my Innarn blockers and *warped* them," Cyrus added, walking into the office. "He stole the arrow and passed it on to someone from Jinkor."

"Jinkor?" Jonathan repeated. "Could Chamele have something to do with this?"

Milo started thrashing in the chains.

Kneeling, the Guardian stared into the eyes of the Daen, who stopped moving immediately. Without so much as twitching, Jonathan activated the ward around his office, which would only allow Samuel or Shari to enter.

"Release the chains," Jonathan said, his voice deceptively gentle.

It was a credit to Zac that he didn't question the order but did instantly.

The traitor sprung up and made a run for it, slamming into the ward face-first. Knocked backwards, Milo howled and covered his nose.

Shari and Samuel shifted into the room, weapons drawn.

'*We felt the ward activate,*' Shari said.

'*Zac and Cyrus identified and captured the traitor,*' Jonathan said.

Samuel snorted.

Whipping around at the sound, Milo glared at the trio. "You!" He pointed at Shari, revealing the blood streaming from his broken nose. "Couldn't you just stay dead?"

"Sorry?" Shari shrugged and glanced at Jonathan out of the corner of her eye.

"You ruined all my plans!" Milo shrieked.

Suppressing the urge to wriggle a finger in his ear after the high-pitched noise, Jonathan asked, "What plans were those?"

"I was going to move to the mainland and away from Cantash so I could finally, *finally* work on what I wanted to do!"

"What does me being dead have to do with your plans?" Shari asked.

"It's the only way they'll pay me! Your death, or sending trinkets to help them stop you." Milo was trying to look down his nose at them, but tilting his head back just made him sound congested.

"Trinkets!" Cyrus burst out. Samuel put a restraining hand on his shoulder.

"Your devices are hardly revolutionary," Milo sniffed, and pulled a face straight after. Apparently, blood didn't smell so good.

Cyrus growled. "How could you allow Ginorti to suffer like that?"

"I never wanted to be on the islands! I was assigned to Cantash as an uneducated teen, told I'd be able to earn a decent wage and travel the Realm," Milo sneered. "Travelling the Realm doesn't count when you're trapped on the same hunk of dirt. And a decent wage? Cantash isn't even civilised enough to use *money!*"

"So, what, you started stealing things and passing them off as your own?" Zac asked.

"Hardly. I began writing articles, researching, trying to get noticed. It earned me a few measly beads and lots of 'exposure' but nothing else." Milo sighed, then looked at Shari. "I tried everything first. All I wanted to do was to be left alone."

"How long did it take before you started poisoning Cantash's Linked?" she asked.

"Decades. I grew close to the family, hoping that I could convince them to join with the mainland so I could get off, but the first Linked wouldn't listen. She'd say 'Cantash was made to be at sea.'" He snorted. "I fell ill for a while, and when I was coming up with a cure, I stumbled across a tonic that dulled my Innarn. The dose I took was too concentrated, but I figured out the right balance. She was happy to take the restorative tonic."

"And Fenix?" Cyrus asked.

"Like mother, like child," Milo sneered.

Jonathan wanted to punch his smug face.

"How did you meet Chamele?" Zac asked.

"She came for a tour years ago. Saw my potential, wanted to cultivate my genius." Milo straightened his tie and glared at his blood-covered hands.

"How did she do that?" Shari asked, all big eyes and breathy voice.

Jonathan shared a look with Samuel, the corners of his apprentice's mouth twitching as he tried not to laugh at the suddenly demure version of the Altoriae.

"Gave me access to equipment I'd only dreamed of, ensured that *my* articles were placed in front of the right editors. Sent me gifts." Milo stuck his hands in his pockets and rocked back on his heels.

Jonathan smirked.

He could feel the signal trying to get past the wards.

Whoever had crafted it was strong.

But he was stronger.

"That won't work here," Jonathan said.

"I don't know wh..." Milo started.

"You'll have to face the tribunal, traitor." Zac crossed his arms and stared at the shorter man.

"I'm not a traitor," Milo argued.

Shari stepped forward. "You poisoned not one, but two Linked." Another step. "You stole." Another. "You lied." Another. "And did it all intending to harm not only Fenix and their family, but Cantash and Innarnians as a whole." One last step, and she poked him on his blood-stained chest. "What does that make you?"

"But... I'm... You can't do that. Do you know what they do to traitors on Cantash?" Milo shrieked. "They throw them in the volcano!"

"That is a far quicker death than what you deserve," Shari said.

Shifting the entire contents of Milo's pockets to the table behind him, Jonathan lowered the ward and sent a message to Fenix.

Cantash's Linked arrived, hair fluffed out as if they'd been playing with plasma.

"It's true then?" they asked, looking at Jonathan.

He nodded.

Turning around, Fenix strode right up to Milo and punched him, hard. "You... you had no right."

"He's admitted to everything," Cyrus said.

Drawing themselves up, Fenix wiped away the angry tears. "His words were witnessed?"

"They were," Jonathan said.

"How many were his crimes?" Fenix asked.

"Over five," Jonathan said.

Fenix flicked a glance at the Guardian, shock covering their features.

'Two counts of poisoning, lying, cheating, intent to harm,' Jonathan sent to them.

"Our laws are clear. One crime results in counselling, two means service. Three is time. Four is removal, five... Five is death."

"Fenix, you know I would never..." Milo started.

"What? Hurt me?" they scoffed. "Course not. You've just poison me since I was a child. That's not going to hurt at all."

"I was just..."

Fenix made a slashing motion with their hand, and all sounds coming from Milo stopped. They stepped closer to the traitor. "Just be glad I took your vocal cords and not your heart."

CHAPTER TWENTY-NINE

Lissae

Kerday

Third day of the third week of Stormwake

Jonathan sank next to Shari as dangled her legs over the side of the ledge she'd created.

The girl who could barely get dirt to move out of her way had effortlessly created a rock ledge on the side of a mountain. Just so she could sit and pat her palon.

Zoomer was basking in the sunshine, leaning against Shari and getting fur all over her shirt.

With one hand buried in his coat, she really didn't seem to mind.

"The U'sala want to stay on Ronah," Shari said.

"I figured as much."

"What do you think?"

Jonathan looked out at the ocean and tried to get his thoughts in order. "I think the U'sala have proven themselves time and time again to be honourable, and work for the best interests of the Realms at large. Kodan was an exemption to their way of life."

"All it would take for Lissae to fall would be another Kodan, biding his time," Shari said bitterly. Zoomer put his front paws on her leg and huffed into her ear. She laughed.

"You can't hold an entire group responsible for the actions of one being," Jonathan said.

Shari wrinkled her nose. "So you think they should stay?"

"If what you and Samuel have said is right, then the very fabric of Lissae is about to change. We know Yessna. Know that she'll be determined to prove whatever misconceptions you have due to the actions of their candidate are wrong." He took in a breath of sea air. "I think it would be silly to say, 'thanks for all the help,' and shove them back through the gateway."

"Plus, they might help with patrol numbers," Shari teased.

"Well, it won't hurt," he chuckled.

Tania grinned as Oakley jumped from one stone to the next, crossing the wide stream easily.

"Your turn!" Oakley called back.

"Can't I just shift across?" she asked.

Oakley laughed. The first joyful noise she'd heard him make. "Just try," he yelled.

"Why does getting to the heart of an island have to involve some sort of feat of derring-do?" she muttered. Sizing up the first rock, she tried to map the path out in her head. "Fine!" she yelled back.

Leaping out on the first water-smoothed rock was fine, despite having to windmill her arms to stay upright.

"Just keep moving," Oakley encouraged.

Taking a breath, she jumped to the next rock, and the next. Before she knew it, she was on the far bank.

"You did it!" Oakley smiled.

Grinning back, Tania bounced on her toes. "I thought I'd fall in for sure, but that was fun!"

"Just wait until you see what's on the other side of these trees. Let's go." Leading the way along an overgrown path, Oakley pushed through thorny bushes and prickly thickets like they were nothing.

"How is this not ripping your skin apart?" Tania asked, removing another strand of tangled hair caught in a branch.

"I grew up wandering Ginorti's forest," Oakley said, "I was one of a handful of half-satyrs, and we were constantly teased for it as kids. The trees didn't taunt me, so I sought refuge there. In the height of summer, I wanted to wade in the stream, but the sunlight reflecting off the water was blinding, and I ended up over here. I heard some of my tormentors approaching and hid in the trees. Eventually, I stumbled out of the thicket and found this."

Tania almost fell over as the last of the brambles let her free to enter what seemed like a mythical clearing.

Hidden birds were twittering in the trees, the sound of the stream a melody to their chorus. Lush green grass waved in a gentle breeze, lit up by shafts of sunlight streaming through the canopy above. Butterflies danced through the beams.

And in the middle stood a giant, grey boulder. Worn smooth by age and polished by the touch of many hands, the boulder seemed to beat like a literal heart.

Tania beamed at Oakley.

'Well met, Ginorti,' Tania sent, trailing her fingers along the stone.

'Well met, Ronah's Linked. Oakley has finally brought you to meet me.'

Giggling, Tania sat, idly patting the rock.

'*I've been busy,*' Oakley protested.

'*Thought you'd brought Rocky out to play again.*' There was a teasing note in the send.

'*Rocky?*'

Oakley groaned. "After I became Ginorti's Linked, he started training me in Earth Innarn, and I created a special golem I called Rocky. When he was first made, Rocky would stand on my hand and come with me everywhere. He developed a bit of a personality and grew as I did."

"Awww," Tania said.

"Thank you for bringing that up," Oakley grumbled, patting the ground.

'*What are friends for?*' Ginorti asked.

Anika screamed and charged at the Altoriae.

Shari waited until the last possible moment and stepped to the side. "Don't telegraph what you're doing, or your opponent will out manoeuvre you every time."

Pulling to a stop, Anika whirled and lashed out. Shari danced away.

"You've got good form, but your movements are still too big. Too telling. Slow down and breathe."

Taking a breath, Anika shook out her aching limbs. "Remind me why I decided asking you to join the training was a good thing?" she asked.

"Because you caught me moping at home feeling sorry for myself?" Shari quirked her lip.

Rolling her eyes to hide her smile, Anika huffed. "It's totally not because you're good at what you do, right?" She lunged, hoping to catch Shari off guard.

No luck.

"Not at all." Shari didn't even have her weapons out.

"Can I see your claws?" Anika asked abruptly, dropping her daggers.

"They aren't claws," Shari said. "They're blades." Obligingly, she materialised the glove, and the dual blades glinted in the light.

"Looks like claws to me," Anika said.

"When I first started patrolling, I tried out a bunch of different weapons, but they were all too big and unwieldy. I settled on a sword but ended up losing it in a battle. Came up with the idea of these because the glove would have to be forcibly removed." Shari twisted her arm, so the blades glinted in the light.

"And they retract?" Anika asked, grabbing Shari's arm and inspecting the blades closer.

"Sometimes. Depends on the situation," Shari said.

"What about a blade coming from under your arm? Hidden, but flick your wrist and it's out. I could build it in to the next dress," Anika mused.

"I think you'd work well with something like that. I'm so used to my 'claws,' I'd probably end up slicing my hand every time I used it." Shari grinned and banished the glove.

Anika let go of Shari's arm and picked her daggers back up. "Yeah, 'cause you're so bad at learning new... wait. You think I could use it?"

"Every time you unhook the daggers from your heels, you're wasting precious seconds. Mind you, they're an awesome idea. I just don't know how practical it is on a battlefield," Shari said.

"I think I'm going to have to sit down. Shari Dawn, complementing me twice in one day," Anika said, her smile belying the sarcastic tone.

"Ha ha. Very funny. I'm quite nice, you know."

Batting her lashes, Anika teased, "I bet you say that to all the beings you fight."

Wrong thing to say.

Shari's face shut down, the expression wiping clean away.

"Sorry, I didn't mean..." Anika said. She wanted to wring her hands but couldn't when she was holding sharpened blades.

"It's alright. Just reminded me of... something else." Shari's face was still eerily blank. "Want to go again?"

"Sure."

This time, when Anika charged at the Altoriae, Shari blocked her.

Asterion tidied the stack of paper on the Guardian's desk. He'd only been an assistant for a short while, but there was a sense of peace in finding a place to belong.

They'd all but forgotten he was in the room when Milo had been brought in. Had meted out their justice like it was the easiest thing in the Realms. He'd been horrified and astounded at the same time. No red tape, no waffling, no pleading ignorant to the laws, as so many did on Atlantis.

Mind you, Canak-Maku was a different story. There, crime wasn't really a thing they worried about. If the leader of a group was displeased with you, he'd gouge your heart out and eat it in front of a crowd in a show of strength. Asterion had learned to watch his words and actions extremely carefully.

That caution helped when something in the pile from Milo's pockets started beeping.

Lifting a hand to the crystal around his neck, Asterion said, "Guardian, I think you need to see this. Come to your office, please."

'*On my way*,' Jonathan's voice sounded in his head.

Collis chuckled at Tania as she chased Esse around the yard.

"Come back here, you ornery blue hen, or I'll add you to the soup!" Ronah's Linked was yelling.

The chicken seemed quite aware of what was going on. Esse would run just out of reach, pause, and start running again right as Tania would lean down to grab her.

"If you didn't insult her, she might be more inclined to be held," Collis offered.

Tania huffed at a silvery hank of hair that had fallen over her face. "You try then!" She plopped to the ground, sweaty and exhausted.

Kneeling, Collis held out his hand.

Esse twisted her head and stared at him for a moment, then clambered into his arms.

"That... you..." Tania pointed at him, aghast. "Chicken whisperer!"

He chuckled again and took Esse back over to the hen house, locking her securely inside. "Don't worry. I'll look after all our chickens." His back stiffened as soon as the words left his mouth.

"Is that what the soul-matched do?" Tania asked, her voice small.

Collis sat on the grass beside her. "Not always. When I see my future, you're in it. I know everything has changed for you in such a short time. And I'll wait until you're ready."

"To do what?" Tania asked.

"Anything," he said. *Everything*, his heart sang.

"Right now, I just want to hold your hand and lay in the grass," Tania said, gripping his hand and lifting it up.

"Sounds perfect."

They fell back together and watched the clouds rolling overhead.

Narday
Fourth day of the third week of Stormwake

Jonathan looked at the device making noise and poked it with one end of his pen. He'd called the Altoriae and the technomancer to come have a look. Despite testing it since Asterion notified him of it yesterday, Jonathan still couldn't make heads or tails of it.

"I do not know what this is," he admitted to Shari.

Temira walked into the room and froze. "Don't poke it," she snapped. Wrapping her Innarn around it, the technomancer lifted the device away from everything else. "It's a small, timed…"

It exploded.

"… bomb," she finished, as the contained blast subside.

"Glad you got here when you did," Asterion said.

"Me too." Jonathan looked at Temira. "Why would Milo have that in his pocket?"

"It's an old trick the Vitaemancers used. Not as elegantly executed, of course." She winced at her word choice. "They would carry something in case of capture or torture. And use it as the last resort."

Asterion shook his head. "I don't understand."

"The blast on this would have put a big enough hole in a being that they wouldn't survive. Not even with my intervention," Temira said.

"He intended to die rather than reveal his secrets?" Asterion asked.

"Milo wasn't exactly withholding anything when we questioned him," Shari scoffed.

Jonathan whistled.

Her head snapped around.

He poked glumly at the singed papers on his desk. "Or someone wanted to ensure he couldn't sell them out."

CHAPTER THIRTY

Luerix

Jonathan stepped through the double doors of the museum and into the Ducibus' Hall, his patrol group not far behind.

'*You found Shari.*' It was the Ducibus who had been with Pala.

'*Yes, she's home safe,*' Jonathan sent.

The being under the hood hummed, and the Guardian had the familiar feeling they had met before the hallway. Ze sent, '*Don't let her patrol. Not until the Xande...*'

Static filled his mind as Pala descended on the other Ducibus. The hooded beings faced each other, the buzz of sending so thick it was almost audible.

'*Forgive my apprentice,*' Pala said.

Apprentice...

Surely not...

It couldn't be...

"Jon? We good?" Zac asked.

His mate's voice broke whatever thought he'd been about to have, and Jonathan nodded. "Yes." He glanced at the Ducibus. *Why there were two?* "Anything we need to be aware of, Pala?"

'*Be on guard,*' Pala sent.

"Always." Jonathan grinned. Turning, he addressed the group. "Come on. With me. Remember, Darker Realms only until we get word it's safe."

Striding through the halls, Jonathan searched for a stone door. They were patrolling Luerix tonight, a Realm slightly Darker than Lissae. Fiona usually took care of the Realm, but she hadn't made contact for a while. Jonathan would give her until the next joining before he reached out to see if she was alright. If he contacted Fiona too soon, she was likely to go into hiding too deep for even him to find.

"Shields up, everyone," Zac said.

As Jonathan opened the gateway, he felt the rush of Innarn as shields of all types were crafted.

Stepping through, he shivered.

Something about Luerix had changed since the last time he had visited.

The monolithic standing stones ringing the gateway were the same. The purple of the grass and trees hadn't changed, but the air felt charged, like a storm about to hit despite there not being any clouds in the sky.

Plasma sizzled along his veins as he took another step into the circle.

'*It's a trap,*' he sent to the group.

Automatically, Edward stayed behind, keeping the gateway open.

"Don't come any closer!" a cracking voice said.

Jonathan froze.

From behind one of the standing stones, stepped a young teen wielding a pitchfork. He had a nasty wound on his temple and ash coating his face.

"Well met. I am Jonathan from Lissae. Do you require aid?"

"Aid?"

The pitchfork was wavering, not due to Jonathan's subpar negotiation tactics but exhaustion.

"Help," he tried again. "Looks like you've got a nasty bump." Jonathan ran his fingers over his own temple.

The boy propped the handle on his hip and used his free hand to brush his head. Wincing, he drew his hand away and looked at the blood. All colour drained from his face. "Thought it hurt," he said and collapsed.

Shifting the pitchfork out of the way before the teen could cause himself further harm, Jonathan pushed his Innarn out to scan the area. *'No one else is around, but that doesn't mean they weren't waiting just out of range of the scan. Zac, with me. Two of you go see if you can find out where the boy's village is. Everyone else, check around the gateway and figure out why there is so much excess plasma.'*

Cautiously, Jonathan approached the fallen boy.

When he got close enough, the Guardian could tell there was a lot more wrong with the teen than he had first thought.

'Broken leg, concussion, at least two fractured ribs, and the fingers of his right hand have been shattered.' Zac looked at Jon. *'Do I heal him here, or take him back?'*

Jonathan sighed. Injuries like that would heal better on Lissae, where the teen wouldn't be forced to return to work straight away. But they'd long had a policy of not taking in off-Realmers for healing. Not since one had tried to slit Holli's throat and escape the Healers Centre. *'Here.'*

Zac nodded and got to work.

Flicking his Innarn out, Jonathan checked on the others, making sure that they stayed in contact.

'*Nothing around that could cause the plasma,*' Terrance sent.

'*Found the village,*' a scout reported. '*Appears abandoned.*'

"They found the village," Jonathan repeated softly. "We can move him there after you're done.

The boy opened his eyes and sat up with a pained gasp. "Don't go to the village!"

"Why not?" asked Zac.

"Mother is there."

"Mother?"

'*Found the source of the Plasma,*' another scout sent. It felt like he was running. '*I'd strongly suggest leaving.*'

Jonathan turned to look around. His team were some of the most seasoned patrollers, and they didn't get spooked easily. What could have them so...

"Oh."

"Mother has come," the teen said.

A giant whale was swimming through the sky, her tail and fins flicking as she rode currents of Plasma through the air.

Right towards where they were standing.

'*Move. Everyone back to the gateway—now!*' Jonathan sent. "Move," he barked when Zac stayed by his patient.

"Almost done," Zac said.

Eyeing the speed that the whale was coming in at, and their distance from the gateway, Jonathan estimated they had nine seconds, especially since the whale was getting lower in the sky by the moment.

"Eight," he said.

"Not helping," Zac sing-songed.

"Seven."

After grabbing a vial out of his pouch, Zac shoved it in the boy's hand. "Take this."

"Six."

"Jonathan," Zac warned. The boy downed the vial, and Zac stood.

"Five."

"You need to shift him," Zac demanded.

"Four. Where?"

"Here," the boy grabbed Jonathan's arm, and a picture shot across his mind. A glowing green lake nestled in a peaceful valley, deep in the heart of Luerix's major continent.

"I bid thee well." Jonathan shifted him out.

"Two," Zac said, and grabbed his arm.

With the whale closing in on them, they sprinted for the gateway, Jonathan shifting the others in as they went.

"Hurry!" screamed Edward.

The sky above them was dark, and a low, mournful noise rattled his bones as Jonathan dived through the gateway last.

Edward slammed it shut. The hall shuddered for a moment, before the stone door that had led to Luerix shattered.

The patrollers stood staring at the rubble in stunned silence.

"What just happened?" Terrance asked.

'You shattered my gateway!' a Ducibus howled. 'Do you know how difficult they are to repair? Do you know how long it takes? Out. Out!' Ze started blasting the entire group with stinging jabs of Innarn, following them the whole way back to the Lissaen gateway.

Just as they stepped through, he caught a tiny golden flash slipping through the closing double doors, but when Jonathan blinked, it was gone again. A trick of the light.

Safely back on Lissae, Jonathan looked over the group. Edward's lips were twitching, and Zac had his fist pressed against his mouth.

"What happened?" Terrance asked again.

Zac started coughing.

Jonathan looked at him suspiciously but turned to answer Terrance. "We just outran the Sky Mother of Luerix."

"It was a whale," a scout said, deadpan. "A whale. In the sky. Biggest creature I've ever seen."

Edward started guffawing. Zac snorted and joined him, as did several of the scouts.

"What was a whale doing in the sky?" Terrance asked.

"Swimming," the same scout said, the corner of his lips twitching.

"We outran the Sky Mother."

Dizzy hilarity overtook the groups, and their contagious laughter swept Jonathan up. He looked over at Zac, who was clutching his side and leaning against Edward, panting for breath.

"A sky whale," he said, and set the group off again.

Lissae

Rasshday

Fifth day of the third week of Stormwake

Skye marvelled at the change in Grace.

As they walked down the main street of Ronah, dressed in the clothing Anika had created, a passer-by might look at the two of them and not know one had suffered the most traumatic events Skye could imagine.

Until Grace growled at them, of course.

"Grace?" Skye asked.

"Yes?"

"Do you think you could stop growling at people?"

Pausing in the middle of the footpath, Grace tilted her head at Skye. "Why?"

"You're scaring them."

"*They* scare *me*," she said with a shrug.

"There are lots of times when I'm frightened, but growling could drive away the ones who would help." Skye plucked a flower from a bush and twisted the stem through her fingers.

"Scared you away?" Grace rasped.

Skye wanted to lie but figured it would only hurt Grace later. "Yes, probably. I thought you were a pile of rags."

Grace giggled, and her smile lit up her entire face.

"Smiling is contagious, you know? If you smile at someone, they'll catch it and pass it on to someone else," Skye said, grinning back at her.

Tilting her head again, Grace beamed at the next person who passed, and they smiled back. "True," she said.

"Better than growling?" Skye asked.

"Maybe," Grace allowed.

Progress.

Vebaday

Sixth day of the third week of Stormwake

Samuel lifted a cushion and peered under it. "Where are you?"

There was a knock at the door. "Lost something?" Shari asked.

"The hatchling." He scowled and threw the cushion behind him. "I think ze got out," Samuel admitted.

"Does ze have a name yet?" Shari asked. She was leaning in the doorframe and had yet to come in.

"Not yet, which will make it that much harder to find."

'*Portal*,' Sneeze sent.

Another cushion in his hand, Samuel froze. "What?"

Sneeze bit his ear, hard. '*Portal*.'

Dropping the now shredded cushion, Samuel carefully removed Sneeze from his favourite chew toy and held him at eye height. "The hatchling is at the portal?"

The draci bobbed his head.

Shari cursed and shifted before he could even blink.

"Now I know why there were no windows in the hatchlings' quarters," Samuel groaned. He put Sneeze on the table. "You're in charge. Watch the big ones."

A shower of sparks later, he was gone.

Shari shifted to the museum with every intent of going through the double doors and searching every hallway one by one.

Jonathan and his patrol group were all but rolling on the ground laughing, and she didn't want to disturb them.

Silently creeping to the side of the room, Shari startled. A Ducibus was waiting for her.

A pale hand crept out of the robes and beckoned as Samuel shifted in next to her.

"What are you doing?" he hissed.

"Following my gut," she whispered back and tugged on his hand.

Samuel followed her obediently as she crept after the Ducibus, who led her through rooms and down halls she'd forgotten about. In the corner of a dusty room, a massive statue of a crystal being stood, it's back against the wall.

"I don't remember seeing that before," Shari murmured.

The Ducibus turned around, and even though Shari couldn't see the expression beneath the deep hood, she had the feeling ze was glaring at her.

'*Frointh.*' The Ducibus patted the statue's knee.

Something in the walls made a grinding sound, and Shari's jaw dropped as the statue slid along the wall, revealing a hallway behind it.

Sitting at the end of the hallway was the golden hatchling.

"Oh, there you are," she cooed.

'*Come here, little one,*' Samuel sent.

'*Can't,*' the hatchling replied.

"Why not?" Shari asked.

The hatchling twitched a wing and whimpered. Ze had got stuck between a gap in two rocks.

Samuel made to brush past Shari but hissed the moment his hand crossed the threshold. He glared at the stone as if he could will it to combust.

'*Only someone of the Altoriae's bloodline,*' the Ducibus sent, then gasped, doubling over in pain. '*Got to go! Good luck, Shari!*' And ze was gone before she could blink.

That send had almost sounded like… but, no. Surely not?

"Samuel?"

Cradling his injured hand, Samuel scowled into the room.

The hatchling howled and twisted, jerked backwards against the far wall, whimpering.

"Please go get zir," Samuel said through gritted teeth.

Shari, brows furrowed in worry, nodded. Cautiously stepping into the room, she took in the cobwebs covering the carvings on the walls and the fancy pillars on either side of the archway. Watchful of the uneven stones on the floor, she finally made it to the end of the room.

"Well met, little one," she crooned. "Let's get you free." Softly stroking her hand up the wing. The claw at the top had got caught behind one of the loose bricks. "Okay, are you ready?"

The hatchling nodded.

Pulling at the brick with one hand, Shari carefully freed the spike. "All better. Just don't come in here by yourself again, alright?"

Shaking out zir wings, the hatchling jumped into the air and hopped ungainly for the doorway. Shari pushed a current of Air underneath ze, and the hatchling chittered in excitement as ze road it to the door.

Shari strode after zir. "I wish you had a name," she said, and swore as she tripped over a loose stone. Scowling at her scraped palms, it took Samuel's indrawn breath to realise something was wrong.

Blue, glowing symbols appeared in front of her.

"Don't move," Samuel said, his hand outstretched and face worried.

"What's wrong?" Shari asked, keeping as still as possible.

"Those are symbols from the Dark Realms. What did you say just before you tripped?" he asked.

"I said 'I wish you had a name.'" The symbols in front of Shari started flashing and changing until they settled into one shape.

"What does it say?" Shari asked.

"Kemanyr," Samuel said. "Means clever one."

Grinning, Shari stood. "Safe to move?" she asked.

Kemanyr dived and slipped through the doorway, sighing in relief and curling up in Samuel's arms.

"Yes."

"What does Tormorylth mean?" she asked.

"Strength and tenacity," he said. "Although if you need to know what Jetonyx means, I fear for your intelligence."

"Hmmm," Shari said. "Fast black. No. Fast shadow?"

The grinding noise started again, and Shari was still a fair way down the hall.

"How about you live up to his name?" Samuel asked.

As the back of the statue started closing over the exit, the room grew darker.

Chills skated down her spin, and she sprinted, Samuel's worried gaze on her the whole time.

Sliding sideways, Shari held out her hand.

Heedless of the burning, Samuel grabbed the offered limb and pulled her through the gap with such force that the trio landed in a tangle of limbs and wings.

Samuel was broadcasting, and Shari had the impression that he didn't mean to at all. Neither did she think he'd intended to hold her as tight as he was.

Over and over, he was thinking, '*Never again.*'

I'm here, Samuel. I'm not going anywhere, Shari wanted to say.

They both knew that she didn't always have a choice, so the Altoriae bit her lip and remained silent.

Zoeday
Seventh day of the third week of Stormwake

Captain Rappen poked the mirror. "Hello?" he growled.

Still no response.

It had been days since the tiny man had pushed the golden arrow to his side of the mirror, and he wanted more.

More weapons, more tactics, more ways to make all Innarnians pay.

But the man on the other side of the glass wasn't cooperating.

"Hello!" he yelled, banging his fist.

The door on the other side of the glass opened. "Who's yelling in here? Milo?"

It was an older man, his hair still thick but closer to silver than white, the wrinkles on his face deepening as he drew closer. "Huh. Didn't know I looked so young!"

"You look older than the hills," Captain Rappen spat.

"Oh, rude too. Best just cover you up." Turning, the old man grabbed a swath of fabric before moving even closer.

If things can be pushed from one side, surely they can be grabbed from the other as well?

Pressing his hand against the glass, the captain kept pushing.

Cold enveloped his fingers and palm, the back of his hand, and up to his wrist before the man on the other side shouted in alarm.

But he didn't move away.

After grabbing a fistful of shirt, Captain Rappen pulled, the clouds in his head urging him on.

With a garbled yell, the man landed at the captain's feet.

"Welcome to Jinkor," he said, and watched in satisfaction as the clouds dove and started sucking the Innarn right from the aberration.

The mirror could prove more helpful than he'd thought.

Portal
Outside Zuefie's door

Having finally fulfilled its purpose, the body of the host was failing.

Jerking through the halls, parts of it were being left behind. Sloughed off green skin, falling muscle, and an organ or two was abandoned, but they…

just...

    needed...

        to...

            open...

                the...

                    door...

Bones wrapped around the handle. The body faltered and fell, slumping against the only exit.

The weight of the flesh slowly pushed the door ajar.

The fog drifted into the portal. It hung for a moment, thick in the air, tiny flashes of lightning snapping through the white.

More of the mist gathered, and hooded figures scattered as clouds streamed out.

The Xanderri were free.

Discarding the host, ze joined the others.

It was time to take over Lissae.

CHAPTER THIRTY-ONE

Lissae

Adonday

First day of the fourth week of Stormwake

Thunder rumbled, and Shari jerked, sloshing the dangerously hot liquid over her hand.

Swearing as she flicked it away, Shari ignored the gaze of the U'sala leader burning into the back of her head. She and Jonathan were gathered in the mayor's meeting room with the U'sala who'd been staying in the castle.

Shari clutched her cup of azehal closer and breathed in the sweet, spiced scent.

"You and I have travelled through Realms which would make your golden priest cry," Yessna said. "I have seen you dig through the flesh of your kin in order to kill a monster, and not flinch. Why does noise from the sky make you scared?"

"The Xanderri, the Innarn eaters, they don't have bodies. They're just cloud. And whenever the biggest, densest cloud sent, it rattled your soul as though it was thunder right next to your ear," Shari said.

Across the table, Jonathan's brow furrowed.

"But we're not here to talk about my trauma today," she said. "We're here to talk about the U'sala."

Yessna snapped around and faced the Guardian. "Can we stay?"

Jonathan sighed. "Yes. Those of the U'sala who want to call Lissae home may stay."

"And may we leave..." Kerk started.

"... and come back..." Drah added.

"... at any point?" Kerk finished.

"Yes," Jonathan said. "Like all residents of Lissae, there are duties you must abide by. Each being who wishes to stay must swear to protect the Altoriae at all costs, assist her, answer her call, ensure a safe place for her to train, and help to maintain peace amongst Ronah's residents."

"Not Lissae's residents?" Yessna asked.

"No. Although if you wanted to settle on, say, Ginorti, it would change to Ginorti's residents," Shari said.

"So, we have a choice?" Nerina asked.

"Yes," Shari grinned.

There was a silent conversation around the table before Yessna nodded. "We accept."

One by one, the nine U'sala rose and swore to uphold the oath that Jonathan repeated for them.

"Now, do any of you feel up to patrolling?" Jonathan asked with a bright smile.

Shari groaned.

Yessna bared her fangs in a grin.

The Guardian was delivering assignments for the night.

Collis nodded at Remmy, who stepped up for their patrol group.

They were one of three groups left. The Returned waited alongside the U'sala and six members of the Altoriae's Guild.

Not including the Altoriae herself, who was leaning against a pillar with her arms crossed.

He couldn't decide if she looked petulant or bored.

"We got Vinneča," Remmy said.

"Yes, the Returned are looking at Vinneča. The U'sala will patrol Maru. Guild, you have Fiotealar. Questions?" the Guardian asked.

"Can the U'sala and the guild swap?" the Guardian's Apprentice asked. "The Yoxant might be more inclined to allow non-Lissaens on their Realm after what happened last time."

"What happened last time?" asked a massive, broad-shouldered woman with a pack on her back, the pouches on her belt bulging. She was standing with the U'sala, and if Collis had to hazard a guess, he would say she was their healer.

The Apprentice sighed as if the question was an imposition. "The Guardian caught a chakram with his throat."

Collis sucked in a breath and stared intently at the Guardian's neck.

The man in question laughed hollowly. "It wasn't that bad. Not even a scratch."

"I had to restart your heart," Shari said from the sidelines. "With Plasma."

A Ferah laughed. "Plasma." She nudged the U'sala's healer, who chuckled as well.

"If you want to swap," the Guardian sighed. "Feel free. Those three Realms are the last on the roster tonight. Anything else?"

Everyone shook their heads, too stunned to speak.

Collis looked at Remmy and raised a brow. After a nod, they joined the swarm heading for the Ducibus' Hall, batting at the thick mist that lay on the other side of the double doors.

Glancing behind, he smiled at the Altoriae, who was watching them with worry written over every line of her body.

Yessna looked at the ragtag members of the Altoriae's Guild. Despite all of them favouring the same black leathers as their leader, they were as different from each other as night and day.

"Are we swapping?" Yessna asked.

A girl with fiery red hair glanced at the others and shook her head. "We're game to tackle the Realm that almost killed the Guardian."

Baring her fangs, Yessna dipped her head. "Perfect. We haven't visited Maru in far too long." She started down the hall.

"Remember," Kerk called behind them.

"Catch with your hands..." Drah added.

"... not your neck!" The twins laughed as they scurrying after her.

Amara looked back at the others and grinned with a confidence she didn't feel.

"We'll be fine, right?" she asked as they found the right turn and started walking along the hall.

Elani rolled her eyes and nodded.

Glancing at the white-knuckled grip Elani had on her bow did not fill Amara with confidence.

"Right." Standing before the brass-studded wooden door, chilled fingers of foreboding creeping across Amara's skin.

I shouldn't go in there.

But she was a patrol leader. Had fought hard to be one. Overcame the death of her parents, being thrown out of her hometown, and a horrendous boat ride across the largest waves she never wanted to see again.

Stepping through one more door shouldn't be so hard.

"What are you waiting for?" Raven grumbled.

"Just making sure you're awake," Amara said with forced cheerfulness, and opened the door.

Collis roared and smacked the butt of his staff into the guts of the squat quadruped.

Zir skin greyed even further, and slime spewed from zir mouth, all over the end of his staff.

Slamming the staff into ze again, Collis nodded in satisfaction as zir arms pinwheeled, eyes crossed, and ze fell in a heap.

Looking at the splintering wood of his staff, Collis groaned.

"We should have offered to swap!" Remmy called out.

Ashlen grunted and lopped the head off another being. "What are these called, anyway?"

"We are the falkirut of Vinneča," a larger, greyer, slimer being gurgled at them.

Timon yelped as one tried to bite his thigh. "We're just making sure the gateway is clear."

"What are you?" a falkirut asked.

"We are the Returned of Lissae."

"Liss... aye," ze croaked. The others took up the call, and soon the entire swamp was filled with the name of their Realm.

"We want Lissae," a shorter falkirut asked. "You will take us there."

"No, thanks," Denesska said and swung her double-headed war hammer like a mallet, sending the being flying.

Ze landed with a squelching sound in the mud.

"Don't let them through!" Ashlen yelled. A falkirut spat directly into his face, and Ashlen screamed, clawing at his skin.

"So dramatic," Denesska said, and banished the slime.

"Shari is a bad influence on you," Timon said.

"Oh, it's not the Altoriae," Denesska said. "It's Collis's soul-match."

Groaning, Collis flipped his staff over and blasted a falkirut with one end and jabbed it into the back of another, who was trying to sneak past him and through the gateway.

The U'sala were having a blast.

Literally.

Felton was in his element as he fiddled with another ball of twigs and leaves, shaping it with his Innarn so it hid the explosives within. '*Incoming,*' he sent, and lobbed the ball overhead and into the waiting swarm of oversized insects.

"I do not remember Maru having a bug problem," Yessna grumbled, sending needle-sharp fur flying into the multi-faceted eyes of the closest insect.

Even when it fell, chittering, its head was up to her waist, and it was easily twice as long as Yessna was tall.

"Can't we just tell the Guardian it's overrun?" Kibon asked as he let loose another lot of arrows. "Where's Henot?"

A cackle from the middle of the swarm made Yessna groan. '*Get out of there, you ridiculous gnome!*'

As usual, Henot didn't listen.

'*You're not even a snack to these bugs! More like a berry,*' Kibon sent.

'*Callin' me fat?*' Henot asked.

'*Nope. Callin' you tiny,*' Kibon shot back.

Yessna groaned. '*Stop riling him up,*' she signed in veti cant, knowing Henot was too far away to see.

"But it's so much fun," Kibon chucked.

The two were closer than the twins but could make the other madder than a hungry fulni.

"Where are the twins?" Yessna asked.

'*I found a foot!*' Henot sent.

"A foot?" Felton yelled.

'*I think it's Drah's!*'

Nerina sighed. '*Bring it here then.*'

Amara flinched as the door banged closed behind them.

Fiotealar didn't seem like anything out of the ordinary. A grove surrounded the gateway, with a paved path starting at the edge and leading away. No undergrowth made scanning the area easy.

'*Do you think the apprentice was joking?*' Mu asked.

'*No,*' Amara shivered. '*No, I don't...*' A space between two trees shimmered, and something shot out. "Duck!" she screamed.

The guild dropped to the ground right as a spinning disc slammed into the tree behind her.

Snapping her head around, Amara stared in shock. "Well, that wasn't meant to happen."

"That's a chakram?" Mu shrieked, uncovering his head. Plasma danced along his fingertips as he threw a shield up between them and the not-so-empty-spaces amid the trees.

Swinging her great axe, Amara glared as she glanced around the trees. '*Mu, can you fry the shield?*'

"Are you sure that's a good idea?" Elani asked.

"Need to see where they are." Amara shrugged and ducked again as another disc spun by.

From his prone position, Plasma crackled along the length of Mu's body and shot out.

The shield shimmered and broke apart like a multi-hued cobweb, shattering the illusion of an empty grove.

What lay behind was even worse.

Amara had been expecting an army. Or a patrol group, at least. Instead, there were machines, and as a motor spun, a chakram slotted into place, a mechanical arm pulled back. There was a whirring noise, and the arm flicked, sending the circular death blade spinning through the air.

There were mechanical arms at different heights, and with the blades failing to hit anything so far, it seemed to activate something, and lower arms pulled back.

"Up! Get up!" Amara reached down, grabbed Mu by the scruff of his neck, and pulled him up, using a blast of Fire Innarn to give them clearance off the ground as the chakram spun past, brushing the sole of their boots.

"Lucky," Raven said.

Amara turned to grin at him and tripped.

Fell.

Flick!

Something hit the top of her head, hard, and everything went dark.

Temira looked up as the hidden door in her lab opened and a Ducibus guided someone through.

"Move. Move!" A man was carrying Amara in, her red hair contrasting with the silver disc lodged in her skull.

"What do we have here?" her assistant of the day, Zac, asked.

Temira froze. Limbs were easy, organ repair was a breeze, but brains...

"We were on Fiotealar," a weeping boy said. "She saved me. Can you save her?"

The beings in the room turned to face Temira expectantly.

'*Give me the crystals, now,*' she sent to Cyrus.

'*You have crystals, technomancer,*' he sent back, the laugh in his send at odds with the scene in front of her.

Pulling on clean gloves, she huffed. '*The femto-crystals. I know you kept a sample. Give it to me.*'

'*Temira. There is no way I can give you those,*' Cyrus sent. He shifted in next to her, mouth opened to lecture, and looked down. "Oh."

'*They are the only chance to save her.*'

'*But the devastation if even one is still...*'

'*One girl or the Realm.*' Temira sighed. She knew the answer as well as he did. But this girl had been kind to the feared technomancer, and for that, Temira wanted to help her more than ever.

'*We have to try without the crystals.*' Cyrus sighed as he snapped his gloves on.

Nodding, Temira set to work even as her heart dropped. "Three cylinder fives, gauze, and..." She had learned long ago that asking for a body bag too soon made others upset. "And a pack of swabs."

Zac snapped up the supplies.

Carefully separate the bladed disc from the skull.

Squeeze cylinder five into the gaping wound.

No heartbeat.

No breath.

"Restart the heart," Temira ordered.

The assistant scurried to comply.

Ignore the sobs from behind.

"It won't start," Zac said.

'*I know.*' "Try again."

"Still nothing."

"Try *again.*"

"Temira."

Sigh.

'*She's gone.*'

The sobs grew louder.

"I'm sorry," Zac was saying.

Taking her gloves off, Temira turned.

"Your friend is gone," the technomancer said.

And for once, when the others wept, she joined in.

CHAPTER THIRTY-TWO

Lissae

Inthday

Second day of the fourth week of Stormwake

Shari felt it as soon as the guild returned to the castle.

The entire patrol group had slumped shoulders and teary eyes. Raven's hands were covered in blood, and most damning, they were missing someone.

"Where's Amara?" Shari asked, already knowing the answer.

Mu burst into tears.

Bowing her head, Shari's hand flexed at her side. She should have been there with them, could have prevented another senseless death.

"I formally suggest that the Realm of Fiotealar be declared a no-go zone. They've rigged it so their portal is well-defended, and unless there is some..." Raven raised his hand to run it through his hair but stopped when he saw it was still coated in blood. Shaking, he shoved it in his pocket. "Emergency. They should be left alone."

"What happened?" Shari whispered.

"She saved me," Mu sobbed. Elani wrapped a comforting arm around him. "But we couldn't save her."

'*Chakram to the top of the skull,*' Raven sent.

Glancing over at him, shocked, Shari noted his red eyes.

Despite wanting to ask questions, she bit the inside of her cheek. "Clean up and meet back in the kitchen."

"I just want to..." Raven started.

Shari stared at him, hard. "Kitchen," she repeated.

Gulping, Raven nodded and slouched out of the room. The others followed.

'*Jonathan? Do you know?*' Shari sent. There was a vague sense of sleeping, and Shari didn't have the heart to wake him. Entering the kitchen, she looked around. What did you cook when no one felt like eating but they had to? When the grief was raw and all-consuming?

A bottle of calromata caught her eye.

Amara's favourite.

Scrambled eggs and hot sauce sounded good. And easy.

Mechanically, Shari got all the ingredients down and put everything together. The smell of frying onions drew the others in.

"What's this?" Raven asked.

Shari glanced at him as she stirred the cooking eggs. "You've just had the worst patrol of your life. Food, cry, sleep."

For a moment, she thought he was going to argue, but he bit his tongue and slumped onto a stool at the table.

The sizzle of the food and the scraping of the pan was all the noise in the kitchen for a long while.

"It's my fault," Raven said hoarsely.

"How?" Shari asked, careful to keep her back to him.

"She grabbed Mu—saved his arse with an incredible jump. I called her lucky, and she grinned at me. Tripped over her feet and..." He broke off.

This time, Shari looked over.

His face was blotchy, and his eyes were red-rimmed but dry. Devastation was written in every line of his body.

"I know that expression. Wore it for months after... after Mitch died. Right in front of me. And there was nothing I could do." Shari turned back to the eggs, fighting her own tears. "Don't keep it in. Don't think you're the only one who misses her. And don't ever, *ever* think it's your fault."

Raven sniffled. "Is Mitch yours?"

"The Mind Healer says no. Jonathan says no. Most days I do too, now. But it's hard to process," Shari admitted.

"I thought it was going to be a bit of a laugh, you know?" Raven admitted. "The glamourous life of the Altoriae and her guild. Fighting bad guys, coming back and sleeping in an enormous castle, and being lauded for our prowess before going out and doing it all again."

Shari bit back a laugh. "Sorry to disappoint. My life is about as far from glamourous as you can get," she said as she started dishing out the eggs.

"Yeah. There's nothing in the news about returning home hoping the blood on your hands belongs to someone else," Raven said dryly. "And then, when it does, you wish it didn't."

He finally broke.

Flicking a stasis shield over the food, Shari slid onto the stool next to him and waited. Raven was not one for physical contact until he was ready.

To be fair, neither was she.

As the sobs subsided, he leaned against her shoulder. Shari floated a plate of eggs over to him, and another for herself. The rest of the patrol group took a plate as they entered and sat across from each other.

"I'm no expert," Shari said. "I'm still figuring things out myself. But eating something helps. Then cry if you haven't already, and sleep. The rest we can deal with tomorrow."

The others nodded and poked at their eggs.

With a watery grin, Shari floated the bottle of calromata sauce over. She poured some on and sat the bottle in the middle of the table.

Taking a bite, she had instant regret. "This is… how…" Ineffectively fanning her mouth, Shari groaned.

"Calromata sauce is like shoving a thousand of the berries in your mouth at once," Elani said. "I don't know how Amara can stand the stuff."

Raven grabbed the bottle and poured a generous helping onto his eggs. One by one, the others did the same.

Slowly, they went around the table, sharing stories of Amara—how she'd trip over air but still save the day. How she loved the hot sauce that was burning their eyes out. How she'd help anyone in need.

By the end of the meal, they were all sweaty and red faced, with tear tracks that felt carved into their cheeks.

Hearts a little lighter, even if it felt like their insides were on fire, they went their separate ways to rest and recover.

Kerday

Third day of the fourth week of Stormwake

Jonathan looked at Samuel cradling the tiny, gold hatchling in his arms. "We need to talk."

Samuel sighed. "I have no idea how she got out."

"What was she doing in the museum?" Jonathan asked.

"Kemanyr?" Samuel glanced at her.

'*Voices called me.*'

"Did you find them?"

'*Only Frointh. He's been forgotten for so long.*'

"Who?" Jonathan asked.

'*Your deity of crystal*,' Kemanyr sent.

"Deity or not, you can't go into the museum yet," Jonathan said. "The Xanderri are a tremendous threat. If they got hold of you..."

"They won't," Samuel said. "I'll make sure of it."

Nodding, Jonathan rose. "I only want to keep you all safe."

"Not to mention the rest of the Realm from a rampaging Q'Aralide," Samuel said, his eyes shadowed.

"That too," Jonathan tried to smile, but he couldn't. "Being taken over by something and not having any control is terrifying. At least there were plenty of beings to stop me."

"And there are only two, maybe three beings on all of Lissae who could take me down. I get it," Samuel said. "We'll be careful. More than anyone, we've seen what the Xanderri can do."

Chamele glanced up as Captain Rappen enter the room with a chain in his hand.

Jerking along behind him was an older man with a chain around his neck, his eyes blazing with fury and Innarn.

"You brought us a gift," Chamele said. "Don't let it dirty the carpet."

The aberration spat at her.

Captain Rappen punched his beast, hard. "Respect your betters."

It glared out of a rapidly swelling eye. "I don't see anyone better than me here. I see abusers and fearmongers, sipping from teacups and pretending they aren't letting the Realm burn."

"How do you break them?" Captain Rappen asked.

Chamele sighed as she uncrossed her ankles and rose from the chair. "You don't." Adjusting her veil, she spanned the room to a low sideboard and removed a small chest. "Breaking is uncouth and unnecessary, when all we want to know is how to stop them."

Captain Rappen was glaring at her. She could feel it. After taking a small vial out of the chest, she poured it into the teacup and returned to the aberration.

"Here, dear," she said. "Drink up."

Glaring at her, the aberration shook its head.

"We can do this the easy way, or the hard way," she said lightly.

"I'm not drinking anything from you." It scowled at her.

"Don't say I didn't try," she said lightly. Going back to the chest, she put the teacup down and picked up a syringe filled with a muddy, orange substance.

Returning to the aberration, she held the syringe to Captain Rappen and gestured to the beast. "Hold still," she said lightly. "I'm told this will burn."

He started thrashing in his chains. Rappen kicked him to the ground and stepped on his back, applying more than enough pressure to keep the beast still while he injected the concoction.

"I grew up with a volcano as a playground," the aberration rasped. "I'm not afraid of fire."

And then the screaming started.

Narday

Fourth day of the fourth week of Stormwake

The doors of the castle slammed open.

Shari had her weapons out before she'd thought about it.

"Someone took Mick," Fenix said.

"Sorry, who?" Shari asked. She hesitated, trying to decide if she should banish her glove or not.

"A guy in a uniform. Someone with a veil over their face drinking tea from a fancy cup. Tried to make him have some, but…" Fenix broke off, wrapping their arms around their middle.

"Sounds like Chamele has him," Skye said.

"He won't last long," Grace added.

"What do you mean?" Fenix asked, raising a tear-streaked face.

Grace looked away from them. "They never do. The aberrations are only there to see if they can be cured."

"Cured?" Shari asked.

Her cousin glanced at her and nodded. "It's Chamele. She found out by experimenting on me that she couldn't beat the Innarn out of us, so she tried to see if it can be removed. If we can be normal."

Fenix glared. "Normal beings don't go around kidnapping others, beating them up and injecting them with all sorts of stuff!"

"That's all I knew." Grace shrugged.

All the fight dropped out of Fenix. "How do we get him back?"

"If you saved Oakley, you have a way to save Mick, right?" Shari said.

"Don't," Grace snapped. "They'll be waiting."

"I feel so powerless!" Fenix threw their hands into the air.

"Do you have a link to Mick?" Shari asked.

"Yes, that's how I–" Fenix doubled over. "He's… no. They killed him." They looked up, stunned. "Mick might have had a rough time dealing with me, but he never deserved that."

Shari reached out to Fenix, who rushed into her arms. "What will they do next?"

Grace lowered her head. "Chamele will not stop. She'll try again."

"To do what?"

"She wants to cure the aberrations and take over the Shifting Islands. Anchor them to a mainland and strip them of their resources. Chamele will just keep going until she gets what she wants," Grace said.

The Altoriae gritted her teeth. "Not if we stop her first."

Portal

Outside Lissae's door

The Ducibus who usually guarded Lissae's gateway lay on the ground, a drooling mess.

Physical bodies were so untidy.

A group of beings were moving through the hall towards the double doors.

Open them. Ze let the thought whisper along the edge of zir minds as ze lay low to the ground, covering the fallen body of the sentinel.

One paused and looked around. They sniffed at the fog and shrugged before opening the doors and ushering the others through.

The Xanderri swept through the doors and glided into Lissae to join their long-lost kin.

Success.

CHAPTER THIRTY-THREE

Lissae

Rasshday

Fifth day of the fourth week of Stormwake

In the middle of class, Tania doubled over and groaned.

Collis glanced over. "What's wrong?"

"I feel ill. Like I did when Anriluka crossed over," she said, holding her stomach.

"Do you think something similar has happened?" he asked.

"What could be worse than Anriluka?" Anika asked.

Tania glanced at Collis. "I think we're about to find out."

"Go find the Altoriae," Tutor Boyce said, her tone leaving no room for argument.

Arilla blocked the blow with the blade of her sword.

Lenyuu grinned at her. "You're a worthy opponent," he said.

"I just appreciate being a student for the day." Arilla pulled back and struck out.

Blocking easily, Lenyuu grinned, teeth bright against his dark skin. "I'm happy to help."

Anika was running towards them, effortlessly dodging the strikes despite the height of her heels. "Have you seen Shari?" she panted, her eyes clouded with worry.

"No? I thought she'd be at school?" Arilla's heart dropped.

"We can't find her anywhere."

Not *again*.

"We will search with you." Lenyuu's grin was gone, replaced with the fierce determination of a hunter.

Samuel bit back a laugh as Tormorylth tried to show Kemanyr how to control the poison breath.

Shari was curled up next to Jetonyx, both of them studying the script from the Dark Realms. The hatchling seemed to be more inclined to learn it when she was around.

'*Is Shari with you?*' Jonathan asked.

Glancing over to see if Shari had heard the send, he sent the Guardian an image of her, peaceful on the chair.

'*Lock down the house and keep her there. Something is going on, and I don't like it.*' Jonathan sounded terrified.

'*Alright. We'll stay put.*'

'*No matter what?*'

He sighed but twitched the corner of his lips when Shari looked over.

'*No matter what.*'

The students of Ridden Hall streamed out of the school, their eyes glazed and unseeing.

Their heads seemed too full of clouds to stop their bodies.

When Laura brushed against them to find out what they were thinking, only one thought was in their minds.

Find the Altoriae.

She whimpered.

'*Samuel?*'

The Guardian looked at Asterion.

The minotaur bounced as the beings on the other side of the room slammed against the door he was leaning on. "I don't think this will hold them for very long."

"We just need to stall. Give us enough to come up with a plan." Jonathan ran a hand through his hair. He should have been used to this by now. The Eni had tried to take over their children once before. But these clouds were worse. At least the Eni had cared about their host bodies. The Xanderri seemed to have no such compulsion.

"Would a lullaby work?" Asterion asked over the thuds on the door.

"Anything is worth a shot. I remember, when it was time for bed..."

Time.

"Don't move," Jonathan said.

Circling his hands as if he was creating a globe, Jonathan pulled together all the little strands of leftover Time.

"They're getting stronger, or there's more of them," Asterion warned.

"Almost..." Jonathan poked at the ball he'd created. When it expanded, it should be big enough. But with the Innarn eaters, he just needed...

Asterion grunted.

... to make...

The door splintered beside the minotaur's head.

... a few more...

"Guardian!" Asterion cried.

... changes...

Beings thudded against the door and pushed it open.

Done.

"Move!" Jonathan commanded.

Rolling to the side, Asterion was trying to avoid the stampede of teens streaming through the door.

At least it wasn't the little ones.

He looked straight at the clouded eyes of Elizabeth Ribeck and threw the ball.

It smashed against her forehead and broke. Time Innarn spiralled out and looped around all the teens, capturing them in the moment.

As Jonathan shifted Asterion out of the office with him, he could only hope it would hold.

This was one fight he didn't want Samuel or Shari involved in at all, and it was going to take everything he had to keep it that way.

"You killed it," Chamele said. "How are we meant to cure them if you are such an incompetent tester?"

Captain Rappen snarled at her.

"Oh, don't try that with me. I know exactly what the clouds are capable of," she snapped back. "Go fetch another one," she ordered.

"You gave up the right to order me around the instant you let the Xanderri out of your head," Rappen said.

"Hardly. I'm still your superior in every way."

Rappen leaned over her, using his bulk to intimidate.

Chamele blinked up at him. "You forget yourself. I have the one thing we need under my power."

"And what's that?" he said.

Calmly, she pulled a tiny shard of crystal out of the tube in her pocket. And tapped on it five times with a fingernail.

"What's that meant to do?"

She sighed and sank gracefully into an armchair. "The Guardian was the one who stole my personal aberration. It stands to reason that it would be in his vicinity now. I've just sent a message to it that can't be denied. As we speak, my aberration will be wreaking havoc on Ronah and ensuring enough test subjects are captured that it might even satisfy your bloodlust."

The captain laughed, his voice a multi-layered echo. "My kin are here. Time will tell if you hold as much sway over the beast as you think you do."

Skye was sitting opposite Grace in the sitting room, trying a plate of exotic food from Ginorti, when an odd noise rang out.

Grace froze at the second sound. At the third, she looked up.

"Run," she said as the fourth tap echoed.

"What?"

A fifth, and then silence.

Grace had gone as still as stone.

Then she lunged across the table, scattering the platters of food.

Skye shrieked and did what Grace had asked her to do earlier.

She ran.

Collis glanced around, confused, as his entire class emptied, the teacher just as puzzled as he was.

"What just happened?" he asked.

The teacher shrugged. "Eventually, you stop asking questions and go with it."

"I don't know if this time you should go with it," Collis said

A student re-entered the room, dragging an axe behind him, his movement jerky and eyes unfocused.

"I think you're right," the teacher said, and scrambled out of the window rather than try to get past the teen with the axe.

"Want to tell me what's going on?" Collis asked.

"Need to feed," the young man replied tonelessly.

Collis wished he could remember his name. All thoughts came to a stop when whatever was controlling the other students' body took over again and lifted the axe.

"There's loads of food downstairs," Collis tried.

The boy laughed and swung.

Dodging out of the way, Collis blasted him with a bolt of Innarn, sending the student backwards through a desk or two.

"Perfect," he said, smiling through bloody teeth as he got to his feet. Lunging at Collis, the boy ducked, and Collis dodged and grabbed him by the shirt.

A sucking sensation started, all over his skin, and Collis groaned. He tried to bat his attacker away, but was too weak to do much more than flop his hand uselessly against the other's chest.

The teen shrieked. "Why are you so Dark?"

"Oh, no you don't," said a voice from far away.

There was a thud.

No longer supported, he fell to the ground.

"Need a hand?" asked Tania, cradling a thick book.

"How did you know?"

"I felt it happen. And, you know, hantra students." She shrugged and helped him to his feet. "We need to warn Shari."

Collis ran through different scenarios in his head. "No. Not her, and not the Guardian's Apprentice. Can you imagine what would happen if they were like him?" he gestured to the fallen boy.

"Oh. Wait. Not Shari, no, but Samuel." Tania looked at the boy and nudged him with the toe of her shoe. "He was pulling away when I walloped him. I don't think they can handle the Dark. And who does Dark better than him?"

Captain Rappen strode past the sailors preparing the ship.

If the Xanderri inside him didn't feed soon, it was going to eat away at his flesh. Already, underneath his uniform, a large patch of skin was sloughing off.

All it did was make him more determined than ever to get rid of the aberrations.

"Ready to cast off?" Rappen asked.

"Half an hour, and the fleet will be good to go," the skipper confirmed.

He nodded and walked towards the bow. The information that was streaming through his brain was almost too much to handle. The Xanderri had made it through the portal and were using the bodies of children to fight their war.

Rappen wasn't sure if he should be impressed or terrified.

Either way, it didn't matter how he felt.

It was time to end the aberrations.

Every last one.

CHAPTER THIRTY-FOUR

Vebaday

Sixth day of the fourth week of Stormwake

Thunder rumbled outside the window as Jonathan shot out of his house and ran into Zac, almost bowling him over. "Sorry!"

"Why have the kids all gone mad?" Zac asked, looking over his shoulder.

"Innarn eaters. Shari failed to mention they could control others," Jonathan said. "I need to get to the Returned."

Zac yanked on his arm, turning him around. "Wouldn't go that way. There are more kids outside."

"How did you sneak past?" Jonathan asked as Zac pulled him inside.

He held up his arm and pointed to the shiny silver cuff with an etched symbol of Lissae on it. "One of Cyrus's devices. Sucks on any Innarn aimed my way and pulls them in to create a shield. However these things are eating, I'm pretty sure it requires Innarn."

"Shari said they were clouds. Do you think firing those Innarn dampeners the mainlanders used would work?" Jonathan wondered aloud.

"I think it's mad enough to work. Hold on. I have a shortcut to Cyrus's lab."

"Can I come?" Asterion asked. "I don't like the idea of these being weapons." He ran a finger down a horn.

"More the merrier," Zac said, and grabbed hold of his arm.

The three disappeared.

Seated in the grove on Ginorti, Tania looked up as the clouds rumbled.

"Looks like a storm," Fenix said.

Zana stared at the sky for a long moment. "I don't think so. The cloud formations are all wrong. And they haven't moved past Ronah's borders."

"Does anyone else feel like they have indigestion?" Tania blurted.

The others looked at her with varying degrees of amusement.

"No? Just me?" She shrank in on herself.

Collis had convinced her to join the Linked whilst he searched for Samuel, saying she was too Light to risk.

"I'm worried," she admitted.

"That's enough to give anyone ulcers," Cyrus said, lounging back on his boulder. Something in one of his pockets chimed, and he bolted upright. "Someone is in my lab." Eyes unfocusing, he shook his head. "It's the Guardian, a minotaur, and Zac?"

"Do you think they've been taken over?" Tania asked.

Cyrus snorted. "Not unless clouds can curse like sailors."

"That doesn't sound like Jonathan," Tania said.

"But it sounds like Zac. I'm going to shift them here. Everyone ready?" Cyrus asked.

Fenix and Zana nodded, grim-faced and shields springing to life. Tania wavered for a moment.

Oakley nudged her shoulder and smiled. "We're right here."

Gamely, Tania nodded as well. "Alright."

The trio of lab prowlers landed in the middle of the clearing in a shower of orange sparks.

"Want to tell us what's going on?" Cyrus asked. His words were calm, but his expression promised violence.

"We want to shoot the Innarn dampeners at the Xanderri," Asterion blurted, then pointed at Jonathan. "It was his idea."

Jaw dropping, Cyrus looked at the Guardian. "Are you *mad*? That could kill Ronah!"

"No, it won't, because Tania can stop the crystals from ever hitting the ground." Jonathan looked directly at her.

"I don't know if I—" She started to say.

"I do. I believe in you." The Guardian looked at him earnestly.

A warm feeling settled in Tania's chest. "Alright. But can we get the Returned to help as a backup? I don't want a single speck of dirt to come into contact with those."

"Now we just need to get someone to act as bait," Zana said.

Jonathan sighed. "I'll..."

"Stay out of harm's way and stop being a self-sacrificing fool? Great idea," Zac said, deadpan.

Tania snorted.

"I'll do it," Oakley said.

Variations of no were called out.

"We did not get you back just to lose you again!" Cyrus said.

"Who would be a big enough draw for all of those?" Zac asked, gesturing to the fluffy white clouds circling her island.

"Sam," Tania mused. "Samuel would be perfect. He's got loads of Innarn, and he's so Dark that it would take them a while before they could feed on him."

"Do you really think that's a good idea?" Jonathan asked. "What if they try to control him instead?"

She snorted and slapped a hand over her mouth in embarrassment. "Can you really see anyone trying to control Samuel?"

"True," Jonathan said. "Let's join him."

"For the record, I think this plan is incredibly risky and I don't know if I like the fate of the entire Realm depending on your apprentice," Oakley said. "But I'm in. Let's go kill some clouds."

Jonathan winced.

Even in the safety of his new home with the hatchlings, Samuel looked like he was ready to rend flesh from bone. "You want me to what?"

"I honestly think you have the best chance of survival," the Guardian said.

"You want me to stand in the middle of the island and hope some Innarn-eating clouds will notice me?" Samuel asked.

"No," Shari said. "Absolutely not."

"If this works, Samuel won't actually be in danger," Jonathan said.

Shari bit her tongue, but her thoughts were so loud, he heard what she wanted to say anyway. *'That's what you thought about Mitch.'*

Flinching, Jonathan looked away and ran a shaky hand over his face. "Shari, I..." What could he possibly say to that?

Samuel crossed the room and knelt at Shari's feet, looking up at her. "I trust Jonathan."

Shari spent a long time searching his face, before giving an abrupt nod.

Carefully, Samuel removed Sneeze from his shoulder and held the little draci out to her. "Look after them all for me?"

Sneeze bit down on Samuel's thumb but walked over onto Shari's waiting hands. "I will. All of them."

"I'm coming back, Shari," Samuel said.

"You'd better."

Samuel hadn't been gone ten minutes when there was a rapid knock at the door.

"Jetonyx, don't you dare open that door!" Shari called. The house Ronah had created for the Q'Aralide was massive, and it took her forever to get from one side to the other.

'*Could be a snack,*' Jetonyx sent.

"No! We don't eat people!" Shari started running and slammed into the larger hatchling's rear as he jerked back.

'*Spiky,*' Jetonyx moaned and shuffled back inside.

Cautiously, Shari peered her head around.

Yessna, her fur singed and whiskers quivering, stood panting at the door. "Shari! The odd girl at the castle who looks haunted but has your eyes. She's attacking beings."

"Grace?"

"She's too strong. Took out Drah with one blast. He'd just recovered, too. We can't stop her," Yessna admitted.

"And you think I can?" Shari wasn't up to full strength yet, but if Grace was using her Innarn on people, she had to do something. "Jetonyx, you're in charge. Make sure Sneeze and the others are safe." She carefully put the draci on the hatchling's snout and slipped out the door before he could stop her.

"Stay inside!" she warned, ignoring his grumbles. "Now, where's Grace?"

"At the castle." Yessna made to join her.

"Guard the hatchlings for me?" Shari asked.

The leader of the U'sala hesitated, then nodded. "As you will it."

Beaming to hide how unsure she was, Shari shifted away.

She landed in a nightmare.

The dining hall of the castle had all but been destroyed.

Bodies had been flung here and there, some at an angle that would make a healer wince, and others were showing signs of life, groaning and grumbling as they pulled themselves out from under upturned furniture.

Food covered the walls, and Shari was glad that what she had first thought was blood was actually some sort of tomato-based sauce.

"Anyone know which way she went?" Shari asked.

Someone pointed a shaking hand towards the front doors.

"Of course," Shari grumbled, and shifted outside.

First glance, and it looked like carnage.

Grace at the other end of the street, a menace with streams of Innarn flowing around her so thick, not even the descending clouds could touch her.

The clouds.

Shari whimpered as thunder rumbled along her bones.

Despite the distance between them, Grace whirled as if she'd heard. "Stop me!" she screamed.

Wrinkling her nose, Shari lost precious seconds. The infliction on the words was all wrong.

Then there was no time to think. A bolt of earth Innarn shaped like a knife was streaming straight at her. She barely got out of the way.

"Please," Grace sobbed even as she flung another bolt. "Stop me."

"Who's making you do this?" Shari asked.

Fire joined Earth, turning the raining shards of rock into heated missiles. Shari hissed as one landed too close for comfort. Sweeping her arm out, she pulled Water from the air and poured it onto the spot fires Grace had created.

Big mistake.

Two big mistakes.

One, she'd taken her eyes off Grace, and now her cousin was about to ram right into her. And two?

She'd used Innarn.

Samuel was standing not even a click away, and she'd used Innarn so close to him that the clouds which had been slowly lowering towards him were now streaming her way.

Grace screamed again, and she took a flying leap, Plasma crackling around her balled-up fist.

Shari waited until Grace was at the height of her jump, and struck.

Boulder to the gut.

Her cousin went flying and crumpled in a heap.

"Grace!" Shari screamed, running to her side.

Eyes fluttering open, Grace's head lolled to the side. "Made me do it," she muttered. "Chip in my brain."

'*Holli. Emergency! Serious emergency!*' Shari sent, eyeing the clouds as they slowly got lower.

The healer shifted right next to her. "Where are you hurt?"

"Not me–her," Shari said, nodding to Grace.

"Who is this?" Holli asked.

"Grace. My cousin."

The Healer took in the battered form of her newest relative. "How did this happen?"

"Sometimes," Shari said, "families are hard work." She looked over at the other girl, who looked surprisingly peaceful. "Grace said there's a chip in her brain."

"A chip?" Holli sounded doubtful. "I can scan, but it would be better at the centre." Running her hand over Grace's head, Holli bit her lip. "Here!"

"Can you get it out?"

"Thank Lissae for shifting, yes," Holli said. She held out her empty palm, and the next moment, there was a gooey bit of crystal sitting on it.

"Destroy it," Shari said.

"I'd like to do that," Grace said hoarsely, shaking her head and lifting herself onto one elbow.

"Pleasure is all yours," Holli said, handing it over.

It was astounding that a tiny piece of crystal could make one being cause so much terror and destruction.

Frowning hard, Grace stared at the chip, and it shattered.

Immediately, Innarn backlash smacked into all of them, sending the three tumbling.

Captain Rappen grinned as an uncharted landmass appeared on the horizon. With the force of the clouds pushing the ships to breaking point, they'd travelled around the Realm quicker than he'd hoped.

Now all he had to do was to break through the outer defences, and the cloud inside his head could feed.

CHAPTER THIRTY-FIVE

Samuel stood in the middle of Ronah, feeling like a fool. '*How long do I have to stand here for?*' he asked.

'*Until the clouds try to eat you,*' Jonathan sent.

'*There's something I never thought I'd hear,*' Samuel sent back.

'*Something I never thought I'd say.*'

A ruckus outside caught Samuel's attention, and he tuned out the Guardian for a moment, trying to see what it was, but the fence was in the way.

Wisps of clouds were trailing lower in the sky.

'*I think it's working. Are you ready?*' Samuel sent.

'*We are.*'

The voice was not the one he expected. '*And who is we?*'

'*The Xanderri.*'

Clouds were still well above the top of Ronah's castle but were getting lower.

'*Sounds thrilling,*' he sent drily. '*Tell me more.*' "Hurry, Jonathan," he muttered, hoping the clouds didn't have ears.

Shari slammed her back against Grace's and froze as they stood over Holli's prone form.

"I'm going to shift her back to the Healers Centre," Shari said.

"Well, do it already," Grace snapped, pushing hard against her and mumbling something.

The backlash from the crystal chip was acting like a beacon for every kid with clouds in their brains.

And they couldn't do a thing to hurt them.

Eric, tiny little Eric, was toddling towards Shari, arms outstretched, movements jerky and eyes unseeing.

"How are we going to stop them?" Shari asked.

"Like this," Grace said. In a blink, they were airborne, hovering well above the heads of the kids.

Stopping, the kids dropped like puppets with cut strings, and clouds streamed from their mouths as the Xanderri fled their hosts.

"Don't let them get you," Shari warned Grace.

"I don't know how to stop them," Grace said. She finally started trembling.

From above, the path of destruction that her cousin had wrought was even more devastating.

I can't let the Xanderri inside her head.

"Grace, do you trust me?" Shari asked.

Her cousin huffed.

"There's some place safe you could go, away from all of this." Mentally, Shari started locking up the bereni tree in her sanctuary.

"Nowhere on Lissae is safe," Grace moaned.

"It's not on Lissae," Shari said. "Do you trust me?"

'Yes.'

Immediately, Shari shifted her into the relative safety of her sanctuary. Now all she had to do was not die, and they'd be fine.

"Tighten the net!" Tania called. "It's almost time."

The Returned were helping to weave a net with holes small enough to catch the shards of crystal Cyrus was planning to deploy.

Talhan's Linked had given them the smallest sample he had, and the utter nothingness emanating from it was enough to make her skin crawl.

Was this what life was like for my father?

She shook the stray thought from her head.

"Is everyone ready?" she asked Collis.

He glanced along the line. "Yes."

"Alright," she said. '*Cyrus. It's time.*'

'I *dislike this*,' Tormorylth grumbled from her splayed-out spot on the ground.

For the tenth time in the last three minutes.

Jetonyx sighed. '*You don't have to like it. You just have to stay here.*'

Standing, Tormorylth stretched out her wings. '*I have an idea,*' she sent, mischief sparkling in her eyes.

'*No. No ideas, just staying put and not getting into trouble,*' Jetonyx warned. The last time he'd disobeyed an order, he'd been thrown out of Altum. He wasn't keen on repeating the experience.

Poking her tongue out, Tormorylth walked over to stand just next to the window as if she was merely looking outside.

Narrowing his eyes, he stared at her.

Behind him, something shattered. Whipping around, Jetonyx scanned the area for intruders.

Tormorylth's giggle sounded in his head as the hatchling slipped out the window and into the sky.

'*Come back!*' he demanded.

'*Make me!*' she sang at him.

Growling, Jetonyx streaked past their guest and through the door before she could stop him.

Flapping hard, he caught up to his younger nest mate. '*When Sanithane tells us to do something, we need to... Are you even paying attention to me?*'

Hovering over the mountains separating the water and the sand, Tormorylth was staring at something. '*Is the ocean meant to burn?*'

'*What? Why?*'

'*There's smoke.*'

'*I'm sure it's fine,*' Jetonyx sent.

'*Is not. I'm telling Sanithane.*'

'*No! We're not meant to be. Oh, for the love of Altum, come back!*' Jetonyx flew after her, grumbling the entire way.

Samuel looked up as a shadow flew overhead. The hatchlings were out and flying right towards the cloud bank of Xanderri.

'No!' he screamed. Without a second thought, he changed form and sprang after them.

Grinning, Captain Rappen stepped onto the tree-covered island. Clouds swirled low around him, drifting through the foliage as tendrils of fog.

The aberrations wouldn't be able to hide from him now.

CHAPTER THIRTY-SIX

Arilla's grip tightened on the handle of her sword as she tried to hide her horror. Mainlander troops were leaping off the boats, and scrambling for footholds in the steep sides of the mountainous wall.

Kneeling, Arilla laid her palms on the rocky ground. "Ronah, I know you might not hear me, but we need help." She glanced around. Most of her sword class had been asked to wait here on the beaches, as it had been deemed safer than the middle of town. "Can you bring my swords here? Please?"

"What are you doing?" Anika asked.

"Hoping Ronah can hear me," Arilla admitted.

For once missing her signature shoes, the teen dropped beside her. "What if we all ask at the same time?"

Looking over the edge at the troops, Arilla shrugged. "Can't hurt." Jumping to her feet, she called out, "I need your help. Put your hands on the ground and say, Ronah, we need our weapons."

"We're Blanks," someone down the line said. "She won't hear."

"We have to try," Anika argued.

"Please," Arilla said.

Mutters of reluctant agreement sounded from all around.

"On three. One, two, three."

"Ronah, we need our weapons."

Nothing happened.

"Again!" Anika cried.

They tried again.

Arilla could make out details on the soldiers' uniforms. "Again!"

Their voices rang out.

As the first soldier came within striking distance, Arilla rolled away and jumped up with a sword in her hand.

A quick glance showed the others held theirs as well. Anika was cheering as she parried a mainlander.

Steel clashed, and there was no more time to think.

It was her turn to help keep Ronah safe.

Kerk was a screaming ball of rage, slashing through anyone in a uniform.

He and the other U'sala had felt an unnatural pull towards the beaches, and on following the insistent feeling, had discovered the Blanks fighting back beings in blood-red uniforms.

Bloodlust had beckoned, and Kerk answered with delight.

Until a uniform wearer came at him from the side and buried a sword up to the hilt in his gut.

Grinning, Kerk whirled, separating the uniform from the head in one swift stroke.

"Let Drah know I'm still one up on him," Kerk said, and fell to the ground, his eye staring sightlessly at the descending clouds.

Oakley crouched in the branches of the tallest tree and peered down at the captain who'd caused him so much pain.

Centring himself, he let his eyes slip closed.

'*Ginorti, can I have your help, please?*'

'*My Linked needs me?*' Ginorti trembled beneath him, as the captain stumbled and swore.

If Oakley's smile had a bite to it, his island wouldn't tell.

'*I'd like to see Rocky.*'

'*Rocky is no toy,*' the island warned.

'*Oh, the time for toys is long gone,*' Oakley said. He slipped a little of what had happened to him on the mainland into his thoughts.

The ground rumbled, and an absolutely massive version of Rocky appeared behind the uniformed beast.

Showing some semblance of intelligence, the captain froze and turned slowly.

Rocky lumbered forwards.

Before Captain Rappen could try any of his 'special treatments', the golem made of stone smacked him across the face with a hand larger than the man's head.

The ground rumbled behind him. As he turned around slowly, Captain Rappen's mouth dropped open.

An absolutely hulking stone being stood before him. He had no idea what he'd done to annoy the creature, but Rappen had the sudden urge to beg for forgiveness.

Such an urge had nothing to do with him being wrong, and everything to do with the stone fist aimed at his face.

Rappen went flying. With a sudden ripping sensation, his thoughts were his own again. White vapour poured from his mouth and streamed into the sky.

From far away, a voice said, "Take his body and dump it in a boat. There's no way I want that foul excuse of a man dying on my island."

Cold, stone hands lifted Rappen, and his head lolled back, the Realm going black before he could so much as curse.

'Uh, Shari?' Tania sent. 'Do you know where Samuel is?'

"No?" Shari asked.

'Where are you?' Jonathan sent.

'Outside the training grounds,' Shari admitted, sharing a look with Grace.

'And Samuel isn't there?' Tania's send was rising in pitch.

'Is he meant to be?'

'He's our bait. Everything is concentrated on the grounds. We don't have time to recalibrate...'

'Bait for what?' Shari cut in.

'The Xanderri,' Jonathan sent.

The Altoriae froze. Glancing up at the clouds properly, she noted that despite all the colours, there was a distinct lack of grey. Thunder rumbled, and she shivered.

'Shari?' Concern was clear in the Guardian's voice.

Squeezing her eyes closed, Shari took a breath. 'I'll do it.'

'But...'

'Grace will stop me if...' Shari couldn't finish the thought.

'Are you sure?' Tania's voice sounded small, but it could have just been the crushing thoughts threatening to overtake her mind.

Straightening her shoulders, Shari nodded. 'Do we have a choice?'

Not waiting for an answer, she marched into the training grounds and stood in the middle. There was the occasional glint of a weapon catching the dying light in the stands, and the Altoriae was thankful there was more than one backup plan to take her out if needed.

Sighing, she shivered, and Grace appeared by the entryway, arms wrapped around herself.

"Ready?" Shari called.

Her cousin uncurled and nodded.

Looking up at the clouds that were almost close enough to touch if she were to stand on tiptoe and stretch, Shari shivered again and tried not to tremble under the weight of those watching.

'*Alright*,' she sent to Tania.

There was a beat.

'*Ready*,' Tania sent back.

There was nothing for Shari to do but close her eyes and trust.

Cyrus hovered over the bench.

"Don't bump it by accident," Temira scolded.

'*Ready*,' Tania sent.

Smashing the button that would launch the crystal into the air, Cyrus held his breath and hoped.

'*Ready*,' Tania sent.

She felt Cyrus push the button.

Felt the Returned leap into action, sending their Innarn flying out to power the net they had crafted.

Felt the Altoriae trembling.

Tania froze, not even daring to breathe.

The crystals hit the cloud, and the Xanderri, beings of pure Innarn, exploded into a rainbow mist.

Passing through their victims, the crystals slammed into the net.

Straining against the deadening of their Innarn, the Returned groaned under the pressure.

Shifting in next to them, Tania added what she could to the net.

"Ronah," she whispered. "It's not enough. I'm sorry."

The net sagged.

Shari was waiting to die. The Xanderri here on Ronah, their thunder tearing through her veins and rattling her bones, surely meant death.

Chancing a glance up, Shari flinched as the rain of orange crystal pierce the clouds and shatter them. Gasping for breath as the freezing water fell through the net, Shari shook her hands in a futile attempt to get rid of some of the liquid.

Pushing her Innarn out, Shari searched the skies.

She could have cried with relief.

There was no sign of the Xanderri.

More than anything, Shari hoped they were all dead.

"It's not enough. I'm sorry," Tania was saying.

Shari stepped up next to her. "Want a hand?" Shari poured her Innarn into the net. "Grace!" she called over her shoulder.

Warily, her cousin skittled over next to her.

"We need to capture this crystal and put it..." Shari paused.

"In a ziom box," Tania said. "See it?" She flicked a picture through with her send.

"Let's do this!" Shari grinned. There was nothing like sending bucketful after bucketful of dangerous crystal to a safe spot on another Shifting Island to burn off the adrenaline of not dying.

CHAPTER THIRTY-SEVEN

anithane flew through the skies above Ronah, each claw holding a squirming hatchling by the back of their neck.

'If you so much as think about sneaking out again, you won't get any snacks for a week!' he scolded.

Landing roughly, he shoved them through the door and stomped inside.

'You're not going to get rid of us?' Jetonyx asked, his voice smaller than Kemanyr.

'Why would I get rid of you?' Sanithane asked.

'Because we disobeyed.'

Samuel bowed his head. *'If you break the rules or go against what I say without a good reason, then you will be punished. But that will happen under my guidance and watchful eye. None of you are going anywhere for a very long time.'*

The three hatchlings shrieked and tackled him, landing in a happy pile of gold and black limbs.

Cyrus patted the ziom box containing the Innarn-dampening crystals. "This isn't going anywhere."

"I'll make sure of it," Temira said darkly.

From amongst the other Linked, Tania burst into tears and moved towards Temira, flinging her arms around the technomancer.

Catching Oakley's gaze, he had to turn away. It took more effort than he had left to keep a straight face. Cyrus coughed to cover up his chuckle.

From the glare Temira gave him, he hadn't succeeded.

Shari looked at Jonathan as Grace gave a small smile and crept from the room.

Even after saving Ronah, her cousin was still timid.

"She had a chip in her brain, Jonathan," Shari said softly. "How do we know there isn't something else?"

"If Holli found it, maybe she could give Grace a checkup and see if there's anything else out of the ordinary?" the Guardian suggested. He let his head fall against the back of the couch.

"Tired?" Shari asked.

"Saving the Realm is hard work," Jonathan mumbled.

"You're telling me," Shari grumbled.

"Bed, both of you," Arilla said.

Shari looked up. Her mother was covered in blood.

"Mum!"

"Oh, don't worry," Arilla grinned. "Most of it's not mine."

Pulling the excess blood away from her mother, Shari sighed. "I don't know how you do it."

"Do what?" Arilla asked.

Jonathan turned his head enough for her to know that he was listening.

"Stand back and watch. Seeing you like this is hard," Shari admitted.

Arilla brushed a strand of hair off Shari's face. "It doesn't get any easier," she said.

"Speaking of difficult, what do you think of Grace?"

"I think she needs our help," Arilla said firmly.

She chanced a glance at Jonathan, who gave a slight nod.

"Alright," she sighed.

Shari just hoped she wouldn't regret trusting her cousin.

GLOSSARY

A

Aberration – A slur used by mainlanders to refer to Innarnians.

Adonday – First day of the week on the Realm of Lissae. The other days are **Inthday**, **Kerday**, **Narday**, **Rasshday**, **Vebaday,** and **Zoeday.**

Altoriae – Protector of the Realm of Lissae. Traditionally a female role, although there has been one male Altoriae. Previous Altoriaes have included Kay'imi, Muran Curtis, Jali Thorne, and Fiona MacAde. Forces of nature cannot kill her. They must swear to uphold the seven duties of the Altoriae.

Altum – The home Realm of the Q'Aralide.

Apprentice, The Guardian's – The Guardian's Apprentice is to take over the role of Guardian once the current holder of the title falls in battle or dies of old age.

Arustos – A small mammal native to Cantash. These tree custodians live in hollows near the base of trees. They have a pointed snout, dirt-coloured scales, sturdy back legs, sharp teeth, and a strong tail. They use their forelegs to grab onto bugs, which their companion Caelonis fries for them.

Azehal – A drink favoured by the Guardian. A rutenberry-flavoured stimulant drink, typically served with sweetener and milk.

B

Beads – A form of currency on Lissae created out of **Ziom**. The technical name is **Ziom beads**.

Bereni trees – Trees that are grown to be used as buildings. The size and design of the tree can be controlled by an Innarnian or by one of the sentient islands.

B.I.R.D. – Stands for "Bio Instructor for Relative Distance." Designed by Xani of Talhan to ensure beings would stop bumping into things if they were absorbed in their crystal slab. The B.I.R.D. device acts as both a guide and a guard.

Blank – A person who can't use Innarn.

C

Caelonis – A tiny bird native to Cantash. They can produce a jet of flame from their beak. They typically use the flames to fry beetles for their arustos companions.

Calromata – Red, opaque berries with the approximate heat level of lava. Favoured by the Daens and native to Cantash.

Canak-Maku – A Grey Realm, which is home to the minotaurs.

Castle, Ronah's – The centre point of Ronah and the traditional home of the Altoriae, the Guardian, and their respective families.

Crystals – Hold energy, which is turned into electricity. Often installed in clusters to gain more power and last longer. Different coloured crystals do different things. White Crystals are used for communication. Black Crystals gather power, and Orange Crystals connect currents to create fences. Crystal necklaces are given to young children and Blanks for them to manipulate the crystals.

Curses – Several curses are common on Lissae, including: Adeon's fire; By the Life of Lissae; Ke'ra's Flash; Zoemer's Rocks; Rasshnae's Floods; Vebnah's Breath; Na'reh's Ghosts. Other curses from the Realms include: ketarr; dathae; tuzar's arse; tongue of a Ne'fora; whale's arse; basalt-chewing, hemmit-loving buzzard; cestoray; slime vattar; hanotqe; slime-filled cedore; feseor; gozochas; thrice-damned; fizzpot; trusnuck.

D

Daen – A short, fierce, and loyal race with amazing control over the Fire Element.

Datzal – A Grey shapeshifting race conquered by the Q'Aralide and used as spies by the Queen.

Deities – Lissae has six Deities who are said to have lived on Akoren. See: **Beings and Creatures: Adeon, Ke'ra, Na'reh, Rasshnae, Vebnah,** and **Zoemer** for more details.

Dento – A fixed island on Lissae. Home of the Kumaru.

Draci – Tiny dragon-like creatures that grow no bigger than a human's palm. The draci are native to Cantash, and those who have not found a being to bond with live in the gardens.

Ducibus – The Ducibus guard the gateways between the Realms. No one really knows what they look like, as they all wear dark cloaks. There is a theory that they come from different Realms and comprise many races. They ensure the safe travel between Realms and that those who aren't meant to get through, don't.

Ducibus' Hall – The place between Realms, guarded by the **Ducibus**. Also referred to as the **portal.**

E

Elders – Those who have, through age and experience, survived the Realms long enough to guide their people. They also act as advisors to the mayor.

Elements – Lissae has seven major elements that Innarnians can manipulate: earth, air, fire, water, plasma, spirit, and technology.

Eni – Malicious shapeshifters, able to permanently assume the form of influential figures to summon others of their kind to possess the subjects they have gained. Seriously Dark beings, the Eni are rarely seen out of the Dark Realms. The Eni mentally 'piggyback' their prey before assuming their form. They were wiped out by the thirteenth Altoriae during an unsuccessful attempt to take over Lissae. References from the Eni's time on Lissae can be found in the **Eni Inside**. See **More to Read.**

Eobustus – Native to Cantash, the coal-black equines with manes of fire are a physical representation of energy and heat transference. They use heat from their surroundings to gather energy, then convert that energy into other things—movement, Innarn-boosting, running without rest. They are the fastest creature in all the Realms—provided they've had a good feed of magma or the sun is at full strength.

F

Falkirut – of Vinneča. Short, squat, slimy grey beings.

Femto-crystals – The latest in healing technology for Talhan. They can help a patient recover from any damage they've sustained and decrease recuperation time.

Ferah – Humanoid beings with cat-like features, including fur, tail, whiskers, and claws.

Fiotealar – A Grey Realm, known for its technological prowess. Home of the **Yoxant**.

Fulni – An animal similar to Earth's buffalo, but carnivorous and with two heads. The last fulni herd went extinct over two hundred years ago. Their tails are attached to a major artery, and if the tail is removed, they will bleed out in seven seconds.

G

Gilfress Elixir – Made from the roots of the gilfress plant, the elixir was created by Zana, Rakemyst's Linked. It has the colour of honey and viscosity of water. It has a spicy scent, and acts as a pick-me-up for the drinker.

Ginorti – One of the sentient Shifting Islands on Lissae. He is home to the Satyrs.

Glamour – A type of Innarn used to hide or disguise things. Typically cosmetic in application, glamours are favoured by those with heavy scarring or blemishes.

Golem – A creature made of stone, dirt, or clay.

Guardian – The rank for the person who oversees training and caring for the Altoriae, and for Lissae. In cases of emergency, the mayor and elders defer to the Guardian.

H

Hantra – Earth spirits summoned by the Wisara. Unable to be controlled or stopped by the Shifting Islands as they were given bodies made of the earth. They are slow-moving and persistent, their only goal to do what the summoner has told them to. The only way to kill a Hantra is to remove both arms before decapitating it. Raising the Hantra is taboo on any of the Shifting Islands.

Hazelcrown – The second month of autumn on the Realm of Lissae.

Healers – Similar to Earth's doctors, they heal patients who are sick or injured, usually using Innarn, although they also use the old methods.

Healers Centre – Also called the **Hospital**. A place on Ronah or Rakemyst to go when sick or injured.

I

I bid thee well – A traditional phrase when two or more people part ways.

Inthday – Second day of the week on the Realm of Lissae. The other days are **Adonday, Kerday, Narday, Rasshday, Vebaday,** and **Zoeday.**

Ilutri – Winged humanoids from Lissae. They are usually found on Rakemyst and are high-level Innarnians. They include some of the finest archers on the Realm.

Ignis Academy – one of the schools on **Cantash**.

Innarn – (said Inn-*ar*-n) Predominately elemental magic which is present in all Realms to varying strengths. Innarn is split into three major groups: Dark, Grey, and Light. Each variant of Innarn has its own specialties. See **Elements** for more information. There are other disciplines of Innarn, including Animal, Crystal, Mental, Realm, Time and Travel.

Innarnian – (said Inn-*ar*-ni-an) A person who can use Innarn.

J

Jinkor – A fixed island on Lissae.

K

Kerday – Third day of the week on the Realm of Lissae. The other days are **Adonday, Inthday, Narday, Rasshday, Vebaday,** and **Zoeday.**

Kumaru – Tree-like humanoids from Lissae. They are usually found on Dento and are high-level Earth Innarnians. They pride themselves on their connection with Earth and Spirit Innarn. A long-lived race, the Kumaru rarely step off-Realm.

L

Linked – A soul joined with that of one of Lissae's Shifting Islands. As the Shifting Islands are sentient, it was decided long ago that they should link with a being on their island to ensure that they remain in touch with the current needs of their population, and not remove themselves from the trials and tribulations of everyday beings.

Lissae – A Grey, sentient Realm who is defended by the Altoriae. Comprising six continents, seven sentient Shifting Islands, and multiple fixed islands, she is home to ten races. She is said to be a Mother Realm. There are two moons in her orbit.

Lissaen – A person who lives on Lissae.

Luerix – A Grey Realm slightly darker than Lissae. Monolithic standing stones ring the gateway. Home of the Sky Mother.

M

Mainlanders – A name for those residing on the mainlands or fixed islands of Lissae.

Maru – A Grey Realm, slightly darker than Lissae. Currently has a bug problem.

Mother Realm – The only Realm capable of giving birth to new Realms. Highly guarded and sought after.

Motus – The movement used to create Innarn. One must have thought, intent, and movement correct for the Innarn to work. Motus can be an individual construct, or a widely recognised form. Forms of motus used: Air; Sleep; Wind Blast; Wall of Stone.

N

Narday – Fourth day of the week on the Realm of Lissae. The other days are **Adonday, Inthday, Kerday, Rasshday, Vebaday,** and **Zoeday.**

Nightcrest – The first month of winter on the Realm of Lissae.

Nine Hells – The name given to a particularly nasty set of nine Realms.

Nittany – A Grey Realm with a forest around its gateway.

O

Ofanahni – Native to Bazaven. The Ofanahni are typically oppressed by the Sylpans, whose brutal and inconsistent justice system makes their lives difficult. A group of Ofanahni refugees has settled in the desert region of the continent set aside on Lissae for refugees.

Osin berries – Small, sweet, yellow berries.

P

Palon – Native to Lissae, the palon is a small, six-legged creature descended from wolves. They have soft fur and long tongues, with a preferred diet of insects.

Patrol – Any Innarnian resident over fifteen is required to help the Guardian and the Altoriae patrol the Realms to watch for any potential threats. The Linked, elderly, and Blanks are not required to patrol.

Persea – a green stone fruit, native to Ginorti. Goes well spread on toast with a touch of lemon and salt.

Pocket Realm – A small Realm that is attached to a larger one.

Ponton – A Grey Realm, slightly Lighter than Lissae.

Portal – The place between Realms, guarded by the **Ducibus**. Also referred to as the **Ducibus' Hall.**

Q

Q'Aralide (said Que-*ral*-die) – A vicious Dark race who wield Spirit, Earth, Plasma, and Air Innarn. Approximately thirty feet tall, their social status depends more on their colour and abilities than anything else. Apart from their Innarn, their breath is something to watch out for, as it can strip the flesh and the life from someone in just one exhalation.

Quass juice – a sweet, bubbly, orange drink, served cold.

Quiver and Quill Tavern – The tavern run by the Altoriae's parents on Ronah.

R

Rakemyst – One of the sentient Shifting Islands on Lissae. She is home to the Ilutri.

Rasshday – Fifth day of the week on the Realm of Lissae. The other days are **Adonday, Inthday, Kerday, Narday, Vebaday,** and **Zoeday.**

Realms – Planets which inhabit various parts of the multiverse on three main levels: Dark, Grey, and Light. Although there can be many sub-levels and a mix of Dark and Grey or Grey and Light within the same level. Dark Realms are places with little to no natural sunlight. Most lights in these Realms are made by Innarn. Grey Realms are places with a similar amount of light to Lissae and Earth's equator. Light Realms are places where there is an abundance of natural light.

Returned – The name given to those from Ronah who survived being eaten by Anriluka.

Rezem – A building built out of a mound of earth. The size and design of the mound can be controlled by an Innarnian or by one of the Sentient Islands.

Ridden Hall – The school on Ronah.

Ronah – One of the sentient Shifting Islands on Lissae. She is home to a variety of races and the traditional home of the Altoriae. Traditionally, Ronah selects a being to be her spokesperson. Ronah is one of the six gateways to the Realms.

Rutenberry – The frosted, dark-purple skin of the rutenberry hides the chocolate-like fruit inside. It can be eaten raw, although the skin can be bitter. Skinned, mashed, and cooked, it can be added into cakes, biscuits, and other sweets, including drinks.

S

Satyrs – A humanoid race from Lissae with legs and tail similar to a horse. They are usually found on Ginorti. They include some of the finest crack troops on the Realm.

Sedolic – Green, scaly, dog-like animals with two large pincers at their front that are a favoured food of the U'tan.

Send/Sent – The word used for telepathic communication.

Sentient – Able to perceive or feel things, capable of thought and communication.

Sentinel, The Shifting Island – The major source of news for the Shifting Islands of Lissae. Available on your crystal slab with the low-cost subscription of 3 ziom beads a day!

Shifting – The Innarn art of mental teleportation from one space to another.

Shifting Islands – The name of the group of islands that travel around Lissae's seas, seemingly on a whim. They are sentient beings who care for the residents who make them their home. See: **Akoren**, **Cantash**, **Ginorti**, **Rakemyst**, **Ronah**, **Talhan**, and **Vannali.**

Shiovion – A Light Realm in the third band.

Shiovionian – A being from **Shiovion.**

Sky Mother – of Luerix. A gigantic whale who rides currents of Plasma through the sky.

Spirit Realm – A Realm that is found alongside Lissae, where the spirit or souls of the deceased go when their physical bodies are no longer needed.

Stormwake – The final month of autumn on the Realm of Lissae.

Sulanta – A fixed island on Lissae.

Suncrest – The final month of summer on the Realm of Lissae.

Sunfall – The first month of autumn on the Realm of Lissae.

T

Talhan – One of the sentient Shifting Islands on Lissae, and the only one to start with an all-human population. He now accepts immigrants from all races on Lissae.

Techno Centre – Located on Talhan, it is the hub for all of Lissae's crystal and technological advances. The building also holds the Healing Centre, and the labs of the technomancer and Talhan's Linked.

Technomancer – The head of the Techno Centre has been given the nickname of technomancer due to the number of times her advances have brought the seemingly deceased back to life.

U

Uleulan – A race of four-armed humanoids from Lissae. Usually found on Sulanta, they have distinct features: a single, large eye and translucent skin. Amongst them are some of the Realm's high-level Water and Spirit Innarnians.

Ulnan – Temira's home Realm. It was destroyed, and all that remains is a burnt door in the Ducibus' Hall.

Ulnanian – A race from Ulnan. The only known surviving member is Temira.

U'sala – A group of beings from all over the Realms who have banded together to protect the Realms from creatures who wished to change them for their own benefit. Currently led by Yessna. The numbers of the U'sala vary because of the high turnover rate.

V

Vannali – One of the sentient Shifting Islands on Lissae. She is home to the Weavers.

Vebaday – Sixth day of the week on the Realm of Lissae. The other days are **Adonday**, **Inthday**, **Kerday**, **Narday**, **Rasshday**, and **Zoeday**.

Veti Cant – Or Cant, is a sign language that uses hands and facial expressions to communicate. It is often helpful when overcoming language barriers. There are variations for beings with more limbs, but the essentials of the Cant remain the same.

Vitaemancers – A type of Innarnian found on Ulnan who can control the blood inside another being or creature, dictating their every move. Vitaemancers can also cure diseases and successfully treat blood conditions.

Vendalbara – A continent on Lissae.

Vinneča – A Grey Realm.

Vladine – Refugees from the Grey Realm of **Vinneča**, now living on Lissae.

W

Wards – Innarn shields designed to protect specific areas.

Well met – A traditional greeting throughout the Realms.

Wisara – Primarily ocean-dwelling beings whose bodies, although humanoid, look like the tangled roots of lotus flowers. Their 'hair' is the leaves of the lotus, and the flowers act as adornments. Wisara can change form to a more traditional humanoid shape and inhabit land areas in either form. They move around as travellers and trade between the continents and islands of Lissae by walking the ocean beds. They are the perfect oversea (or in this case, undersea) merchants, as storms have little to no effect on them. Custom dictates that the Wisara are offered fish and bread and other items to restock their larder by the towns they visit. As payment, the Wisara would tell the Tales of Lore. Only the eldest of the Wisara is given the title of **Lore Keeper**, although anyone could tell the tales.

X

Xanderri – A cloud-like race relying on the bodies of their hosts to move around.

Y

Yaqueona – An oblong-shaped red, gourd, best served stuffed or roasted. Native to Cantash.

Yoxant – Beings native to Fiotealar. Incredibly gifted in Techno Innarn, they are the creators of some of the most sought after technology in the Grey Realms. The Yoxants are more than willing to fight to keep their technology out of the hands (or claws) of others. Their preferred weapon is the chakram.

Z

Ze/Zir/Zim – A gender-neutral pronoun.

Ziom – The hardest metal in the Realms, found on Lissae. Used for the creation of housing frames, precious jewellery, and weapons.

Ziom beads – A form of currency on Lissae. Also referred to as **Beads**.

Zoeday – Seventh day of the week on the Realm of Lissae. The other days are **Adonday**, **Inthday**, **Kerday**, **Narday**, **Rasshday**, and **Vebaday**.

Zuefie – Home Realm of the Xanderri.

BEINGS AND CREATURES

Annotated by the Guardian's Apprentice, Samuel.

Adeon – The God of the Element Fire and husband of Ke'ra.

Aharny – An Ilutri Travel Innarnian, formerly working out of Dento.

Akoren – One of the sentient Shifting Islands on Lissae. Originally home to Lissae's deities, now ze is inhabited by a few, select representatives of the races that came from the other Shifting Islands.

Amara – of Ronah. Formerly of Cantash. Former candidate for the Guardian's Apprentice. New member of the Altoriae's Guild.
How does she manage to constantly trip over? air?

Andrew Shansky – Eric Shansky's father.

Anika Thorne – of Ronah. Student at Ridden Hall. Blank. Stylist to the thirteenth Altoriae. *And the Guardian. And me. I feel like I've been branded*

Glad she's gone. Ugh.

Anriluka – of Rataeo. This U'tan is older than Lissae's calendar. She almost devoured Ronah's entire population before Muran Curtis' Guardian banished her back to her home Realm. Anriluka was finally defeated by Shari Dawn, the thirteenth Altoriae, in the spring of 4059.

Arilla Dawn – of Ronah. Mother of Shari Dawn, wife of Calem Dawn. Owner of the Quiver and Quill Tavern.

Ashlen – One of the Returned, and a member of the Altoriae's Guild

Surprisingly helpful and unbiased. Would make a good coatrack.

Asterion – formerly of Atlantis. A former professor who donated his mind to become myth embodied. Currently residing on Ronah.

Belfar – of Rakemyst. Mate of Wolf Dawn. Second in command of Elder SilverCloud's guards.

Ben – of Kenorvia. Elder.

Calem Dawn – of Ronah. Father of Shari Dawn, husband of Arilla Dawn, son of SilverCloud, and brother of Wolf Dawn. Owner of the Quiver and Quill Tavern. *He thought I wanted to do what with his daughter?*

Cantash – One of the sentient Shifting Islands on Lissae. He is home to the Daens.

Captain Rappen – of Jinkor. Under Elder Chamele's command.

Chamele – of Jinkor. Elder. *Surely Lissae wouldn't mind if I ate this one?*

Charin – of Rakemyst. One of the patrol members in Wolf's group. Spouse of Varlee.

Collis Iuvo – of Ronah. Unofficial leader of the Returned. Sworn guardian and soul-match of Ronah's Linked. Member of the Altoriae's Guild.

Crystal Intelligence – of Lissae and Atlantis.

> *Should say – of trouble and mayhem. Never trust a talking crystal. And for the love of the Nine Hells, never take a machine from Atlantis!*

> *Her bells are both a blessing and a curse.*

Cylanthar – The Q'Aralidé deity of destiny. She makes her presence known by the ringing of bells when events which have the potential to change her disciples' lives occur.

Cyrus Petram – of Talhan. Talhan's Linked.

Danielle Williams – Shari's great grandmother.

Dealon – of Ronah. Formerly of the Wisara. Former candidate for the Guardian's Apprentice. New member of the Altoriae's Guild.

Denesska – of Ronah. One of the Returned.

Derri – Co-founder of the Xanderri race.

Drah – of the U'sala. Twin brother to Kerk. *Currently missing a foot.*

Edward Thorne – of Ronah. Husband of Harmony. Elder of Ronah. Grandfather of Anika Thorne.

Elani – of Ronah. Formerly of Ginorti. Member of the Altoriae's Guild.

Elizabeth Ribeck – of Ronah. Classmate of the Altoriae.

Ember Sparks, Professor – of Cantash. Head of Ignis Academy.

Esse – Tania's escape-artist chicken. *Snack with blue feathers*

Eva – of Talhan. Orphaned. Femto crystal tester.

Felton – of the U'sala. Explosives expert.

Fenix – of Cantash. Cantash's Linked.

Frointh – Forgotten Lissaen deity of Crystal.

Ginorti – One of the sentient Shifting Islands on Lissae. He is home to the Satyrs.

Grace – of Jinkor. Former slave of Chamele. The Altoriae's cousin.

Gwyn – of Vendalbara. Elder.

War is never easy for the Healers.

Healer Holli Doonavan – of Ronah. Head Healer.

Helk – Master Warrior of the Q'Aralide. *As annoying as he was, Helk didn't deserve the death he got.*

Henot – of the U'sala. Gnome.

Jetonyx – Whereabouts unknown. Kin to Samuel.

Alive and well. I'll consider not making you my next snack

Jonathan Buan – of Ronah. The Guardian to the thirteenth Altoriae. Owner of Books 'n' More. *The Realms may just freeze over. The Guardian is starting to trust me.*

Kay'imi – The first Altoriae. She lived until she was 1217 years old when a lone Ahana archer killed her.

Kemanyr – newest Q'Aralide. *Recently hatched. With colours. And a penchant for escaping.*

Ke'ra – God of the Element Plasma and husband of Adeon.

Kibon – of the U'sala. Long-range weapons expert.

Laura – of Ronah. *Tiny little Dark thing. Actually seems concerned for my safety*

Lissa – Sarina's daughter. Cousin to the Altoriae. More commonly known as **Grace**.

Liza Hollingsworth – of Ronah. Daughter of General Morrow. Wife of Jordan, mother of Caleb, Christopher, Alistair, Tania, and Jessica. Headmaster of Ridden Hall.

Lizbeth Ribeck – of Ronah. *My friend. Hurt her, and I will peel your skin off, piece by piece and make you watch while I rip your still-beating heart from your body*

Louise Shansky – of Ronah. Eric Shansky's mother.

Mick – of Cantash.

Milo – of Cantash. Self-appointed secretary to Talhan's Linked.

Mu – of Ronah. Formerly of Nindonia. Member of the Altoriae's Guild.

Na'reh – Goddess of the Element Spirit and wife of Vebnah.

Nerina – of the U'sala. Healer.

Oakley – of Ginorti. Ginorti's Linked.

~~Oalark~~ – Queen of the ~~Qualansha.~~ *Could she not have mentioned her life force with Altam? A little warning would have been nice. Still not sad she's gone.*

Pala – Leader of the Ducibus and sentinel of Lissae's gateway.

RainbowMist – Deceased wife of SilverCloud, mother of Calem and Wolf Dawn, grandmother of Shari Dawn, thirteenth Altoriae.

Rakemyst – One of the sentient Shifting Islands on Lissae. He is home to the Ilutri.

Rasshnae – Goddess of the Element Water and wife of Zoemer.

Raven – of Ronah. Formerly of Freeson. Former candidate for the Guardian's Apprentice. New member of the Altoriae's Guild. Excellent tracker.

Reah – of Talhan. Recently lost her sight.

Remmy – of Ronah. One of the Returned.

Ronah – One of the sentient Shifting Islands on Lissae. She is home to a variety of races and the traditional home of the Altoriae. Ronah's current Linked is Tania Hollingsworth. Ronah is one of the six gateways to the Realms. *For a hunk of sentient dirt, she is a surprisingly competent architect.*

Samuel Caragnton – currently of Ronah. Formerly of Altum. Golden Priest of the Q'Aralide. The Lissaen Guardian's Apprentice.

Sanithane – See **Samuel Caragnton**.

I have the remainder of my kind with me.

How did I become the patriarch of an entire race?

Sarina – Mother of Lissa. Aunt of the thirteenth Altoriae.

Shadow – of Ronah. The only creature to be one of the Returned. See **Zoomer**.

Shari Dawn – of Ronah. The thirteenth Altoriae of Lissae and creator of the Altoriae's Guild. *Safe. Home. And mostly intact.*

SilverCloud, Elder – of Talhan. Father of Calem and Wolf Dawn. Grandfather to the thirteenth Al~~toriae, and~~ Head Elder of Talhan.

Skye – Former aide to Elder Suni. Current carer of **Grace**.

Sneeze – ~~One of Cantash's draci.~~ *My draci. Can you train them out of chewing on ears?*

Suni – of Lawrgaea. Elder. Falsely accused of being an Innarnian and summarily executed whilst she slept.

Talhan – One of the sentient Shifting Islands on Lissae, and the only one to start with an all-human population. He now accepts immigrants from all races on Lissae.

Talofa – of Ronah. Formerly of Sulanta. Member of the Altoriae's Guild.

Tania Hollingsworth – of Ronah. Ronah's Linked. Daughter of Liza, stepdaughter of Jordan. Sister to Caleb, Christopher, Alistair, and Jessica. Soul-matched to Collis Iuvo.

Telnarik, Lord – of Shiovion. Leader of the Sentinel Division.

My apologies for the destruction of your Realm. My race is... horrid

Temira – of Talhan. Formerly of **Ulnan**. Also called the technomancer, Temira is Head Healer and head of the Techno Centre.

Terrance Thorne – of Ronah. Anika Thorne's father.

Timon – of Ronah. One of the Returned.

Alive and well. Be grateful Liza keeps up my rotenberry

Tormorylth – of Altum. Tiny Q'Aralide. *supply so I don't have to eat you for not bringing her back.*

Tutor Boyce – of Ronah. Teacher at Ridden Hall.

Vannali – One of the sentient Shifting Islands on Lissae. He is home to the Weavers.

Varlee – of Rakemyst. Third in command of Elder SilverCloud's guards. One of the patrol members in Wolf's group. Spouse of Charin.

Vebnah – Goddess of the Element Air and wife of Na'reh.

Voxis – of Rakemyst. Silver-winged Ilutri youth. Nephew of Zana, Linked of Rakemyst.

May he rot in the bowels of the Altum beast for all eternity

War'Jan – Former leader of the Q'Aralide. Now deceased.

Wolf Dawn – of Rakemyst. Mate of Belfar. Brother of Calem Dawn, and uncle to the thirteenth Altoriae. Commander of SilverCloud's guards. Previously known as LoneWolf Dawn.

Wubi – of the U'sala. Wielder of the spiked chain.

Xan – Co-founder of the Xanderri race.

Xani – of Talhan. Also called the technomancer, Xani was Head Healer and head of the Techno Centre. Deceased. Better than most mortals.

Yessna – Commander of the U'sala.

Jonathan's... something?

Zac Husdon – of Talhan. Formerly of Ronah. Techno apprentice.

Zana – of Talhan. Talhan's Linked. Eldest of the Linked, and an accomplished diplomat.

If you thought corpse form was bad,

Zirgha – Ambassador of Otike. this is worse. Whatever this is.

Zoemer – God of the Element Earth and husband of Rasshnae.

Zoomer – Shari's palon. The only creature to be one of the Returned. See **Shadow**.

MAP OF GINORTI

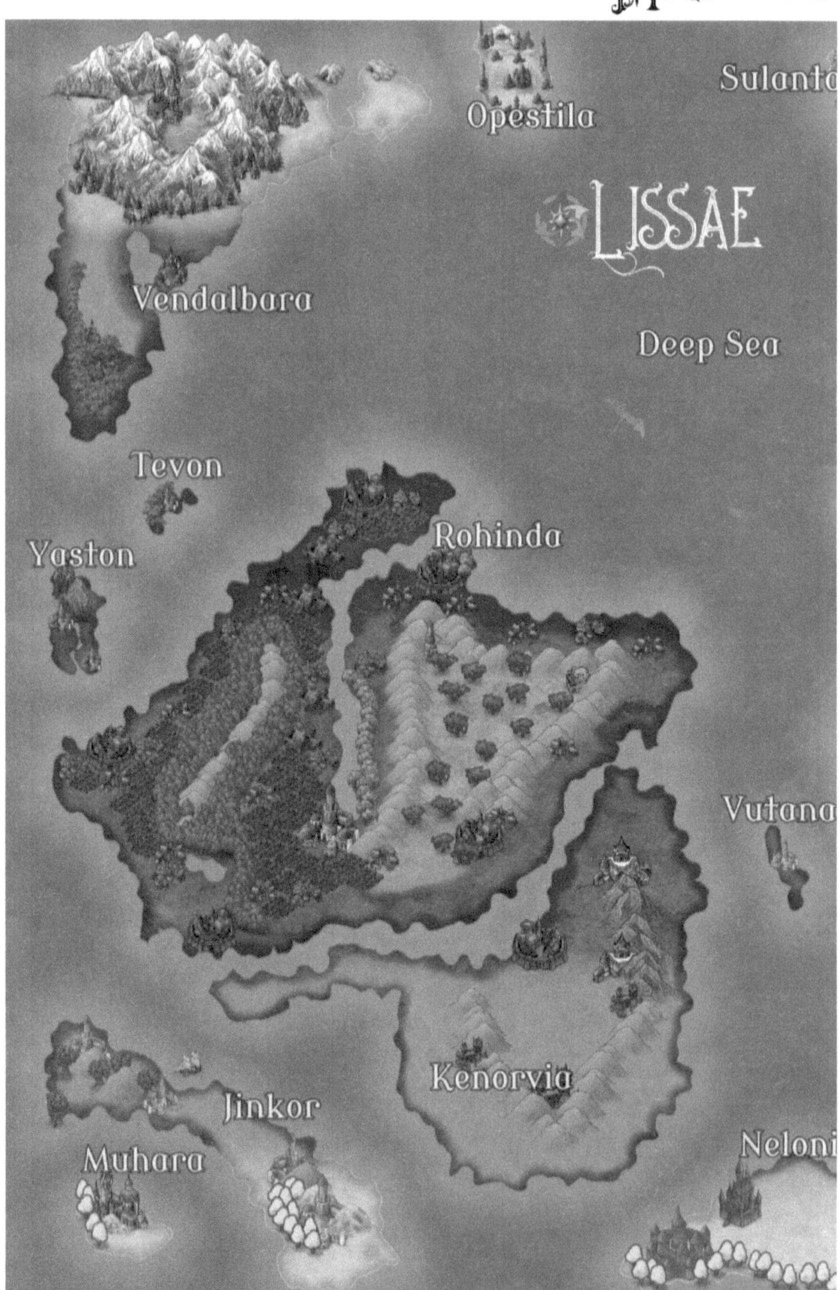

MAP OF
Sulanta
Opestila
LISSAE
Deep Sea
Vendalbara
Tevon
Rohinda
Yaston
Vutana
Kenorvia
Jinkor
Neloni
Muhara

LISSAE

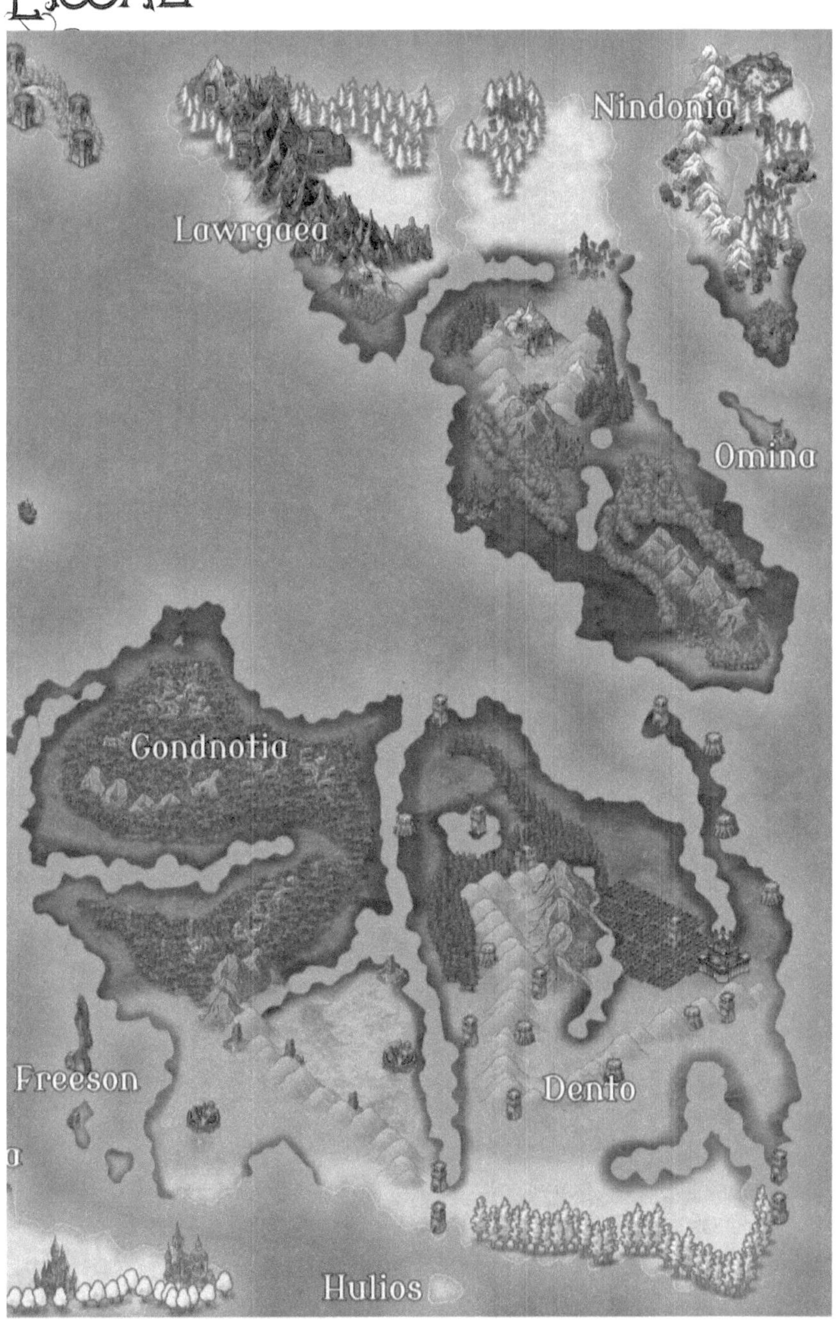

ENJOY THIS BOOK?

You can make a big difference

Reviews are the most powerful tools in my arsenal when it comes to getting attention for my books. They help me gain visibility, and they can bring the Realm of Lissae to other readers who may appreciate the journey.

If you have enjoyed this book, I would be incredibly grateful if you could spend just a few minutes leaving a review (it can be as short as you like) at your favourite bookstore, or on the Goodreads page. You can jump right to the page by clicking below.

Find it in your preferred bookstore - books2read.com/ginorti

Goodreads - goodreads.com/book/show/62811457-ginorti

Thank you very much.

ACKNOWLEDGEMENTS

As always, I owe the many talented people who have come together to make this fantastical world alive on the pages.

One of the most frequent questions I get asked is: "How long does a book take to write?" The answer varies depending on the book and the author. Ginorti took an insane amount of time. How long?

Seven.

Weeks.

No sleep, back to coffee, and making sure that I was up before the sun to get it finished. I truly cannot thank my lovely family and friends enough for giving me time to write.

Jodie, Ruth, Kathy—my beta readers extraordinaire! Thank you for prodding at things to make Ginorti a better book. Sorry about the cliff-hangers. You slammed through the roughest of drafts and kept me encouraged.

My beautiful editing team—thank you Anna from CREATING ink for fine-tuning the manuscript, and Tracey for the check-ins.

I can't thank Vanesa enough for the stunning covers she continues to create! Lissae wouldn't look the same without you.

Special thanks to Cyrus, Lisa, Kathy, and Michelle for some of the new character names.

Jodie—you continue to amaze me. You got through the beta reading so quickly, set up all the event stuff on top of everything else you do. There aren't enough words to say how much I appreciate you.

Husband of mine, the original technomancer. You are the best sounding board I could ask for. I love you. Here's to another 20 years (with fewer electrocutions, I hope).

My Ren, your concept of energy vampires created the Xanderri, and I feel like the world should be more terrified because of it.

Corin, you refined the idea and made it worse. I love it! You continue to enrich my world just by being you. Never stop.

Ruth (aka Mum), thank you for being so thorough in such a short timeframe.

Danielle, your encouragement has shaped the worlds both in the book and the one outside it.

Oak, thank you for your enthusiasm for Lissae, and for letting me use your name. I hope I made book Oakley half as awesome as you were expecting.

My gremlin army, you keep me young. And wondering exactly what 'slay' means when Shari isn't the one doing it. Or is she? I'm confused.

To the amazing team at Sunshine Coast Libraries who always seem so excited to hear about what I've been up to in the writing world–endless gratitude for all your encouragement, particularly Christine, Rohin, Karen, Patricia, Amanda, and Jo.

To the developers who created and maintain 4theWords. Your amazing website helped to get this book, and so many others, finished.

I cannot forget you, the reader! Thank you for exploring the Realms within these pages. Until next time, I bid thee well.

ABOUT THE AUTHOR

R. Lennard is the Australian author of the young adult fantasy series *Lissae*. She is an avid fantasy and sci-fi reader, and in her spare time, she works as a librarian. She enjoys learning about ancient civilisations, cosplaying, and drinking endless cups of tea.

Residing on the beautiful Sunshine Coast in Queensland, Australia, Rebecca enjoys the natural beauty of both the beach and the bush. She lives with her family and is ruled over by her cat.

Rebecca is a fan of many things, and used to drive her husband nuts by being able to tell him 'who dun it' within the first few minutes of an NCIS episode.

To find out more about Rebecca, head to rlennard.com

After More to Read?

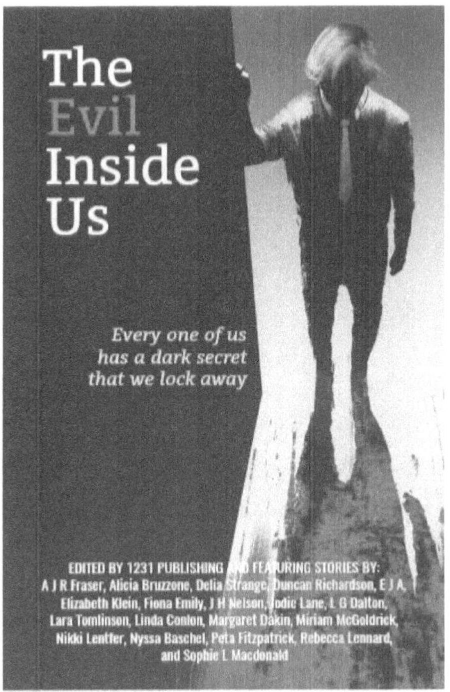

The *Eni Inside* is a short story prelude to the Lissae series included in the 3rd Australian Pen anthology, *The Evil Inside Us.*

The headmaster of Ridden Hall, Lawrence Anderson, went out on patrol, but never returned. Instead, a being bent on taking over Lissae came back in his place.

Full of stories about dark secrets, you'll want to join the masses and buy your copy of *The Evil Inside Us* now!

Available at: lissae.com/short-stories

What would you do when you had nothing to lose?

Orphaned, Jonathan Buan travels halfway around the Realm to defend his father's honour.

He finds more than he expected—more pain, more death, and more people to call his own.

Can he save them all, or will he become a demon's snack?

Find out what Jonathan was like before he became the Guardian.

Buy *Guardian* to bend the elements to your will today!

Available at: lissae.com/short-stories

How do you live after being eaten by a monster?

After he died, Collis found himself in a nightmarish Realm full of creatures who wanted to eat him. Waking up after the fiftieth time he'd died wasn't any easier than the first.

Stuck in a pocket Realm, Collis and the residents from Ronah must defend themselves against the deadliest creatures from across the Realms. But survival comes at a cost.

And if they die? They reform. Over and over. Just how are they going to escape?

Find out in *Returned*.

Available at: lissae.com/short-stories

A misplaced arrow could cause a war...

Wracked with guilt, Shari must face the joining of two Shifting Islands with her sword at the ready.

But as the search for the Guardian's next apprentice is still underway, fear strikes her heart. Not all the candidates are who they claim to be. And a fearsome new foe is out for revenge.

Can Shari lower her defences enough to let someone else in? Or will the decision cost her more than she's willing to give?

Buy *Rakemyst* and fly into Lissae today!

Available at: lissae.com/rakemyst

His choice could change the very fabric of the Realms...

The most feared being to walk the Dark Realms was once a mere hatchling. Scrawny, weak, and half-mortal, Sanithane strives to gain enough power to ensure his tormentors never bother him again.

But when his Queen sets an impossible task, Sanithane has to choose—his kin, or his life?

Find out the story behind the Golden Priest in *Shadows*.

Available at: lissae.com/short-stories

Something is watching them from the shadows...

After a devastating betrayal, Shari longs for life to return to the way things were.

But she has little time to dwell on normality. A disturbing new foe rises, and former enemies become allies in the fight to save Lissae.

Juggling school by day and patrolling by night, it will only take one slip up to bring everything crashing down. Shari must battle her way to the heart of her problems... or die trying.

Buy *Talhan* and discover the heart of Lissae today!

Available at: lissae.com/talhan

There's something hiding in the Dark.

It's seeking Shari relentlessly and it's got only one thing planned for the Altoriae…

When a spy impersonates Shari, Samuel is summoned home to chair the Dark Conclave. It's the most dangerous meeting in all the Realms; a place where blinking out of turn will lead to being eviscerated, and Shari, it's number one enemy, accompanies Samuel under the guise of protecting him.

While Shari is away, the mainlanders have declared war, and Jonathan alone must confront them. With trouble brewing on both sides of the gateway, how will Shari overcome the Darkest of Realms and keep Lissae intact at the same time?

Buy *Cantash* and fan the flames of Lissae today!

Available at: lissae.com/cantash

READING ORDER

Guardian

Ronah

Returned

Rakemyst

Shadows

Talhan

Guild

Cantash

Sanctum

Ginorti

Tempest

Akoren

Weaver

Vannali

Lissae Chronicles

Grace

The Altoriae's Handbook

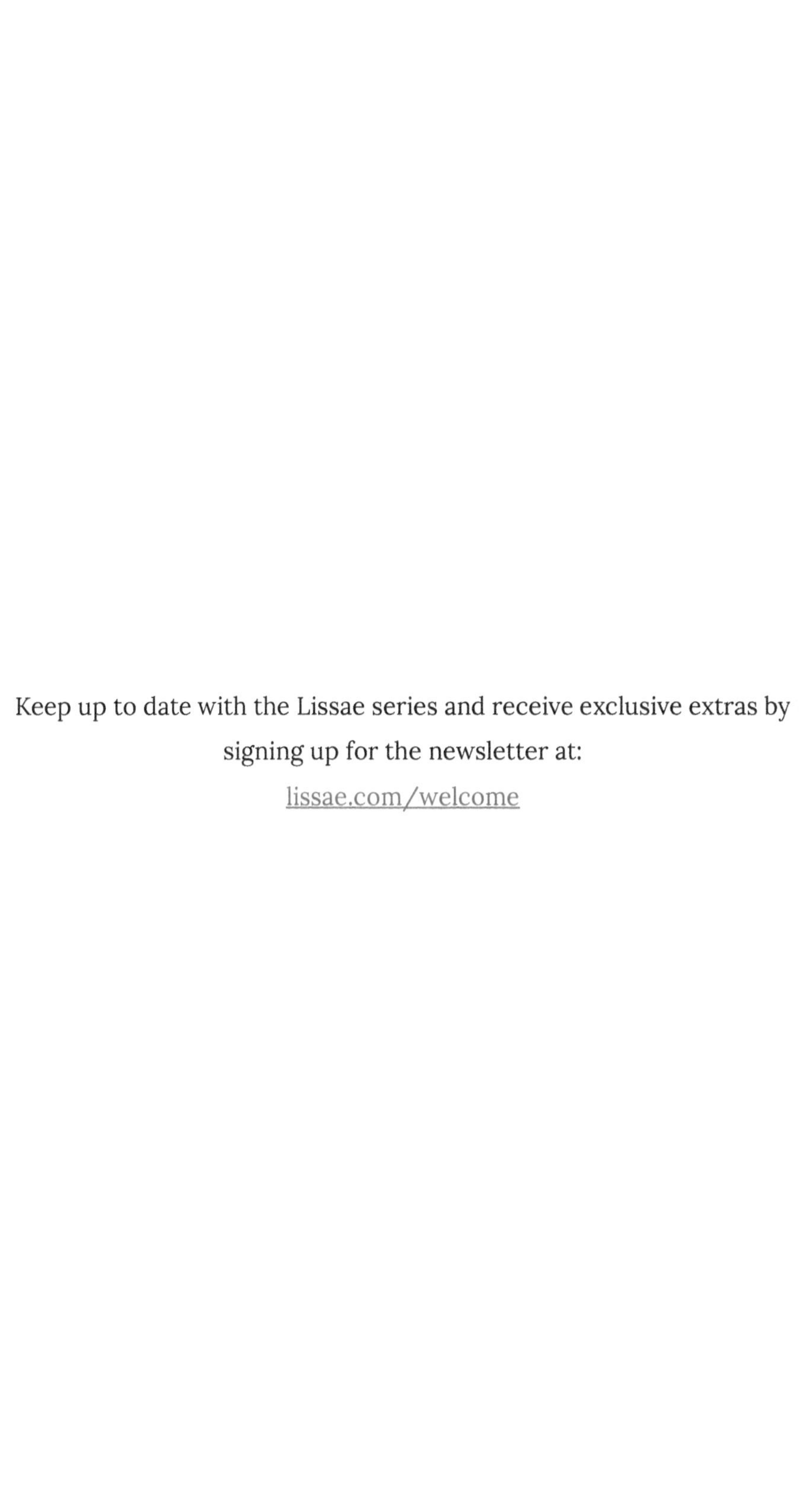

Keep up to date with the Lissae series and receive exclusive extras by signing up for the newsletter at:

lissae.com/welcome